MONTANA MAVERICKS

Welcome to Big Sky Country, home of the Montana Mavericks! Where free-spirited men and women discover love on the range.

LASSOING LOVE

After years away, some of Bronco's most memorable sons and daughters have returned to the ranch seeking a fresh start. But there are some bumps along the road to redemption. Expect the unexpected as lonesome cowboys (and cowgirls) discover if they've got what it takes to grab that second chance!

Tori Hawkins's heart belongs to the rodeo, and Bobby Stone is fine with that. Why not enjoy a simple friendship with a beautiful woman? No ties, no lies and no chance of anyone getting hurt. The longer they keep company, however, the harder it is to ignore the truth: falling for each other could be the best mistake they ever make...

Dear Reader,

Three years ago, Bobby Stone faked his own death and walked away from Bronco, Montana. Last winter, when he discovered a twin brother he never knew existed, Bobby finally came home. But the lonesome cowboy has kept his secrets to himself.

That is, until he meets barrel racer Tori Hawkins, part of the famed Hawkins sisters rodeo family. Suddenly, he finds himself opening up—to a point. He and Tori have only until the end of summer to be together and then she'll ride off without him. Unless he can face his past and unlock a very guarded heart...

I hope you enjoy Bobby and Tori's story. It's full of romance, emotion, questions, family ties, cannoli, and unexpected hopes and dreams. I love to hear from readers, so feel free to check out my website, melissasenate.com, for my contact info and to learn more about me and my books.

Happy reading,

Melissa Senate

A Maverick Reborn

MELISSA SENATE

HARLEQUIN

SPECIAL
EDITION

Special thanks and acknowledgment are given to
Melissa Senate for her contribution to the
Montana Mavericks: Lassoing Love miniseries.

HARLEQUIN®
SPECIAL EDITION™

Recycling programs
for this product may
not exist in your area.

ISBN-13: 978-1-335-59414-3

A Maverick Reborn

Copyright © 2023 by Harlequin Enterprises ULC

For questions and comments about the quality of this book,
please contact us at CustomerService@Harlequin.com.

Harlequin Enterprises ULC
22 Adelaide St. West, 41st Floor
Toronto, Ontario M5H 4E3, Canada
www.Harlequin.com

Printed in U.S.A.

Melissa Senate has written many novels for Harlequin and other publishers, including her debut, *See Jane Date*, which was made into a TV movie. She also wrote seven books for Harlequin Special Edition under the pen name Meg Maxwell. Her novels have been published in over twenty-five countries. Melissa lives on the coast of Maine with her teenage son; their rescue shepherd mix, Flash; and a lap cat named Cleo. For more information, please visit her website, melissasenate.com.

Books by Melissa Senate

Harlequin Special Edition

Montana Mavericks: Lassoing Love

A Maverick Reborn

Dawson Family Ranch

His Baby No Matter What
Heir to the Ranch
Santa's Twin Surprise
The Cowboy's Mistaken Identity
Seven Birthday Wishes

Furever Yours

A New Leash on Love
Home is Where the Hound Is

Montana Mavericks: Brothers & Broncos

One Night with the Maverick

Visit the Author Profile page
at Harlequin.com for more titles.

For my mother

Prologue

Six months ago

At nearly forty years old, Bobby Stone discovered he had a twin brother he never knew existed. This—a brother, family, *connection*—was what finally brought Bobby back to Bronco, Montana, today.

But nothing in Bobby's life had ever been easy and the homecoming was gonna be a doozy.

Because everyone thought Bobby was *dead*. And had been for over three years now.

He'd let them think that. Back when he thought there was no one who'd care. He'd seen a short article about his presumed death a few days after he'd disappeared. People thought he'd fallen off a cliff while walking in the woods at night, ruminating on all that was wrong in his life. Like his marriage—his shot at thinking he could believe in love—which had ended in divorce. His old backpack, his wedding ring and disturbed brush had been found by the edge of the cliff overlooking a hundred feet into dense brush and the river—and folks figured Bobby Stone was truly gone. He didn't think anyone had been grieving his loss.

Until just a few days ago.

He'd come across a social media post from a man named Sullivan Grainger. Last summer, Sullivan had come to Bronco, Montana, looking for the twin brother *he'd* only just found out he had. But when he arrived in Bronco, he discovered his long-lost twin—Bobby Stone—was dead, or presumed dead, anyway, since his body had never been found.

Gone—and forgotten.

That had pissed off Sullivan Grainger, Bobby was surprised—and touched—to learn in the long social media post. The man had decided to force the residents of Bronco to remember his twin—by making folks think they saw a ghost when they saw Sullivan skulking through town at night. By secretly creating strange happenings, including putting up signs with Bobby's picture that read REMEMBER BOBBY STONE.

Turned out there was one person who did remember Bobby—and fondly. His former friend Sadie Chamberlin, who owned the gift shop in Bronco. *Former* because Sadie was his ex-wife's sister, and when his ex had asked Sadie to choose between them during the divorce, of course she'd chosen her sister. She'd had to, and Bobby got it, but it had stung. Sadie had been determined to solve the mystery of the Bobby Stone lookalike and the weird occurrences and had unmasked the culprit—Bobby's twin, Sullivan Grainger. And then she'd fallen in love with him.

Hell of a story. And now it was time for another. Because Bobby was, right this moment, standing in the shadows on Commercial Street on this cold February night in Bronco. He figured he'd go to Sadie's shop, Sadie's Holiday House, and maybe he could approach her first. Sadie had been a good friend, despite everything—and boy, had there been a lot of *everything*, but he felt like he owned her an explanation.

That he was alive.

For a moment, though, all Bobby could do was look around, take in the sights, the shops and side streets that were so familiar.

He'd come home.

A chill raced up his spine and he shoved his hands into his coat pockets.

When would he finally get to meet his brother? His *twin* brother. Tonight? Tomorrow? Would Sullivan be furious when he discovered that Bobby wasn't dead, after all? Would the relationship be over before it even had a chance to begin?

He didn't know anything. Nothing new.

He kept walking toward Sadie's Holiday House. And as he neared the store, a man came out. A man who looked just like him, so much so that Bobby stopped dead in his tracks and gasped.

For a moment Bobby was speechless. And choked up. This was Sullivan Grainger. His twin. His reason for coming home. His reason *period*.

"You don't know me," Bobby called to him, not even

sure what was coming out of his mouth. "But I think you might be my brother."

Oh, and by the way, I'm clearly not dead.

Bobby waited as the guy turned. His heart started to pound, blood rushing in his head.

The man stared at him, drew a bit closer and stared some more, all kinds of emotion plain on his face. And then he slowly shook his head with something of a smile and said, "Welcome home, Bobby Stone."

Relief flooded Bobby to the point that his knees wobbled. Sullivan's reaction was a surprise. Bobby didn't detect anger in Sullivan Grainger's expression or tone. Some shock, yes. But there was mostly curiosity on the man's face.

The questions would come, he knew. From his twin—from everyone. *What happened on the night you disappeared? Where have you been? Why didn't you tell anyone you were alive?*

In three years Bobby had barely thought about any of that. He'd just focused on getting by.

But now he had questions too. About his family. About how newborn twin brothers had gotten separated and why.

Did Sullivan know? If he'd found out about Bobby in the first place, he must have done his research.

All Bobby knew for sure was that his entire life was about to change.

Chapter One

Once the folks of Bronco, Montana, heard that Bobby Stone was not dead after all, and back in town, they wanted the story. But Bobby didn't want to talk about it. Not six months ago when he'd come home. Not now. So when the answers they sought weren't forthcoming, from Bobby himself or through the gossip mill, he quickly became persona non grata.

There's goes that good for nothing Bobby Stone, he heard a woman whisper on his way into the Gemstone Diner the other night.

Maybe it's his twin, the man with her said. *Remember all that stuff Sullivan pulled to get people to remember Bobby?*

Well, Sullivan did think Bobby was dead, she responded, *like everyone else.*

They both shook their heads.

Bobby had pulled his Stetson down lower on his head

and retreated, not going into the diner when he had a mad craving for their chicken-fried steak and garlic mashed potatoes. He'd gone home and shoved a frozen version in the microwave and eaten alone on his small patch of patio.

Fine. Bobby knew he deserved the "welcome" he got from Bronco—which had been ongoing since February. Spring and most of summer hadn't thawed the deep freeze. At least Sullivan was in a better position. Being the fiancé of the well-liked woman who owned everyone's favorite gift shop had done wonders for Sullivan getting a pass. Plus, once folks had heard the basic rumors that the twin brothers had been separated at birth and hadn't known about each other till recently, they felt more kindly toward both Bobby and Sullivan.

Bobby now knew that story—how he and his twin had gotten separated at birth and why. He didn't like talking about that, either. And neither did Sullivan. So folks were doubly mad about not getting those juicy answers.

"That," Bobby said now to Bucky, one of his favorite horses in the stables at Dalton's Grange, where he worked as a cowboy, "is why I like living and working on a big ranch like this. Cowboy code—which includes not asking too many questions."

When he'd visited the ranch last winter about a job, the wealthy Dalton clan, no strangers to rumors and gossip themselves, had hired him after hearing what little of his story he'd tell, which wasn't much. Bobby had his own small cabin on the property and did work that suited him. He moved cattle, he kept the herd fed and their water trough filled and he did his rotation on barn and stable mucking, appreciating the mind-less physical labor. Sure, his fellow cowboys had asked what happened the night he supposedly died and where he'd been. But when Bobby had responded, each and every time with, *I really don't like talking about it*, they respected that and tipped their hats. He had told his bosses that he'd worked on a big spread in another state and his experience spoke for itself once he was in the job at Dalton's Grange. Neal Dalton, patriarch, still a bit rough around the edges despite winning millions gambling a few years ago, often gave Bobby a literal pat on the back and said, *Whatever your story is, glad you're back in Bronco, son*.

And every time, Bobby Stone, who'd never had a fa-ther, who'd barely had a mother, got choked up.

Now, though, he had a brother. Family. Bobby had felt like hell when Sullivan had taken him out to see Bobby's grave in Bronco Valley. His *grave*. He'd seen the headstone as they'd approached. Etched with his name, Robert James Stone, his birthdate and the date he'd disappeared, and he'd almost bolted—that was how shaken he'd been by it.

But Bobby Stone, *that* Bobby Stone, the man he'd been, was dead and gone.

Now, he was someone new. Or trying, anyway.

Hell, if Sullivan had gotten through seeing the grave of the twin brother he'd only recently discovered, his *own* birthdate right there, etched into the stone, then Bobby owed Sullivan to get through it, to stand there and see it. Accept it.

The brothers had taken down the headstone together, carrying it to Sullivan's truck to get it demolished—

with Bobby planning to keep a small piece as a reminder, a "memory stone" of sorts, to never let himself get pulled into that kind of despair again. He felt good about that. And *really* good knowing that things would be okay between him and Sullivan. They would work through the past and present and future together.

Damn, that was good to know, to believe.

As he headed down the long aisle to put the rake and gloves away, he could hear a woman's voice coming from the next aisle. She was talking to a brown and white quarter horse, one of the new boarders in the stables. As someone who talked to horses himself, he got it. They were good listeners. He took a rake from one of the huge lockers when he heard her say, "I don't know, Bluebell. I just don't know."

From where he stood a good fifty feet away, he could see her by the stall, but she clearly didn't know he was there. She was a newcomer to town, part of the famed Hawkins Sisters rodeo family, in Bronco for the rodeo at the end of the month. He knew that because he'd seen posters downtown advertising the event with a photo of her and her sisters and cousins. Just the other day he'd come across her for the first time, surrounded on Main Street by a bunch of middle school girls who'd screamed, "It's a Hawkins Sister!" as they'd run over to her. She'd graciously signed autographs with a warm smile and answered their questions.

He also knew, because once again he could barely drag his gaze off her, that she was beautiful. Tall and slender with long dark brown silky hair. Delicate features. She wore a Western-style shirt and form-fitting jeans with brown riding boots.

She slipped the horse an apple slice. "One day, Bluebell," she continued, "you wake up and you're forty. Just like that. And single, but that's absolutely fine. I've got my family and the rodeo and my side job, which is going great, by the way." The horse gave a little neigh and she added, "That you wishing me a happy birthday? It was two weeks ago but I'll take it. Or do you just want another apple slice?" She smiled as she gave her another, then leaned her forehead against the long brown nose and let out a sigh.

Now he felt bad about eavesdropping on what was clearly a private conversation and moment.

She had a side job? He wondered what it was. And when she found the time. Those Hawkins Sisters, all of them, worked and trained hard, competing in rodeos not only all over the American West but the world. Bobby knew that their seventy-something-year-old matriarch, famed retired rodeo queen Hattie Hawkins, had a bunch of daughters who'd become rodeo stars, forming the original Hawkins Sisters, and then *they'd* had a bunch of daughters who'd kept the family tradition going. This beauty was one of that third generation.

He wondered if she was dating anyone, though "single" probably meant no. Not that he was in the market for a relationship. Since he'd been back in Bronco, he'd lain pretty low, despite Sullivan and Sadie often offering to fix him up. No thanks. Even if anyone *would* dare date the infamous Bobby Stone, dating was all about questions, and he couldn't exactly sit across from a woman at a restaurant, or go on a walk or for coffee, and keep dodging what she wanted to know or changing the subject. People had big questions for Bobby that he just wasn't interested in answering. So he kept to himself.

But this woman had his attention. Just basic attraction. But when was the last time he was attracted to *anyone*?

Then again, he'd heard the Hawkins Sisters were fiercely independent and lived on the road. Maybe she was all about the cowboy—cow*girl*—creed and wouldn't ask personal questions. And maybe she'd be open to just some very causal dating.

"I'm also forty and single," he said before he could stop himself, stepping into view. "May my age change each year, God willing, but not my marital status."

He heard her slight gasp before her gaze landed on him. Big brown eyes took him in, slightly narrowing. Did she recognize him? Was she about to tell him it was no wonder a man who'd faked his own death would eavesdrop on a woman's private conversation with her horse?

"Got something against marriage?" she asked, a challenging twinkle in her sharp gaze.

He leaned the rake against the locker and headed over to where she stood in front of the stall. She was even prettier up close.

"Well, I *am* divorced," he said, surprising himself since he didn't like talking about that, either. Even with Sadie, his ex-wife's sister. Maybe especially with Sadie. She knew how hard he'd tried. And failed.

"I've never been married myself," she said. "I've had a bunch of relationships but nothing that would lead to marriage—except once when I was really young, barely out of my teens. That relationship ended when he told me he just couldn't see *never* kissing another woman as long as he lived." She shook her head. "I stopped falling for good-looking, smooth-talking cowboys after that. So, I'll be on my way." She gave the horse another pat and turned to go.

At least she thought he was good-looking.

But smooth-talking? Bobby had to smile. He was anything but that.

"Strong and silent is more my style," he said. "I'm surprised I even said anything to you at all. Guess I didn't feel right about overhearing you without letting you know I was in earshot."

She turned back to him, leaning against a post. "What broke up your marriage?"

Whoa. What happened to the code of the West? Was she even allowed to just come out and ask that?

"I want to know if I'm also talking to a guy with a roving eye," she said. "That'll be the third strike. Good-looking, smooth talker *and* a cheater? If that's the case, I'll cut my losses now and pretend we never had this conversation."

"Cheating had nothing to do it," he said, more grimly than he intended.

Unless you counted with vodka and gin. His ex had been an alcoholic, but he was hardly going to bring *that* up with this woman.

What he hadn't known until he'd returned to Bronco was that his ex-wife had died in a car accident six months after his disappearance. It hadn't been alcohol related. Dana had been trying to get sober and had lost her life to a random accident.

He let out something of a hard sigh. The pretty woman

he'd been talking to was watching him, waiting for him to…say something.

"As you can see," he said, "I'm great at flirting and small talk." He shook his head and rolled his eyes at himself. "No wonder I've been on my own for over three years," he added quickly, trying for a lighter tone. "But the single life suits me. Living on my terms and no one else's. Nothing to ask of someone. Nothing to be asked."

She tilted her head slightly, her silky hair falling. "Well, damn, that sounds…lonely, if you ask me."

He gave a slight shrug. But she wasn't wrong. "You make enough mistakes, you accept that you're better off solo. Cowboy. Lone wolf. But don't feel too bad for me. I've got a twin brother and we're close."

It felt good to say that. That first night he'd come home, back in February, he and Sullivan had stayed up all night talking, ruining Sullivan and Sadie's planned Valentine's Day dinner—a very special Valentine's dinner, since they'd gotten engaged that night—but neither had minded. Bobby had asked Sullivan if he knew anything about how they'd gotten separated at birth, if they'd both been adopted, clearly by different families, and Sullivan had told him one hell of a tale, which he'd learned from their estranged aunt, their mother's sister who'd left town and their lives soon after they were born. Sullivan had tracked the woman down with Sadie's help. They hadn't kept in touch, more owning to the aunt's physical and emotional distance, but Sullivan had given Bobby her contact info on a slip of paper. Bobby, true to his nature, and maybe nurture, wasn't interested in talking to the lady. He had the facts of his birth and the separation. He didn't need more.

It had taken Sullivan hours to come out and ask what happened the night Bobby disappeared, but Bobby just couldn't bring himself to talk about it. *You're better off not knowing,* he'd told Sullivan. *I'm better off not remembering.* And Sullivan had given him a respectful nod. What they *had* talked about was the family they had in common since it turned out that Bobby had actually been raised—till age ten, anyway—by their biological mother, and then his grandparents, while Sullivan had been adopted by another family at barely an hour old. There wasn't a part of their birth story—the how and why—that didn't have both brothers shaking their heads. That neither liked talking about it wasn't a surprise. Bobby tried not to think about it and did a pretty good job of it.

Bobby snapped himself out of his thoughts. "My twin, Sullivan, is engaged and his fiancée is a good friend too," he added.

He was so glad to have Sadie's friendship. They'd talked some about the past, about the ups and downs of their friendship, about his ex, her sister, and the two of them were solid.

"A twin," she said. "Lucky you. Though I do have four sisters and we're all pretty close in age. One's getting hitched at the Bronco Summer Family Rodeo at the end of the month. Chaps and spurs welcome."

He laughed. "My brother is getting married in December. I have no doubt I'll be asked to wear a monkey suit."

She smiled. "I'll bet you clean up well."

He held her gaze, their chemistry, the unexpected flirtation warming his heart and every other part of him.

Dammit, but he did want to step forward and touch her, put a hand to her cheek with the question of a kiss in the air between them. She'd answer with her eyes and step closer, their lips would meet and…

And forget it. Once she found out who he was, she'd regret this conversation and any kissing. He should probably say he had to get going.

Instead he kept talking. Because he could not drag himself away no matter what his head told him.

"The wedding talk is endless," he found himself saying. "I'll be over for breakfast at my brother's place, and we'll be having pancakes and bacon and debating whether Canadian bacon is really just *ham* and suddenly he'll ask if he should wear his dress cowboy boots or real shoes. As if I'd know? On and on. In fact, this morning, he called to ask if I thought they should offer a vegan option for the reception dinner. Apparently, they can't decide. I said 'Sure, why not?' just to shut him up about the wedding already."

She laughed. "Yup, same thing in my family group chats and group texts. My sisters and cousins and aunts and grandmother are all really independent women but they're in *love* with love. And weddings are all about love."

They might start out that way, he almost said, but didn't. He'd already made it clear he was cynical on that subject.

"You're a Hawkins, right?" he asked. "I saw you in town the other day mobbed by screaming preteen girls."

"Sure am," she said and he could hear the pride in her voice. "Tori Hawkins," she added, extending her hand.

He swallowed. He was expected to shake her hand and give *his* name.

He shook because he wanted to feel her hand in his. It was hard and soft at the same time. A woman who knew her way around reins and ropes.

But he didn't give his name.

He just…couldn't.

Bobby Stone. Yeah, that guy.

Even a newcomer to Bronco has probably heard about him. The man who'd faked his death for over three years.

He couldn't bear the expression on Tori Hawkins's face changing—cringing—when she put two and two together. He'd see the questions in her eyes: *Why'd you do it? What really happened in those woods, on that cliff? How could you let people think you were dead?*

Given that Tori had already demonstrated how blunt she was, she might just come out and ask.

And some things were better kept buried.

"Well, I'd better get back to work," he said fast, tipped his hat with a nod and then hurried around the corner and practically ran out of the barn.

Once again, regret being the story of his life.

Chapter Two

Jeez, was it something I said? Tori wondered, completely confused as the hot cowboy took off on her.

She shook her head and sighed, moving closer to her horse. "See, Bluebell? This is why I'm forty and single. And to think I was about to ask him out. When's the last time I did that? Years ago." She frowned. "Dang. There was something there, Blue. Right? I wasn't imagining it? He and I were really *talking*. Not about the weather or how great horses are. Really talking. And was he beautiful or what?" Those intense brown eyes with the hazel flecks, slightly long chocolate brown hair, the contrast to the fair complexion, his rugged jawline with the slight five-o'clock shadow… Yes, he was beautiful, all right. He was at least six two, maybe six three—long and lean and muscular.

Bluebell nudged her for either more conversation or another apple slice.

"Sorry, that's enough apple or you'll get a belly ache," she told the quarter horse.

She figured she'd wait a minute or two or three to see if her cowboy came back. She hadn't even gotten his name before he'd fled. Why had he left so quickly, anyway? She could see the interest in his eyes. On the long flight to Bronco from Australia, where she and her sisters had been touring in rodeos, she'd decided to find herself a summer boyfriend, an August boyfriend, a sexy one like the man who'd just disappeared on her. A real relationship just wasn't in the cards for her. Men made demands, like her second big relationship when she was in her early twenties. *If you loved me, you'd give up the rodeo and be happy because you have me*, he'd said. *You're gone too much and I'm expected to be faithful?*

Uh, yeah, she'd told him. *If you love* me.

She'd tried again, falling for an accountant of all things in her midtwenties. He'd surprised her—and not in a good way—by buying a small ranch for the two of them and tacking up a sign over the barn that read The Future Home of the Tori Hawkins Horseback Riding School. It was his way of getting her to quit the rodeo and stay in one place. Tori had never been interested in teaching riding—barrel racing maybe, once she'd retired like her aunts and grandmother, but that was a long way off. Still, she'd looked long and hard at that sign, knowing that her yes or her no to that man, to the life he was offering, meant something really fundamental. A person said yes to this or no to that and a future was built. She'd said no and back then it wasn't even hard, despite how much she'd liked the accountant, how touched she'd been that he wanted a life with her, that he was trying with that sign.

Because what *she'd* wanted most of all, was the rodeo and her family. Being a Hawkins Sister had her heart, had always been her dream since she was a little girl. All she'd ever wanted was to be like her mother and aunts and her grandmother. In the arena, her and her horse. Her own woman.

But now, as she'd told Bluebell, she was forty and single. Which really was fine; Tori liked her independence. Sometimes, though, maybe more than sometimes, she wished she had a partner that wasn't a horse. A partner to trust with her secrets and hopes, a partner she could turn to, a partner to share her everyday life and future with.

Since the accountant, there had been a couple more relationships, but they'd gone sour too and after that she'd kept her love life to a *like* life. Dating just casually. Sometimes she'd get so smitten over a man that she'd give a relationship a shot to see if it could go anywhere, but invariably the response was the same. *You're just not around... The rodeo comes first with you.*

She'd talked about it with her relatives. Her cousin Audrey, who was getting married at the end of the Bronco Summer Family Rodeo in a few weeks, had said: *When love lassoes you, that's it, you just know, and you'll both make compromises. It's not love if one of you has to give up your life.*

Her cousin Brynn, who'd gotten engaged and settled down in Bronco last year, gave a big nod to that. *Sometimes you find what you want changes*, Brynn had said.

Her grandmother—the famed rodeo queen and legend Hattie Hawkins—had pulled Tori into a hug and advised her to just follow her heart wherever it led. *The heart tells the truth*, Hattie had said.

Right now, her heart was in the arena and traveling all over the world—and in her side job, something new and exciting in her life. For the past six months, Tori had been writing articles for *Rodeo Weekly*, a well-respected online and in-print rodeo magazine with a huge circulation. Her pieces focused on women in rodeo, highlighting up-and-comers, champs and trailblazers like her grandmother Hattie. Between the rodeo and her side job, Tori was fulfilled. And busy. Was there time for a sexy short-term boyfriend, anyway?

For that guy who just hoofed off, I'd make time.

She gave Bluebell a long stroke on her pretty nose and turned to go. Her cowboy wasn't coming back. She'd find him again, though. This time tomorrow, maybe.

"Saw you talking to Bobby Stone," a male voice said.

Tori whirled around. Coming up the aisle was a blond man she'd never seen before, holding a saddle and wearing a diamond-studded belt buckle and expensive cowboy boots. He looked to be in his late thirties. He stopped and stood a bit too close to her, and Tori took a step back.

Bobby Stone? Was that the name of her cowboy? Why did it sound familiar? She tried to place the name, but the blond man was talking again.

"You're new to town—a Hawkins, right?" He gave her a flirtatious smile, his gaze dropping to her chest before going back up to her face. *Ugh.* "Trust me," he added, "you want to avoid Bobby Stone like the ole plague. After what he pulled?"

Tori heard footsteps and a throat clearing. Walking toward them was Deborah Dalton, the matriarch of the Dalton family that owned this ranch. She was in her sixties with ash-blond bobbed hair and a warm manner. It had been Deborah who'd given Tori a tour of the stables a couple days ago when she'd made an appointment about boarding Bluebell here for the month.

Deborah lifted her chin, staring down the blond man. "Is there a problem I should know about, Mr. Kennely?" she asked.

"No problem," he said, tipping his hat at Deborah. "I'm just *saying*. Warning the newcomer to town about a guy like that." He shook his head for good measure.

Deborah's eyes glinted. "We value you as a client who's been boarding your horse here for years, but we also value our employees who've become like family to us—such as Bobby Stone."

The man's cheeks reddened a bit and he turned and huffed off.

Deborah rolled her eyes and turned to Tori. "Ms. Hawkins, I'll just say that among the best advice I was ever given was to pay no mind to gossip and to make up my own mind about people."

Tori smiled. "I couldn't agree more."

But just what did her hot cowboy "pull"?

If her interest had been piqued before, now she wanted to know everything about the man with the intense brown eyes. She said another goodbye to Bluebell and headed down the aisle when her gaze caught on something glinting by the door. A watch. She bent down and picked it up. A man's watch with a round white face, roman numerals, black leather strap. Nice enough but utilitarian. She turned it over and gasped. On the back was engraved *Bobby Stone—2/14*.

She stared at the watch, at the date, wondering what it signified. Valentine's Day. Maybe it had been a gift from his girlfriend. She frowned at that thought. Given their conversation, she didn't get the feeling there was a woman in his life.

Maybe it was the budding reporter in her, but Tori was going to get Bobby's watch back to him—and find out what the 2/14 meant. And what he'd "pulled."

She *had* to know.

But more, she had to see him again.

A hopeful caterer looking to get hired for Sullivan and Sadie's wedding had dropped off a three-course feast for two at the home the happy couple now shared, and since Sadie was working at Holiday House and staying late to do inventory, Bobby got lucky with an invitation from Sullivan for dinner. He'd suffer through wedding talk and filling out Sadie's ranking sheet of the courses for a catered meal any day. He'd never been much of a cook, even when he'd had to be because his ex had been drinking and forgotten she'd put something in the oven or on the stove top. Quite a few pasta pots had been ruined and small fires started. Takeout had always been his thing. But a home-cooked meal? By a real chef? Oh, count him in.

And *especially* after a long day at work doing manual labor as a ranch hand, which he truly enjoyed. Sullivan was doing the same job at another big ranch in

Bronco—the Flying A, owned by the Abernathy family. The Abernathys had offered Sullivan a full-time job and had also put him in charge of installing wind turbines since that had been his line of work back in Columbus. Their jobs were now another thing they had in common.

When Bobby had arrived at Sadie and Sullivan's place a little while ago, he'd been thinking this would be a funny story to tell Tori Hawkins. Wedding prep palooza complete with little ranking cards for each course. But after taking off on her the way he had in the stables today, he had no doubt any interest she'd had in him—pre-identity—had fizzled. He frowned. He'd lost his chance with the one woman he'd found himself really attracted to. And his watch too. He glanced at his empty wrist as Sullivan heaped salad onto his plate. It must have come loose and fallen off when he'd been mucking out the stalls today. Or fleeing from Tori like a man with something to hide. Hopefully the watch, which had sentimental value to him, wasn't buried deep in straw in any one of the fifty-plus stalls. He'd stop in the stables and look for it later tonight before heading home to his cabin.

"This is good for salad," Sullivan said, taking a bite of the weird pile of various lettuces and colorful vegetables on his plate.

Bobby forked a bite. "The creamy dressing definitely helps." A little card besides the salad bowl listed the salad ingredients but Bobby hadn't heard of half of them—what was a sunchoke?—and he considered himself a man of the land, which included being appreciative of what grew from the ground and on trees.

He preferred the next course. A filet mignon that melted in his mouth, asparagus in garlic butter and roasted potatoes drizzled with olive oil and rosemary. This caterer had his vote.

"Will I be invited to the wedding with a date?" he suddenly asked Sullivan. He didn't know who seemed more surprised. Himself or his twin.

Sullivan peered at him. "You seeing someone?"

"No," he was quick to say, forking another delicious potato. "But I did meet someone today."

"Really. Who is she? Maybe I know her."

"I think everyone knows her," Bobby said. "Or of her. She's a Hawkins. New in town. Tori."

Sullivan nodded. "I haven't met her, but I've seen her with her one or two of her sisters. I think a couple are in town with her for the rodeo at the end of the month." Sullivan grinned and wiggled his dark eyebrows. "So when's the first date? I only ask because Sadie will want to know."

He eyed the last piece of steak on his plate, his appetite gone. "It's not like I could ask her out. I couldn't even tell her my name. We were talking for a while at the stables at Dalton's Grange and then she introduced herself. Instead of doing the same like a normal person, I turned and ran."

"You don't have to do that, Bobby. I mean, I know you feel like you do. That everyone's talking about you and whispering behind your back. But you've been back for six months, you're a part of this town. Give people a chance to get to know you again."

"I just didn't want to see her face turn all horrified

at the sound of my name," Bobby said. "It's a really pretty face."

Sullivan smiled. "She made quite an impression on you, I see. This is the first time I've heard you express interest in any woman since you've been back."

Bobby felt himself clamming up. Wanting to change the subject *and* keep talking about Tori at the same time. "There are *a lot* of Hawkinses. Must be something, coming from a big family like that. All those siblings and cousins and aunt and uncles."

"Yeah," Sullivan said. "Must be. Sadie says she and I will just have to make our own big family. You'll do the same."

"Whoa. I probably won't even see Tori again. We're hardly getting married and having six kids."

"Wilder things have happened, Bobby. We're both proof of that."

"That's the truth," he said, finishing the steak, his appetite back.

He glanced at his twin, who looked so much like him. Sullivan's hair was slightly darker, as were his eyes, and Bobby's features were slightly less intense, but otherwise, they could pass for each other, as Sullivan well knew. For the past six months, Bobby had thought a lot about how much he'd missed out on. Growing up not knowing he had a brother, a twin. An only child of a mother who was barely around and had taken off when he was ten, leaving him with his grandparents. His grandmother had been wonderful; his grandfather not so much, but he'd been a long-haul trucker and not around often anyway. And Bobby had never known his father. He hadn't even known the man's name until Sullivan had filled in him. Thanks to his brother finding that biological aunt, a woman named Michelle, who for some reason had estranged herself from her own family—and her nephew.

The story was wild—in a bad way. Their mother, Aubrey, only sixteen years old, hadn't known she was pregnant with twins; no one had. The father, Ken, who she'd been warned against but apparently couldn't resist, had taken off when he learned of the pregnancy. True to form, he'd been jailed shortly thereafter for robbing a convenience store. Pressured by her parents to give her baby up for adoption, knowing there was no future with Ken, she'd signed the papers but then changed her mind and wanted to keep the baby. Her parents had talked her out of it. They wouldn't help her, they'd said angrily. What kind of life could she give a baby at sixteen and alone with no money?

What everyone, including the doctor, hadn't realized was that *another* baby was coming. Twins. The second baby was sickly and not expected to make it more than a day or two. Aubrey's parents had told her she could keep the second baby until he "went with God" if she let the first one go to the good, loving family waiting to take him home.

The second baby was Bobby. Who *had* made it.

And Sullivan had gone off, barely an hour old, with his new family, who hadn't known about the twin. But his parents had never told him he was adopted, either. Sullivan had found out just last year when he'd found his adoption certificate in the attic while looking for some old photos. He would never have known about Bobby if he hadn't looked into finding his birth parents, leading to a genealogy website.

Sullivan had been very upset with his parents for not telling him about his past and he'd even stopped speaking to them for a while. But over the past few months, Sullivan had done some deep soul searching, and he'd worked hard to understand and forgive Lou and Ellie Grainger, who'd adopted him at birth and had raised in him in loving home. Sadie, of course, had had a lot to do with that. At Sullivan's invitation, the Graingers had traveled to Bronco from their home in Columbus, Montana, and the three of them spent some quality time together—really talking about things. Bobby had joined them a couple of times too.

Bobby had understood how Sullivan had felt. Bobby's grandmother, tough and no-nonsense but loving to him, hadn't ever said a word to him about having a twin brother somewhere out there, not even when he was grown. He still wasn't sure what he thought of all she'd withheld. Secrets. Abandonments. Estrangements. Fundamental truths. His grandfather had died when he was a teenager, but he'd only lost his nana a few months after he'd gotten married. Almost as if she'd hung on until he wouldn't be alone in the world without her as his only family.

What Bobby would have given for a brother growing up. Four brothers, like Tori had sisters. That must have been really wonderful. Having a big family, all those people who loved you and cared about you, built-in friends. People who'd be there for you through thick and thin.

Then again, what Bobby knew about family wasn't all that good. People just couldn't be trusted. Though Sullivan and Sadie had been proving time and again over the past six months that there were exceptions.

"You can easily find Tori at the arena in town," Sullivan said, forking a piece of asparagus. He picked up the pen Sadie had left and marked off a five out of five. The salad had gotten a two. The steak a five plus. "It's in the convention center."

"I don't know," Bobby said. "I've got baggage. Maybe too much. Definitely too much."

"What's definite is that you have to start talking about that baggage to help you let it all go," Sullivan countered. "If not with me or Sadie, then maybe with Tori. Sometimes it's easier with someone who doesn't know you."

"Doesn't seem to be easy no matter who it is. I'm too far gone, I think. Too cynical. You and Sadie are definitely meant to be, but that kind of thing is rare."

"Not every relationship of yours will be fraught like your marriage was, Bobby. You just have to give something—someone—a chance."

He thought of Tori's pretty face, her sharp brown eyes and delicate features, her tall, slender body in those form-fitting jeans and knee-high riding boots. But more, he thought of how easily they'd talked, how quickly he'd opened up. Talk about rare.

"So do you know if she's seeing anyone?" Bobby ventured, feeling oddly vulnerable.

Sullivan smiled. "I don't. I haven't seen her around town with anyone but her family. She's a busy one, I know that. Between her job as a reporter and practicing for the rodeo—"

Bobby froze. "Wait. She's a reporter?"

"Well, a journalist. She writes for a rodeo magazine. Sadie loves *Rodeo Weekly*. Just last night she was telling me about an inspiring story Tori wrote about an up-and-coming female bull rider who'd been told she'd never walk after a freak accident as a child and was now making a big name for herself on the rodeo circuit in a male-dominated area."

Bobby shook his head. "Just what I need. A woman who knows how to pry and get people to spill their guts. No thanks," he said, his appetite truly gone this time, despite the waiting course number three, which was red velvet cake. He pushed his plate away.

He wasn't even ready to tell *Sullivan* about what happened the night he'd disappeared. Sullivan and Sadie knew some of the basics, though. Last Christmas, the two of them had been walking in the area where Bobby had dropped the backpack, and Sadie had found Bobby's wedding ring, which was engraved with his and Dana's initials; he'd finally taken it off that night even though he'd been divorced awhile by then.

Sullivan had asked him if he wanted it back, and Bobby had said no. A chill ran up his spine now, and Bobby grabbed his beer and took a long swig, aware his brother had concern in his eyes.

He couldn't let himself start thinking about that night. Or his failed marriage. Or who he used to be. The months he'd been back in Bronco with Sullivan had been good; for the first time, he felt like he truly belonged somewhere. That was the only fresh start he needed.

There would be no romance. Certainly not with professional snooper Tori Hawkins.

Chapter Three

Tori couldn't get back to the small cabin she was renting near the rodeo arena fast enough. She hurried inside, took off her boots and beelined for her laptop on the desk by the window.

She sat down and typed *Bobby Stone*, *Bronco*, *Montana* into the search engine, but then paused, her finger hovering over the enter key. Was she invading his privacy? Should she wait for him to tell her anything he wanted to share with her himself? Well, when would that be? It wasn't like she'd necessarily see him again, though she did board her horse where he worked. Dalton's Grange was a huge ranch, with an enormous stable. He could avoid her if he wanted.

Dammit. Look him up or not?

He'd fled from her rather than give her his name in return. He was hiding something, clearly. And given the sneer on the blond man's face at the stables earlier, what Bobby had "pulled" was something big. Or just...unseemly.

She bit her lip and stared at his name in the search box. Oh hell, if there was something to find out about Bobby Stone, something searchable, like hard *news*, then she should know it. That wasn't gossip, it would be facts. Facts that were out there. She'd draw her own conclusions about it, about him. Like Deborah Dalton had advised.

Plus, she did need to return his watch to him. And if he was some kind of axe murderer, she should know that before she knocked on his door.

She rolled her eyes at herself—and hit Enter.

There were just a few articles. One from over three years ago, about how Bobby Stone, of Bronco, Montana, was presumed dead after a drunken hike in the woods, where he'd allegedly fallen off a cliff. A few days prior, he'd apparently sat down on a "haunted" barstool at Doug's, a bar in Bronco Valley, and legend had it that anyone who sat on that stool would meet a terrible fate. Tori raised an eyebrow at that. She wasn't particularly superstitious, but...

Another hit was a social media post last winter by a man named Sullivan Grainger, who'd discovered he had a twin he never knew existed and had come to Bronco to seek information. He had quite a tale to tell himself. He didn't want to believe his brother, Bobby, was really gone, but he knew he had to face the sad truth.

Then finally, another local article, from six months ago. *Bobby Stone, Not Dead, Returns to Bronco.*

Tori raised an eyebrow at that too, grateful she had

better headline writers for her articles. None of the pieces was in-depth, but she got the gist. Bobby Stone had faked his own death over three years ago, and news of a twin brother he hadn't known about had brought him home.

She was more interested in that latter angle than anything else. People who faked their deaths did so for one of two reasons, she figured. Either they were running from the law or they were running from their past. Nothing in any of the articles suggested Bobby Stone was a criminal. So he'd been running from himself, she surmised. *Wherever you go, there you are*, she thought, echoing one of her grandmother's favorite wise old adages.

She closed her laptop screen, then slipped her feet into her clogs and headed out, Bobby Stone's watch burning a hole in her pocket.

Don't let Amy or Faith see me and ask me where I'm going, she prayed to the universe as she dashed to her car. Her sisters were renting the cabins on either side of hers, and they'd want to know where she was going. The minute she'd say anything about a man—even just returning a watch she'd found—they'd grab her over to the picnic table by their cabins and want to hear everything. And there was a little too much *everything* to tell. Right now, she wanted to keep anything to do with Bobby Stone private until she made up her own mind about him. *Hat tip to you, Deborah Dalton*, she thought as she drove off toward the main road and Dalton's Grange.

When she arrived at the huge ranch, there were employees here and there as she'd known there would be, and asking directions to Bobby Stone's cabin got her what she needed in two seconds. Down the drive, left at the smaller red barn, right at the fork, quarter mile nestled in the tree line. Can't miss the weather vane of the wrought iron steer on the roof.

As she followed the directions, she would have missed the weather vane, that's how dark it had gotten, but the lights were on in the cabin. As Tori parked out front, excitement bubbled up in her belly at just the idea of laying eyes on Bobby again. *Oh stop*, she told herself. *The man has a major past. Just see what comes out of your mouth when you knock, see what comes out of his, and you'll go from there.*

She'd barely closed her car door when the front door of his cabin opened, his tall, muscular form stepping out onto the small porch. He had something in both hands, she realized as she stepped closer. A small paper plate containing what looked like cake. And a fork.

He looked very surprised to see her.

"Found your watch," she said, digging it out of her pocket and holding it up as she neared the three porch steps.

He stared at her, taking in a breath that he let out slowly. "Guess you know I'm Bobby Stone, then, since it's engraved on the back."

"Yup, I do. I mean, I didn't when we were talking— or when I found the watch. But then someone at the stables mentioned your name. And so I, uh, looked you up."

"Just like a reporter," he said. No hint of a smile in his eyes.

"No, not like that. My interest in your story was

strictly personal." She felt her cheeks redden. "I mean, well, I did make it clear that I'm a bit self-protective when it comes to men I'm attracted to." God, now her cheeks were burning. Had she just said that?

And now there *was* a hint of a smile in his eyes.

"I actually looked you up too," he said, taking a bite of the cake. "Meaning I asked my brother if he knew anything about you. He mentioned you're also a writer for *Rodeo Weekly*. I figured that means I should keep my distance from you since you'd be too good at prying personal information out of me."

"I've learned that people who don't want to talk *don't*," she said. "No matter how skilled an interviewer a reporter might be."

"Unless that reporter is so pretty and easy to talk to that a man finds himself saying things he normally wouldn't." He smiled and shook his head. "Like that," he added. "I shouldn't invite you in, Tori Hawkins."

Tingles danced up her nerve endings at the compliments. *Yes, invite me in*, she thought.

"Not even for a bite of that cake?" she asked, upping her chin at it. "Looks like red velvet with buttercream or maybe cream cheese frosting. Both of which are favorites."

"I'd tell you if I knew," he said, the brown-hazel eyes twinkling.

"You can tell me if it's *good*, though." Was this Tori Hawkins *flirting*? Yes, yes it was.

"Oh, it's good. Very good. So good. I really should offer you half."

"Agreed," she said, wiggling her eyebrows. Jeez. She was surprised she wasn't slowly licking her lips.

"Well, look at that. I should be worried. In three seconds you managed to wrangle an invitation inside and get half my dessert."

"Guess that's a yes," she said with a grin as she headed up the porch steps and followed him inside.

She looked around. "Cozy. It's a lot like the cabin I'm renting by the arena." There was a sofa with throw pillows, a low pile Western rug and a stone fireplace with a basket of dried wildflowers in the hearth. No photos on the mantel.

"Ah, now I know where *you* live," he said.

She smiled and sat down on the sofa. "I'm not afraid of you, Bobby Stone."

He held her gaze for a moment. "After what you found out?"

"I assume you had your reasons for walking away from Bronco three years ago," she said. "From what I can piece together, you saw a chance to start over and you took it by disappearing. But the call of family brought you home."

He sat down beside her, putting the plate of untouched cake on the coffee table and pushing it over to her. "I lost my appetite for it," he said. "Talking about that time turns my stomach to cement, even the good part about finding out I had a twin. If you're here to ask questions, Tori, I'm not interested in answering. I am interested in *you*. But not talking about what happened three years ago."

"Fair enough." She picked up the plate and fork and cut a bite. At this point, they'd both made it clear they were attracted. Each of them would do with that what they would—either by baby-stepping it forward or taking a giant step away. "Oooh, this is divine," she said, forking another bite of the rich, delicious cake. "You bake?"

He laughed, the sound so surprising that she laughed too. "Hardly. In fact, when I was at my brother's place for dinner earlier, enjoying a hopeful caterer's trial menu, complete with my soon-to-be sister-in-law's checklists to rank each course, I thought what a funny story it would be to share with you. This is a wedding cake sample."

"It's soo good," she said, taking another bite. "I should tell my cousin Audrey about this caterer but I'm sure the food details have long been settled for the rodeo wedding. The promoters are actually paying for the whole shindig so I'm sure there will be amazing cake and I do love my desserts."

Another easy smile graced his handsome face. "Ditto. Coffee to go with it?" he asked, getting up. "I could use a cup or three."

Oh, did she like this man. Yes, he had a big hazy past and yes, she had questions it would be very difficult not to ask. But he had a warm, easy smile, he was straightforward and her gut told her he was a good guy. "I'd love some."

When he left the room, taking his giant-sized presence and swirl of mystery with him, she had a teeny sense of relief. He was *a lot*. Not in a bad way, though. Not in a bad way at all.

That was her take on Bobby Stone.

She supposed that meant she was choosing to baby-step it.

* * *

Bobby was glad to see Tori still sitting on the sofa when he came back into the living room with a tray containing two mugs of coffee and fixings. He wouldn't have been surprised if she'd had a chance to think on what she'd learned about him and taken off.

He sat back beside her, watching her pour cream into her coffee and plunk in a sugar cube, stirring with a cinnamon stick he'd added to the tray at the last second. Sadie had packed him a cabin-warming bag of stuff when he'd first moved in there, and the cinnamon sticks—and the macadamia nut coffee—were from her store.

"Ah, good stuff," she said, wrapping her hands around the mug and taking a long drink.

He added cream and a cinnamon stick to his own coffee and sat back. This was nice. Having a woman over who wasn't his soon-to-be sister-in-law. Feeling this way…even the butterflies flapping around his stomach. What he mostly felt was awareness of Tori—and anticipation. Of what, he wasn't sure.

"So, I have to ask…" she began, slightly biting her lower pink-red lip. "The watch—the engraving. Your name and then a date—Valentine's Day. Girlfriend give you that?"

He'd have to be careful around Tori Hawkins. He already knew she was an asker. A come-out-and-just-say-it-er. He appreciated that, though. Didn't mean he had to answer. But the question of the watch was an easy one.

"February 14th is the day I came home to Bronco," he explained, picking up the watch and turning it over. "After three years away and living under a fake name.

On the long drive, I stopped for coffee in a touristy town and the general store had the watch for sale. It just called to me—time to start fresh, time to truly start over. The clerk asked if I wanted it engraved and I said sure. I went with my real name and the date I was finally coming home. To be honest, that it was Valentine's Day hadn't even registered."

She reached over and squeezed his hand, her brown eyes full of sweet things, like compassion and understanding. God, he wanted to kiss her. Or just hold her, really.

"I'm glad I found it for you, then," she whispered, her face inching very slowly toward his.

"Me too," he whispered back.

And then they *were* kissing. Her hands snaked around his neck, one of his in her hair, the other touching her soft face. He couldn't get close enough to her.

She wasn't the first woman he'd kissed since his divorce, but this was the first time he felt something more than red hot sexual desire. He liked Tori. He liked her and he wanted to get to know her.

But then suddenly she was pulling back, her eyes slowly opening.

Dammit. It was probably for the best, but he could have kissed her for another five minutes, at least. Her lips had been so soft, so warm, so inviting…

"What time is it, actually?" she asked, grabbing the watch and making a show of looking at it before popping up. A bit nervously. "Wow, almost nine. And I have to be at practice at eight a.m., so…"

He smiled as she practically raced to the door. "I get it."

"Yeah?" she asked hesitantly, tilting her head a bit.

"We're each a little…complicated," he said, walking over to where she stood by the door, her hand on the doorknob, ready to flee.

"That we are," she agreed, looking relieved and impressed that he understood. "I thought forty was supposed to bring wisdom. I feel like a sixteen-year-old right now."

"Me too," he said.

She held his gaze for a moment, her cheeks pinking. "So, I'll just be moseying along now."

"Thanks for bringing back my watch," he added, once again just inches away from her and reaching for the doorknob, his hand landing on hers.

She didn't move for a moment, then he could feel her twist the knob.

"Maybe I'll see you around," she said.

"Maybe you will."

With that, she was out the door and in her car before he could even step out onto the porch.

Yup, they both needed a little time to think. Were they going to actually do this? Act on their undeniable attraction? One night stands and week-long affairs had been as far as he'd gone in almost four years. But there was something different about Tori Hawkins than the women he'd been with it. He knew that already. And that meant he should back away. Walk away.

He was good at that.

He sighed, not sure of anything. What was right, what was wrong. What he *needed*.

Then again, Tori was here for the rodeo and would hit the road in a few weeks.

All this could really be was an end-of-summer fling. He just wasn't sure if that was a good or bad thing.

Because Bobby took things to heart, took things hard. Always had. He wasn't a fling kind of guy. And he couldn't imagine becoming one with a spitfire like Tori Hawkins.

So maybe he'd just better stay away.

As if he could.

Chapter Four

In the morning, Tori was showered and dressed and had just pulled her long hair into a low ponytail when there was a knock on her door and a "We come bearing breakfast!" trill from her sister Amy.

She opened the door to find Amy holding a bag from the Gemstone Diner and Faith carrying a cardboard tray with three medium coffees. Tori grinned and plucked one—they all took their coffee the same way, light and sweet.

"Just what I needed," Tori said. "I was about to brew a cup and make myself a bowl of boring cereal, so I appreciate what smells so good in that bag."

Amy set the diner bag on the counter between the tiny kitchenette and living room and pulled out the sandwiches. "Bacon, egg and cheese on an English muffin for you, T. Egg and sausage for me, and gross turkey bacon, egg whites and cheese for Faith," she added, wrinkling her nose.

Faith sipped her coffee and tossed her long dark braid behind her shoulder. "I love turkey bacon and it's healthier, so there."

"I'm just saying no one should mess with the perfection of bacon," Amy said. "Am I right?" she added, grinning at Tori.

Tori unwrapped her sandwich and took a bite. Mmm, crisp, yummy bacon. "Sorry, Faith, but she's right."

Faith laughed and rolled her eyes and they each took seats at the counter.

Her sisters never changed. Thank God. As Tori took a sip of her coffee, she glanced at the photo of the five Hawkins girls on the mantel of the small fireplace. Tori wished her other two sisters, Elizabeth and Carly, were here too, but they were in Australia on another rodeo circuit. They'd come up for the family wedding in a few weeks.

Tori might only be in town for a month, but if she was going to live somewhere for longer than a week, she liked having the comforts of home around her, and that included pictures of her family and the stuffed koala she'd had since she was three. Tori loved the photo of her and her sisters, taken by their mom in front of a corndog stand at a rodeo in Texas. The Hawkins girls were all adopted, different races and ethnicities—Tori and Amy were white, Faith and Elizabeth were Black, and Carly was Latina—but they looked like sisters. Their expressions, the happy, proud smiles, the way they each had an arm around the next, were all very similar.

They were a tight group and Tori adored her sisters.

Their mom, Suzie, had also been adopted and was one of four multicultural sisters, the original famed Hawkins Sisters. Tori's aunt Josie and her two biological and two adopted daughters, Tori's cousins, were another set of Hawkins Sisters. Tori and her siblings were proud to be following in the family footsteps.

Tori was proud to be a Hawkins, period. She loved being part of a diverse family. Even if the sisters and cousins and aunts *did* look different on the outside, they all had the same big hearts, love of rodeo, and love of family. Tori had always been grateful for them.

The three sisters talked and gossiped and laughed while having their breakfast and sipping their coffee. The three were in agreement that Bronco was a nice place to land for the month even if wedding talk dominated any time the relatives got together.

Amy pulled the orange velvet scrunchie off her wrist and rolled her long blond hair into a messy bun at the nape of her neck. "Hey, Tori, did you score an interview with Kacey Karrow?"

Tori shook her head. "I've tried to find contact info for her, but I've had no luck. No phone, no email, no social media, nothing." Not that she was surprised given that the former rodeo queen had apparently become a recluse and didn't grant interviews. "I'm planning to stop by her house today,"

Faith balled up her sandwich wrapper. "Tell us everything after! I'm so interested in her life and why she left the circuit at the height of her fame."

So was Tori. And so was Tori's *Rodeo Weekly* editor, whose eyes had lit up when Tori suggested a tribute piece on the seventy-five-year-old former rodeo star since Tori would be spending August in the very town where Kacey lived. Tori was hopeful her own rodeo cred, not to mention her being the granddaughter of Hattie Hawkins, from the same era as Kacey, would get her an interview. Hattie had said more than once that she admired Kacey, who'd been trampling over barriers to women in rodeo right alongside her. A woman bronc rider, skillfully hanging on for dear life on the back of a bucking horse, had struck a lot of people as way too dangerous *and* way too unladylike. Still did. But both Hattie and Kacey had persisted and made big names for themselves.

"What a trailblazer Kacey was," Amy said, scooting off the barstool and collecting their wrappers and empty cups. "Just like our grandmother. Kacey might even have been huge like Hattie Hawkins if she'd stayed in the rodeo. I wonder why she suddenly quit and disappeared to a tiny Montana town just when she was making a name for herself."

That was the question. Why? Tori certainly wanted to know. Hattie had no idea herself. Apparently not long after Kacey had left, Tori's grandmother had tried to track Kacey down and see if she could be of any help, but she hadn't been able to even locate the woman and then had decided to respect Kacey's choice to leave the circuit.

Kacey Karrow hadn't married or had children. Had she lived alone all these years? When Tori had first arrived in Bronco just days ago and had asked around about Kacey, some folks weren't even sure she did live in town. But one old-time cowboy she'd met in the diner remembered her fondly and assured Tori she did, way out in a cabin nestled in the woods with three dogs.

Since Tori was planning on knocking on the door, she sure hoped those dogs weren't big and scary. Pugs would be fine. Dachshunds. Mini poodles. *Note to self: bring doggie biscuits when you go to Kacey's.*

She was itching to delve deeply into a human interest story, especially about a legend like Kacey. Tori felt so lucky that she'd found this new outlet for herself. Six months ago, the big 4-0 looming, she'd started feeling a bit restless but couldn't really figure out why. She loved her life, and at first she wondered if it was about being single and that maybe she should start putting some effort into finding a life partner. But on one of those sleepless nights, she'd been reading her favorite magazine, *Rodeo Weekly*, and there was a notice of a contest: a seven-hundred-fifty-word essay on What the Rodeo Means to Me, and Tori's heart had lit up. She wrote an essay about her family, about Hattie being a trailblazer, about her mom and aunts and the original Hawkins Sisters, about the third generation of female Hawkins rodeo riders. She won third place in the contest and was offered a monthly column writing features about women in rodeo. That restless, unfulfilled feeling went away as Tori said an excited yes to the new opportunity. Turned out she had a way with horses *and* words.

"Another reason I'm hoping Kacey agrees to an interview today," Tori said before she could stop herself, "is because focusing on that will mean less time to think about the guy I met." She was surprised she'd brought that up, but Tori was suddenly dying to talk about Bobby—as the first man she'd been wildly attracted to in a long time and as the mysterious cowboy she'd already been warned about.

The room quieted. Two sets of eyes widened, then her sisters pulled her over to the couch and plunked her down between them.

"Every detail," Amy said.

"Where'd you meet him?" Faith asked.

Tori told them everything.

Faith gasped. "We heard all about Bobby Stone just the other night! Remember when we invited you to a fun bar we heard about, but you said you wanted to do some research on Kacey Karrow so you missed a really fun night?"

"Yeah," Tori said, her ears perking up.

"Well, we walked into Doug's bar—total dive but in a good way," Amy began, "with darts and a pool table and a supposedly very good pub menu. The place was pretty crowded, so we figured we'd just eat at the bar. We were itching to try their great buffalo wings. There were two seats available, a barstool and then one to the left of it, but that one was roped off with yellow crime scene tape. Weird, right? So I asked the bartender if we could use that stool, and he said, 'Oh, trust me, you *don't* want to sit in that seat.'"

Faith nodded. "Apparently, it's haunted. Legend says anyone who sits on that stool has something terrible happen to them. Everything from an IRS audit the next day to an air conditioner falling out a window on their head. Oh—and *death*."

Tori recalled a tidbit about the haunted barstool in one of the local articles she'd read.

Amy mock shivered. "But then a guy at the bar said,

'Oh, please. It's all baloney. Bobby Stone sat on that supposedly haunted chair, supposedly died three days later by falling off a cliff, and then shows up alive and well three years later. Come on. It's not haunted or bad luck and if it's the only available chair in the place, someone should sit their butt down on it.'"

Faith shook her head slowly. "Well, I said, '*I'm* not sitting on it.'"

Amy nodded. "And I said, 'Me either.'"

"And the guy said, 'I'd give up my stool and take the haunted one, but…'"

Faith laughed. "Crazy, right? Anyway, a couple got up from a table so we took that. The guy at the bar was still ranting about this Bobby Stone person, about how he faked his own death and then just turned up in Bronco three years later alive and well but wouldn't answer anyone's questions."

"And then the bartender said, 'Hey, Bobby's a good guy. And what happened is no one's business but his own, so let's change the subject to how great Montana State has been playing lately.'"

"Interesting," Tori said casually, as if she hadn't been hanging on her sisters' every word. "The bartender vouched for him?" That made two people.

Faith nodded. "Everyone shut up after that."

"I get why people want to know his story," Amy said, "why he faked his death, where he went. But I agree with the bartender—it's his business."

Tori was very interested in the answers, though. Not just basic curiosity either because she was so interested in *everything* about him. What did happen that night? Why did he choose to walk away from his life? Was it because of his divorce? And where was he the past three years? And what was the story about this separation from his twin brother? Had they been adopted by different families who hadn't told either there was a twin? Had the adoptive families even known that detail? Did Bobby know the story of his birth? Did his brother?

I'm not interested in answering questions, she recalled him saying. *I'm interested in you...*

A little voice inside her said: *He seems like a man who needs fixing*. Hadn't her mother once told her that men who needed fixing didn't actually want to be fixed? She'd claimed that it was more about the woman's need to caretake than anything else and neither would get from the other what they really needed or wanted. Hattie had agreed with a sage nod.

Yes, everyone had baggage. Especially at her and Bobby's age when they had some experience under their belts and had lived and loved and lost. But Bobby Stone's luggage did seem extra weighty.

Tori had never thought of herself as a caretaking type. She barely had maternal instincts. Now that little voice was telling her to stay away from Bobby Stone. But another slightly stronger voice was saying: *There's something between you two. Something that feels too big for either of you to ignore*.

Maybe Tori was overthinking when she barely had reason to. It's not like she and Bobby would see each other again.

"What's he like?" Amy asked. "The mysterious Bobby Stone."

Tori found herself suddenly smiling. "I like him. That's all I know. There's just something *there*."

"Ooooh," Faith singsonged.

Amy's blue eyes twinkled. "When are you seeing him again?"

"That's just it," Tori said. "I don't know. We left it kind of…nowhere. Like maybe we'd see each other around."

"Oh, you'll see him around," Amy insisted. "If you didn't kiss, it would be more of a maybe."

"Totally agree," Faith said with a sure nod. "The kiss seals the deal."

Tori hoped they were right. Because she couldn't stop thinking about him. Or that kiss.

Bobby drove the pickup towing a horse trailer into a spot near the side entrance of the Bronco Convention Center. The foreman at Dalton's Grange rarely asked him to handle a job off the ranch; there seemed an understanding that Bobby avoided town since returning to Bronco, avoided stares and whispers. But this particular request? His entire body had vibrated with the possibility of seeing Tori Hawkins since the rodeo arena, where she was practicing, was in the convention center. She'd mentioned she had to be there at eight, and it was barely eight thirty. Which meant she was here.

Last night, he'd tossed and turned thinking about their kiss. And how badly he wanted to do that again. And again and again. And then he'd think about how she tended to just come out and ask what she wanted to know, that she was a *reporter*, and he tried to put her pretty face and sharp brown eyes and silky dark hair out of his mind.

He'd failed. She hadn't pressed him last night on

what she'd found out about him. But she would eventually—if they were dating. And that was the problem—he didn't want to talk about any of it. The not talking about it would put a wedge between them. It wasn't like you could build a relationship on avoiding answering some pretty basic questions about yourself. Like: Why did you fake your death? What happened that night in the woods?

And how did you and your twin get separated from each other at birth?

Not that those were basic questions. More like very personal ones.

Tori didn't seem like a woman who'd be satisfied with nonanswers. Or answers that shut doors. Despite being fully aware of this, he couldn't resist trying to watch her in action this morning. Maybe he'd hang back so she didn't see him, get his fill of her, not that a few minutes of watching her ride would ever be enough, and then he'd return to the ranch.

The manager of the rodeo appeared by the horse trailer and Bobby opened up the back, handing over the paperwork on the two horses he'd transported from the ranch. Then he headed inside the convention center, a large building with the arena taking center stage now that the Bronco Summer Family Rodeo was just weeks away. There were several areas sectioned off for practice, but he didn't see Tori. He headed outdoors to the open arena, looking around for Bluebell and Tori's long dark hair, and there she was. He watched mesmerized as she skillfully and gracefully guided her horse around the barrels' setup with such speed and precision. One of her sisters—whom he recognized from the poster—was timing her.

"Great!" the sister said, her hair as blond as Tori's was dark.

For the next half hour, he watched Tori race around the barrels, unable, as usual, to take his eyes off her. She and two of her sisters then starting riding together, weaving in and out, gliding past one another. They were mesmerizing.

"That's a wrap for today," the blonde one called out. "Faith and I are getting massages. Sure you don't want to come?"

"I want to go over my notes for the possible interview with Kacey Karrow," he heard Tori say. "You guys go."

And then she was leading Bluebell over to the temporary stables where a cowboy like himself would pick up her horse and others later for the return trip to Dalton's Grange. Bobby had been given the rest of the morning off since he'd gotten up so early to help coral two goats that had managed to sneak away.

Once again, he watched her give her horse a pat and an apple slice, then her attention was taken by the workers across the arena unrolling a poster on a twenty-foot-high billboard facing inward. As they smoothed it across the platform, he could see rodeo star Jack Burris sitting atop his horse, facing Audrey Hawkins, sitting atop hers. *From Rodeo Rivals to I Do! Congratulations to Jack and Audrey, getting lassoed for life at the Bronco Summer Family Rodeo.*

"That's some billboard," he called over to her.

She whirled around, surprise lighting her pretty face.

"Well, I guess we saw each other around sooner than we expected."

"I'm glad for it," he said.

She smiled. "Me too. And yes, the sign is bonkers. Audrey and Jack were pitted against each other at last summer's rodeo, in like a battle of the sexes kind of thing. But they fell in love and decided to join forces instead of compete against each other. Their wedding is a little more public than most but they don't mind sharing their happiness with the world."

"They must be," he said. "Then there's me. As camera shy as they come."

He froze for a second, wondering what the hell was wrong with him. Was he trying to *remind* her that he had something to hide? "So you have a big interview planned for today?" he asked to change the subject fast. "Not that I was eavesdropping again—I swear."

"You so were, Bobby Stone," she said with a grin.

"Well, I was more watching you practice. You're an amazing barrel racer. Wow."

She beamed, and that touched him. She must hear she was great all the time, but she clearly didn't take rave reviews for granted. "Thank you. I appreciate that. For the rest of the morning, I hope to switch hats from barrel racer to reporter. But the former rodeo queen I hope to interview doesn't grant interviews."

He tilted his head, not liking what he was hearing. "But you're still going to try to get her to talk to you?"

"I'm going to try to make her feel comfortable enough to talk to me."

A chill ran up his spine. "Why, though? Why not respect her privacy?"

She lifted her chin. "I do respect her privacy. But I can still *ask*. Sometimes, when people say no, they still might like to be asked again, in a different way. To be invited to share, to talk. She can say no, and if she does, I'll absolutely respect that. But I'm thinking my background and family name may help her feel more comfortable talking to me."

"I'll tell you right now, Tori," he said, "I *don't* want to be asked about my past."

"Understood," she said with a nod.

Now he felt like a jerk. "Sorry for how defensive I am."

She reached over and squeezed his hand. "Here's the thing I get from you in spades, Bobby. You may not want to talk about your past, but you're honest. And I like that. A lot."

Phew. He hadn't blown it.

"That you can count on," he said, putting his hat back on.

She eyed him as if making some kind of decision. "Soooo," she began, "I'm heading over to Kendra's Cupcakes to pick up some treats to bring over to Kacey's house. I hear the cupcakes are amazing. If you've got a little time, maybe you want to join me for one."

Wow. The woman just asked him out. Maybe she'd meant it as a friendly trip to the bakery-café, but it sounded like a date to Bobby. And he was all for it. "I don't get into town much, but even I've been lured there by Sullivan and Sadie's rave reviews."

She grinned. "Let's go."

He knew, right then and there, that there was no turning back.

Chapter Five

When Tori and Bobby walked into Kendra's Cupcakes, she noticed several sets of eyes swing their way.

"Mommy, Mommy—it's a Hawkins Sister! Look!" a little girl about seven or eight exclaimed, pointing. The girl raced up to Tori by the door, her curly red hair flopping behind her.

"Sorry!" her mom said, hurrying after her.

"No problem at all," Tori assured her, grinning at her young fan. She dug her hand into her tote bag and pulled out a Hawkins Sister promotional postcard about the rodeo. All the Hawkinses participating in the August rodeo had signed it. She gave it to the sweet kid.

"Yay!" the girl said, beaming at her postcard. "Thank you!"

"We're huge fans," her mom said. "Our whole family is. Heck, our whole neighborhood is." She smiled and led the girl back to her seat.

"Interesting—in a very good way," Bobby whispered as they headed to the counter and to the end of the short line. "People seem much more curious about the impressive barrel racer than the guy who faked his own death."

Tori gave his hand a quick squeeze, and somehow that brief touch managed to send a few goose bumps along her spine. "It's so heartening how much folks seem to like the Hawkins Sisters. I'm sure Audrey's wedding at the upcoming rodeo has a lot to do with the excitement. And my sisters and I are a new set of Hawkins Sisters. Stick with me," she added, "and you'll have the focus off you in no time."

He squeezed her hand back. "I just might," he whispered.

More goose bumps. She smiled at him and he smiled back, and Tori knew without a doubt that they were on their way to somewhere. *Where* was a big question mark. But something was starting here.

The cute bakery-café was crowded, no surprise on a summer morning. Tori and her sisters had been here three times in the three days they'd been in town—that was how good the treats and drinks were. As they waited in line, Tori was so aware of Bobby beside her. She wasn't one to get nervous or giggly around a man who had her attention and interest, but Bobby really did make her feel like a teenager again with her first crush.

"Oooh, the cupcakes look so good," she said, peering ahead at the display case.

"They do. I'm thinking a maple cream cheese and then German chocolate for the road. Maybe I'll bring a big box back for the ranch hands at Dalton's Grange. Keep up the good will and all."

She glanced at him. "Has the good will been strained from you not answering questions about yourself?"

"Yeah," he said, looking down for a moment.

"Cupcakes will go a long way," she said with a smile, feeling for him. "You lost friends when you came back?"

Was she coming off like a reporter? Asking probing questions that were none of her business? Again, she really just wanted to know more about him.

He'd either answer or not. And that was fine. It would have to be if she did want something to happen between them.

He glanced down again. "I'd already lost my wife and then my closest friend—her sister, Sadie—to the divorce. But yeah, some guys I used to work with at Axle's Auto Repair—I was a mechanic then—kept their distance when I wouldn't talk about what happened. There were no invitations to Doug's like there used to be. But I'd always been something of a lone wolf anyway."

There it was again. The honesty. The willingness to put himself out there with her. There seemed to be a line he wouldn't cross, though—what happened that fateful night.

"You've definitely been through a lot, Bobby Stone," she said.

He was about to say something, but then the man in front of them got his order and left and it was their turn.

"Tori and Bobby," Kendra Humphrey welcomed from behind the counter with a smile. In her early thirties and a single mom of a cute little girl, Kendra wore her long blond hair in a low messy bun that Tori wanted to copy. Because Bronco could be a gossipy town, Tori had heard that the father of Kendra's daughter wasn't in the picture anymore. Couldn't be easy, raising a child on her own and running her own business, but Kendra was always all smiles. "What can I get for you two this gorgeous morning?"

They placed their orders, Bobby indeed also asking for three dozen cupcakes for the ranch staff, Tori selecting four—chocolate chip, pistachio, lemon drizzle and pumpkin spice—to bring to Kacey Karrow's house. If only doggie biscuits were sold here.

"Such a treat to have you in again," Kendra said to Tori as she boxed up their to-go treats. "My daughter and I are so excited about the rodeo in a few weeks. It's all Mila can talk about. She's obsessed with weddings and can't wait to watch Audrey and Jack get married. We're so lucky to be invited to the private ceremony—it's good to be a favorite bakery of the Hawkins Sisters."

Tori grinned. "You've certainly got all the branches of the family hooked."

"The rodeo and wedding is the event of the year around here, for sure," Bobby said. "Even the cowboys at Dalton's Grange have mentioned it." He shook his head with a grin. "'Former rivals will say I do and lasso each other for life,'" he singsonged. "Some days we'll be patching up section of fence or loading horses, and a cowboy will come out with that line for no reason at all."

Tori laughed. "If the promoters even have cowboys tossing around their jingles, you know this rodeo will be standing room only. Good thing I have front row seats to the rodeo as a performer, and an invitation to the wedding as a cousin."

Kendra smiled and slid a big box with the Kendra's Cupcakes logo on it toward Bobby. "Oh yeah, we've had our tickets to the rodeo for *months*. Now, Bobby," she added, "don't eat all these before you get back to the ranch."

He smiled. "I'll try, but they look incredible."

"And here's the rest of your order," Kendra said, handing Tori her box as a barista brought over their treats and coffees on a tray.

They found an open table in the back, Bobby taking the chair facing away from the room. He was quiet as he stirred cream into his coffee.

Tori took half of the scrumptious maple cream cheese cupcake they were sharing. "Mmm, delicious," she moaned when she took her first bite. "So you're going to the rodeo and the wedding?" she asked.

"I love the rodeo. And you're a special draw, so of course I'll be there. Sullivan got us tickets months ago too. I don't know Audrey or Jack, so no, I won't be at the wedding."

"Maybe you'll be someone's plus one," she said, suddenly envisioning him in a tux as she sat beside him in the pretty pale pink dress she'd brought with her for the occasion. Then she realized she was getting way ahead of herself and felt her cheeks burn a bit.

She gave a laugh to cover herself. "I mean, I've heard it's the event of the year. But seriously, it is truly amazing how Audrey and Jack came together after all that rivalry between them. They're so in love."

He glanced away for a moment, his expression darkening a bit. "I guess weddings make me think of my own and that one didn't exactly work out, you know?"

Her heart went out to him and she gave him a sympathetic nod. *Oh, Bobby*, she thought and was quiet for a few seconds. "I've got some real doozies in my romantic past. Nine tenths of the time I'm content being single. But then…"

"Then…?" he prompted, holding her gaze.

"Then all the talk of love and weddings gets me kinda wistful."

He mock shivered. "Not me." He took a bite of his own bagel, cinnamon raisin. "And I should be grateful that Dana and I didn't have kids. I wouldn't have been any good at that."

"Didn't have the best role model?" she asked.

"I never knew my father, so no. I wouldn't have a clue how to be a dad. And my mom split on me when I was ten. At least she left me with my grandparents. I did get lucky there with a loving grandmother." For a moment, he seemed lost in thought, and she wondered what he was thinking about. "But she's gone now, unfortunately."

"I got lucky in the grandmother department, too," she said, wanting to rush over to him and just pull him into a hug. She glanced at him, picturing little Bobby Stone at ten, waiting every day for his mother to come back, asking his nana if she ever would. "You sure haven't had it easy in the family department, huh?"

"Guess not. But I am grateful as hell for Sullivan. If I had to pluck a long-lost twin brother out of the clear blue sky, he's the one to get. Really good guy. He and Sadie both feel like family."

She smiled and reached out to touch his hand, the little electric zap not surprising her. She was so attracted to this man. On many levels.

"Meow. Meooooow."

Tori turned around at the plaintive sound to see a handsome orange cat sauntering right into the bakery, dashing between the legs of the couple who'd just come in.

"Me-owww!" The cat stopped and sat quite regally, looked around, meowed again and then seemed to stare right at Kendra who'd just handed coffee to a customer.

"Oh no," Kendra said, rushing out from behind the counter. "Shoo, kitty. No cats in the shop!" She opened the door. The cat hurried out but then turned to sit by the side of the door and peer in. Kendra smiled and shook her head. "That cat's been coming around the past month—I think Mila has been feeding him and that's what keeps bringing him back."

Tori laughed. "He does look well-fed. Maybe he lives nearby and is just taking a stroll around town."

Kendra pulled her phone out of her pocket, but then glanced out the window and sighed and put it back. "Every time I go to call the local shelter for someone to come get him, he darts off," she said as the cat hurried away into a wooded area. She threw up her hands and headed back behind the counter to tend to the line of people waiting.

"Do you have pets?" Tori asked Bobby.

"Nah," he said, taking another bite of his bagel. "Though to be honest, I've been thinking about adopting a dog someday. I don't know. I work long hours."

"Yeah, I wish I could have a dog but I live on the road." She'd have three dogs, just like Kacey Karrow.

A little one, a medium-size one and a giant. They'd be best buds and all sleep at the end of her bed, which would have to be a king. She smiled to herself, loving the idea of wagging tails awaiting her when she came home. Unconditional love.

"I feel like I do too," he said. "I mean, I live here in Bronco now, but there's something transient about a cabin on Dalton's Grange land that comes with the job. It's not home."

"Your cabin is nice, but I know what you mean," she said. "I live out of hotel rooms and Airbnbs and my relatives' places."

"We're a pair," he said, then seemed to freeze as if he definitely hadn't meant to say that.

In ways we really are, she thought. *You need a dog just as much as I do.*

Or that orange cat.

Or maybe just a friend. But there was nothing "just" about a friend. Because of her lifestyle, her sisters and cousins and aunts and mom and grandmother were her friends. When was the last time she'd had a confidante who wasn't a Hawkins? High school. And that was a *long* time ago.

"Friends, then?" she asked, extending her hand so she could touch him again just as much as to shake on it.

A dark eyebrow shot up. "I want to be your friend, yes. But—" He tilted his head, his gaze intent on hers. "I haven't been able to stop thinking about our kiss, Tori. I want more than friendship. More than chitchat."

She stared at him. Ooh boy. She could spend the day reading into that last line of his. Just how *much more*? "Well, I did say you were honest. But you know

I'm leaving town at the end of August. I'll be heading off to Australia for a couple of weeks, then back to the States to compete in rodeos in the West. That's my life."

He sat back and sipped his coffee, his brown eyes remaining on hers. He was thinking, she could tell. Deciding something. "So we have now," he finally said. "A few weeks. Maybe that's just right for the two of us."

Ah. *That* much more. Which wasn't all that much more.

Then again…

She sipped her own coffee to give herself a minute to think. *Just right*. Like the porridge and chair and bed was for Goldilocks. Cozy, comfy, warm. The rodeo had always felt that way. Writing articles also gave her that feeling. As did spending time with her family. But her relationships with men had been anything but just right. When was the last time she'd even thought about romance beyond an admiring glance at a good-looking man? When was the last time she'd felt butterflies?

You can do this, Tori, she told herself. *You're not some rookie—you have decades of life experience. He'd be sort like a birthday gift…*

"Just right," she repeated. "The Goldilocks fling. Not too hot. Not too cold. Not too big. Not too small. Just right."

He smiled. "Well, romance is a fairy tale. So, yeah."

"I don't disagree," she said.

Tori's gaze wandered from Bobby's gorgeous face to his chest under his green Henley shirt, over his muscled arms. Yup, being in those arms would feel just right for sure. And the way they so easily talked—about very personal subjects—and their chemistry…

Walking away from him wouldn't be easy, even if she did go in knowing their relationship was temporary.

Was she going to do this? Date Bobby Stone while she was in Bronco and then just ride off alone, back into her usual everyday life? They *could* both use some romance in their lives. Maybe this would be a nice way to ease back into the dating world. To recharge their batteries, in a way. They both knew it would end. No hard feelings, no expectations. They'd both be enriched by it and maybe it would help them open up to love again. He definitely needed that. And she...yeah, Tori could admit she often felt lonely.

As if she could resist the idea of more with Bobby Stone.

"I say we seal the deal with another kiss," she whispered.

His smile lit up his handsome face. Then he leaned across the table, his lips meeting hers.

Oh, yeah. Yes, yes, yes. Every bit of her body felt the electric zap from just the press of his mouth on hers. Everything about Bobby Stone had her intrigued. His past. His present. The way he was increasing the soft pressure of their kiss, letting her know there was passion to come. Passion that wasn't meant for a public bakery over a coffee and cupcake.

And in a flash, it was over.

But oh yeah, she had to have *more*.

Chapter Six

Fifteen minutes later, with plans to meet Bobby at the stables at Dalton's Grange tomorrow afternoon to go riding, Tori was on her way to Kacey Karrow's house. Her editor had given her a firm deadline for the article in a week; the magazine wanted to run it to coincide with the Bronco Summer Family Rodeo as a special online feature. Given how Audrey and Mike had become America's Western sweethearts because of all the coverage of their highly anticipated arena wedding, the Bronco rodeo was expected to bring in huge business from across the country. According to Tori's editor, Kacey's hometown connection, the mystery behind her withdrawal from the circuit and a Hawkins Sister writing the article promised to boost readership and hopefully subscriptions.

Getting hold of Kacey's address was easier than

Tori had expected; a simple online search for *Karrow, Bronco, MT*, listed an address from a deed transfer decades ago. Apparently, Kacey had grown up in the house she now lived in.

Tori followed the map app's directions and finally turned onto a dirt road marked by a mailbox with a beautifully painted sunrise over a mountain. A quarter mile up, a small white clapboard house came into view with a steeply pitched roof topped by a wrought iron weathervane, a porch with a padded swing and blooming flower boxes. Three small dogs, adorable shaggy mutts, napped on the swing in the sunshine.

Huh. Maybe Tori didn't have to worry about just barging in. Everything she saw suggested Kacey Karrow was warm and welcoming. *I'll have no problem meeting my deadline*, she thought as she grabbed the box of cupcakes and got out of her car. The three dogs bounded over, yipping their heads off and wagging their tails. She didn't even need doggie biscuits to make friends with them.

"Hello there, cuties," she said to the pooches.

They kept yipping in response. Tori headed up the three porch steps, the dogs beside her. Before she could even knock, the door opened and a rifle poked out at her, followed by a woman in her seventies who had the lovely face of Kacey Karrow, just more lined.

The dogs quieted and jumped back on the swing.

Kacey stayed in the doorway, the rifle aimed right at Tori.

She could feel her eyes becoming saucers. She took a step back and froze, her hands trembling on the bakery box.

"Private property," Kacey said, a long silver braid tumbling down past one shoulder over her Western-style shirt with mother-of-pearl buttons. "I'd turn and leave if I were you."

Tori held her breath for a second. "Can I leave the cupcakes? I hear you're very fond of them—from Kendra's Cupcakes. Four different kinds." Her babbling definitely belied her racing heart over that rifle aimed at her in such close range. Egad.

Kacey's green eyes narrowed. "Why are you here?" she asked, lowering the gun with a hard sigh.

"My name is Tori Hawkins. I'm a barrel racer who performs all over the world with my sisters and cousins—the Hawkins Sisters. My grandmother is Hattie Hawkins, who I'm sure you knew back in the day. Anyway, I also write for *Rodeo Weekly* magazine about women in rodeo, and I want to do a feature on you—the legendary Kacey Karrow, how you got started all those decades ago, why you suddenly left, your thoughts on anything connected to women in ro—"

Kacey held up a hand. "What makes you think I'd give an interview or want to talk about any of that? I'm seventy-five years old, Ms. Hawkins. I quit when I was twenty-five. But fifty years later, nosy folks still come knocking and calling and bothering me." With that, she closed the door in Tori's face.

Drat. Maybe Tori *wouldn't* make her deadline, after all.

"Leave the cupcakes on the porch," Kacey said through the open window beside the door. "On the railing so the dogs can't reach the box."

That gave Tori a smidgen of hope. "Could we talk

just for a few minutes? Off the record?" she called to-ward the window.

The door opened again and Kacey stood there, with-out the rifle, thank God, the stony eyes narrowed again. "What would be the point? Aren't you just after the story?"

"Well, not really. I'm interested in you, Ms. Karrow. You're a legend."

Kacey waved her hand dismissively. "Your grand-mother is a legend. She broke barriers and changed ev-erything for women in rodeo. I left."

"At the height of your fame. I must say, I do want to know why."

Kacey folded her arms over her chest. "That is no-body's business but mine."

"I suppose not," Tori said. She opened the bakery box and held it out. "Chocolate chip, pistachio, lemon driz-zle and a pumpkin spice even though it's August. Every year it takes me about a week to have so much pumpkin spice everything that I can't bear another bite or sip."

Kacey jutted her head forward and eyed the offerings in the box. She stepped out and closed the door behind her, then shooed the dogs off the porch swing and onto the rug at her feet. "Fine," she said, sitting down. "Off the record, though. And just for as long as it takes me to eat that pumpkin spice cupcake."

Tori's heart leaped. Yes! She'd meant what she'd said—she was interested in Kacey even if the woman wouldn't consent to an interview. And who knew—maybe the former rodeo queen would soften toward tell-ing her story. She sat down beside Kacey, who plucked out the dark orange-filled cupcake on its festive parchment paper.

Kacey took a bite. "Oh goodness, that is amazing. I've always had a sweet tooth. My si—" She abruptly stopped talking, taking another bite as if to swallow what she'd been about to stay.

My si, Tori wondered, her reporter's ears on red alert. What was *si*? Sister? Sitter?

She hoped Kacey would continue, but she didn't. She just took another bite, then leaned her face up to the sun for a moment.

Don't press, Tori told herself. *Follow her lead and just move on.* "Me too," Tori said with a smile. "I could eat that whole box in one sitting."

"Well, help yourself to one," Kacey said. "I don't want to be a completely terrible hostess. But feel free to take the lemon—not my favorite."

Tori laughed. "Don't mind if I do." She took the delicious-looking confection and sank her teeth into it, amazed she had the appetite for it after the one she'd shared in the bakery with Bobby.

Kacey sighed. "Well now, I'll have to get us some iced tea. Hope you like it sweet. That's all I have."

"I do," Tori said.

Kacey got up and disappeared inside, then came back a few minutes later with two glasses of iced tea. She set one each on the small tables on either side of the swing. "What's the rodeo like for women now?" she asked. "Same old crap or have things actually changed in fifty years?"

"A little of both," Tori said. "Just like you and my grandmother and my mom and aunts, my sisters and cousins and I speak up whenever we're faced with discrimination of any kind. Last year at a rodeo in Texas, I went off on a pack of good ole boys who tried to not only mansplain me but undercut my win. A few of them actually listened to my rant and took their hats off and apologized."

Kacey lifted her chin. "I'm very glad to hear that," she said, pushing her long braid behind her back. She stared out at the tree line and seemed lost in thought for a moment. Tori was so curious to know what she was thinking about. Her own past run-ins?

"Did sexism have something to do with why you left?" Tori dared to ask.

"Nope," Kacey said, popping the last of the cupcake into her mouth. She dabbed at her mouth with the napkin that had been tucked inside the box. "I mean, I didn't mind not having to deal with all that anymore, but it wasn't why I left. And since I'm done with the cupcake, we're through here."

Tori's heart sank. "I'd love to stay and hear more of your rodeo stories."

"I wouldn't," Kacey said. "Sorry to be brusque, since you seem like a nice gal, but I am who I am." She stood up. "That's a rare apology too."

Tori smiled and took a fast sip of her iced tea, then hopped off the swing, careful not to squish any of the dogs. "Well, I do appreciate that you gave me even a little of your time. It's an honor, Ms. Karrow."

"I prefer Kacey."

"Kacey," Tori repeated, honored to be on a first name basis but knowing better than to gush with this woman. "Can I come back sometime? Off the record?"

Kacey crossed her arms over her chest, and then her gaze seemed to land on Tori's left hand. "No ring. Not married?"

Huh. That was an unexpected question. "Nah," Tori said. "Just never found my person, I guess."

"Interesting," Kacey said. "I'd venture to say someone who hasn't married at your age, which looks to me late thirties, maybe even forty, hasn't because she doesn't *want* to be married. I was the same. Rodeo has your heart, huh?"

"Well, it does. But it's not like I didn't try," Tori said. "With men, I mean. I would have found a way to balance the rodeo and a relationship. But my boyfriends couldn't deal with my absences or the attention I got when I'd return." She frowned, wishing it hadn't had to be that way. "I met someone in town, though," she found herself saying, aware of herself brightening as an image of Bobby Stone floated into her mind. The brown eyes, tousled dark hair. The strong shoulders and the way he fit those jeans. How they talked so effortlessly. "He seems different. But I'm leaving after the Bronco Summer Family Rodeo in two weeks so it's not like our little fling can go anywhere."

"I see," Kacey said, looking quite seriously at Tori for a moment. "Well, I'll tell you what, Tori Hawkins. You bring more cupcakes, and you can come back and chat a bit. Make sure there's a pumpkin spice in the mix."

Tori felt her heart swell. "I'll take you up on that. You can count on the pumpkin spice."

She might not get her article, but there was something wise and shrewd in Kacey's sharp green eyes.

Wisdom. Tori did have her grandmother and aunts and sisters and cousins, but talking to someone who wasn't related to her, who had no preconceived notions or judgments? And a legendary rodeo queen from back in the day? Priceless.

Bobby stepped into Sadie's Holiday House and slipped his large dark sunglasses into the pocket of his denim shirt. He rarely walked on Main Street without his shades or Stetson pulled down low to avoid stares and whispers, and though he'd like to keep his sunglasses on inside the shop, it would just draw more attention to him.

He loved this place. Always had. While Sadie's shop celebrated every festival in the calendar, at Holiday House, it was Christmas year-round—the owner's favorite. No matter the season, there were always trees and decorations and racks of ornaments and interesting hand-crafted true-to-size reindeer for the yard or roof. Time stood still here, and Bobby found that a comfort. He'd returned to Bronco in February and it was now August, so he'd had six months of popping in to see Sadie every now and again, and he loved that though it was nowhere near the holiday season he was surrounded by Christmas.

He passed a table full of fall decor, lots of gourds and ceramic pumpkins. "Hey, Sadie," he called when he spotted his soon-to-be sister-in-law-2.0 pouring candy corn into a glass jar at the counter. With her long blond hair and brown eyes, Sadie resembled her late sister, Bobby's ex-wife. But the two women were so different that seeing Sadie never brought back memories of Dana. He was grateful for that.

Sadie turned with a smile. "Hey there. Want some candy corn?" She waved at the filled jar and scoop and basket of little cellophane bags with orange ties.

"My teeth hurt just looking at those little buggers."

Sadie laughed. "Are you here to invite me to lunch? I hear the diner has a crock of French onion as their special daily soup."

"Actually, I'm here to buy a picnic basket. Sell them?" he asked. "Regardless, I'll not only invite you to lunch, I'll treat."

Sadie narrowed her eyes, which were full of mirthful curiosity. "A picnic basket? *You?*"

"I picnic," he said, looking around for anything resembling a wicker rectangle with handles. He'd realized his mistake too late. He'd now have to explain to Sadie why he *needed* a picnic basket because she'd never stop asking.

"Um, no, you don't," she said.

"Okay, fine. I don't. But I'm going on a picnic tomorrow. A…friend and I are riding out on Dalton's Grange and I plan to stash a picnic basket out on a scenic spot."

Sadie's mouth dropped open. "By friend you mean a woman you're dating."

"Well, it would technically be our first date. Unless you count this morning," he added mostly for himself.

"I most certainly *do* count this morning," she said, her eyes positively twinkling now. "Because someone already reported seeing my soon-to-be brother-in-law kissing a Hawkins Sister in Kendra's Cupcakes. I said to her, 'Oh, you must be mistaken. That couldn't have been

Bobby. He's not seeing anyone.' But clearly you are. Tell me everything!" she said excitedly, eyes widening.

"Does the rumor mill ever stop?" he asked, shaking his head but with a smile.

"No. People like gossip. Especially good gossip like you making out with someone in a bakery."

"It was one kiss," he said. "And very unexpected. I, uh, guess I am sort of seeing someone."

He froze for a second as he realized it was true. They *were* dating. Even if temporarily. And that was a big step for Bobby Stone.

Sadie laughed, then laughed again. "You guess you're sort of seeing someone, huh."

"Fine. I'm dating Tori Hawkins. Just till she leaves at the end of the month. Nothing serious. Nothing to talk about. You can tell the gossipmongers they can move on to someone else's love life. So do you sell picnic baskets?" he added, taking a step and glancing around so Sadie would know he was done with this way-too-personal conversation.

It wasn't that he didn't want to talk about Tori. And dating her. But it was all so new—and felt private and special and very personal. He wanted to keep it all to himself.

"I sure do," she said. "A few different kinds. Right this way."

He followed her to an area with tables still set up for summer, with beach balls and brightly colored beach towels, and a few different picnic baskets.

"This one has everything," she said, opening the top. "Wine holder. Corkscrew. Cute blanket. Napkins. Melamine plates and wineglasses. Cooler compartment with ice packs to keep things cold—perfect if you plan to stash it and then go riding for a while. Containers for the grapes you'll feed her, the cheese and bread and sandwiches…"

Bobby gave a scowl at that but inwardly he was all over the thought of feeding Tori Hawkins grapes, dangling them one by one over her luscious mouth. The picnic basket was exactly what he had in mind. "I should take this one since we might be going on a bunch of picnics over the next couple of weeks."

The grin was back. "Good choice. And you get the *double* brother-in-law discount."

Bobby smiled and gave Sadie's hand a squeeze. Sometimes they joked about how he'd been her brother-in-law when he was married to her sister, and now he was going to be her brother-in-law again because she was marrying his brother. Whenever Bobby thought about that, he was always struck by how unexpected life could be. Like how until six months ago, he hadn't known he *had* a brother. Almost unbelievable. Sadie had gone from his friend to his sister-in-law to his ex-sister-in-law to his former friend to his friend and come December, at the *real* Christmas, she'd be family again.

She took the basket over to the counter and rang it up. "So, you really like this woman."

He reached for his wallet. "I didn't say anything of the sort."

She glanced up, regarding him thoughtfully. "I'm glad you're dating again, Bobby. Even if it's just temporary. A summer romance is a nice way to ease back into things."

He shrugged. "I don't know. It's more about her than easing back into anything."

She beamed. "So I'm right. You do like her."

"Well, obviously. Or I wouldn't be going riding or having a picnic on a perfect spot where the sky turns pink and orange and purple at sunset."

He liked her, all right. A lot. His big plans for them made that very clear—even to himself.

"Your brother's a romantic too," Sadie said. "Says he's not, but he is."

"And on that note, I'll take this and run."

She laughed. "Have a great time, Bobby. Seriously. Have a very good time."

He squeezed her hand. "I don't think there's any doubt about that."

Which was what worried him, he thought as he waited for Sadie to help another customer before they could leave for lunch.

Yes, he did like Tori a lot. And how did you just like someone a lot for two weeks and then say goodbye?

He hadn't really thought through this deal of theirs; he'd only known this morning that he couldn't bear the idea of being friend-zoned by her. He had to kiss her again. And again. And again. He had to touch her. Everywhere.

Hadn't he said he wasn't a fling sort of guy?

One day at a time, he reminded himself. That was how he lived his life these days. That was how he'd handle this temporary romance.

Chapter Seven

*D*on't *knock on the door with a smoothie for me...*
Don't knock on the door with a smoothie for me... Tori
silently chanted as she got ready for her date with Bobby.

A knock came at the door and Tori sighed.

"We're here with a smoothie for you even though you
said not to get you one," Faith called out.

"Chocolate coconut banana," Amy trilled.

Tori couldn't help but smile. Two hours ago, Faith
had texted her and Amy that she was in the mood for
a smoothie and was anyone up for a trip to town, first
to stop at Bean & Biscotti and then a little shopping at
that cute boutique Cimarron Rose that sold chic Western-style clothes and home goods. Tori had said she had
plans and couldn't and was relieved her sisters hadn't
pressed her on what her plans were.

They would want all the juicy details and she wasn't

ready to talk about those details yet. She'd barely talked herself into agreeing to a two-week fling, and her sisters would be full of comments and questions that she didn't want to get inside her head.

Tori opened the door to see Faith holding up her smoothie. "I'll put this in the fridge and devour it later."

"Hmm," Amy said, peering at her. "I see a little makeup. I thought the plans that kept you from going into town with us involved working on your article about Kacey Karrow. But maybe you have a date?" She wiggled her eyebrows.

A hot *date*, Tori silently mused as a mixture of butterflies and excitement took over her stomach. "First of all, my article on Kacey is on hold because she told me she'll only talk to me off the record."

"Oh," Faith said. "So you didn't find out anything? Why she left the rodeo?"

Tori shook her head. "I asked if I could come back sometime, and she said okay, as long as I brought more cupcakes, so maybe she'll change her mind and open up. We'll see."

"Does sound promising," Amy said.

Faith was eyeing her. "So *do* you have a date?"

Tori could feel a smile bursting out on her face. "Fine. Yes, nosybody. I do have a date."

"Oooh," Faith said, as she and Amy pushed past Tori into the cabin with excited gleams in their eyes. "With Bobby?"

Tori nodded, shutting the door behind them and taking her smoothie into the kitchen to pop it in the fridge. "We're going riding at Dalton's Grange."

"Romantic," Amy said. "Good for you, Tori."

I sure hope so, Tori thought. "Well, it's just temporary because I'm not going to be here long. He's gorgeous and we have so much chemistry. Yes, he's kind of a mystery, but my gut says to go with this so I am."

With big smiles and a promise to be called afterward with updates, her sisters left her to finish getting ready. Since the date was an early evening ride on horseback, preparing was a snap. Long ponytail. Riding gear. And yes, a little makeup. Her favorite sparkly nude eyeshadow, mascara and sheer rose lip-balm. Just a sparkle to her otherwise scrubbed-clean face.

As she got in her car and drove out to Dalton's Grange, she thought about how great her sisters were, that they weren't full of gloom and doom about Bobby Stone like that guy at the stables had been. Tori had long been an adult and if her sisters had reservations about his past and what they'd heard about him in town, they'd respect that she was letting herself make decisions about him instead of letting others warn her off him.

He was meeting her at Bluebell's stall. As she entered the barn, she could see him standing by her horse, and as she got closer, she heard him talking in a low voice.

"I stashed the picnic basket by the overlook," he said to Bluebell. "Too much? I figured we'd ride for a while and work up an appetite for dinner and then enjoy it while watching the sunset."

Awww. She slowed her pace so she wouldn't surprise him.

"Everyone likes a sunset, right, Bluebell?" he whispered.

Yup, she wanted to say and fling herself into his arms and kiss him senseless. So the man was a romantic.

She rounded the corner, the heels of her boots clicking, and she heard him whisper, "She's here. Talk to you later."

Be still my weary, wary beating heart, she thought. Did he know the way to that heart was through her quarter horse? As a horse guy himself, he likely did.

"Hi," she called as she walked down the aisle toward him. God, was he handsome. So tall and muscular and hot in his sexy jeans and black Stetson.

"I've been chatting up Bluebell," he said.

I heard, she wanted to say.

"Bluebell and my favorite horse, Bucky, are all set and waiting. Ready to head out?"

"Can't wait," she said quite honestly with a smile.

She led Bluebell out and down the aisle where his own quarter horse was hitched. Within minutes they were trotting out on the gorgeous property, with rolling green land as far as the eye could see, and the majestic mountain range in the distance. There were various ledges and inclines on Dalton's Grange, and at points she could see hundreds of cattle in the pastures. At a sunny and breezy seventy-two degrees right now, the weather was perfect for riding.

They rode for an hour, Bobby slowing to show her his favorite spots, such as one area close to the woods where the treetops created a canopy over a path to make for an enchanted entrance to the forest.

"And right beside it," he said, "is the best spot of all." He dismounted and so did Tori, then he led both horses to a hitching post.

She smiled. The guy thought of everything. "You put that there?"

Bobby nodded. "I come out here a lot. Bucky gets a rest and I stare out at the vista and horizon and it's like what yoga must feel like to some people."

"I do yoga every morning," she said. "So I know what you mean."

There were bushes to the side of the rocky cliff, not too high up but enough that she'd break a leg if she fell. She wondered if Bobby thought about the cliff he'd fallen from the night he'd left town over three years ago. If he'd fallen from the cliff at all. Maybe he hadn't. Maybe he'd just walked away. She wanted to ask so bad that the question was bursting in her throat. Not out of nosiness or even curiosity about it in and of itself, but because she wanted to know *him*. She wanted to know everything about him. Who he was, how he thought, what made him tick.

He reached between the bushes and pulled up the picnic basket he'd been telling Bluebell about. Her heart swelled. *This is who he is*, she thought. *He's a lot of things, obviously. Past and present combined. But this is his heart.*

"A picnic!" she said with all the delight she felt, hoping she didn't have too big a goofy grin on her face.

"I hope you like fried chicken." He brought the basket over to the grassy area by the ledge and set it on the ground, then opened it up and started pulling things out. A red-and-white blanket, which he snapped open and set on the grass by the overlook. "M'lady," he said, gallantly waving an arm for her to sit.

She smiled. "What other surprises do you have in there?"

"The aforementioned fried chicken," he said, pulling

out take-out containers. "Pesto pasta salad. A French baguette. Two kinds of cheese. Grapes and strawberries. And sparkling cider and white wine." A bunch of plates and utensils followed in the center of the blanket. "And no worries—I didn't make anything in here, so it'll actually be good and you won't get food poisoning."

Tori laughed. "Not a cook?"

He handed her a plate. "Actually I can make the basics. I think I mentioned that my grandmother pretty much raised me. When I was around five or six, she started teaching me. She'd always say, 'Now, Bobby, come watch how I make this meatloaf or stew or scrambled eggs so you'll know how when your mama doesn't come home for a few days.'"

Tori paused from opening up the box of fried chicken. "Your mom wouldn't come home for days at a time?"

He nodded. "She finally left when I was ten. My grandmother wasn't always well so she'd assured I wouldn't starve by teaching me to make my own meals. I never had the patience—or interest, really—to cook anything beyond boxed mac and cheese, though. I ate a lot of that."

"I can just see you, standing on a stepstool, stirring that orange concoction in a pot," she said. "I mean, I'm a fan of boxed mac and cheese, but…" Tori hesitated. "Bobby, you must have felt so alone."

He gave something of a shrug. "Well, I did have my grandmother. But yeah, I felt alone. My mother gone. Never knew my dad. My grandfather away for weeks, sometimes months at a time, as a long-haul trucker." He took the lid off the pasta salad and heaped a small pile on his plate, then added a drumstick. "You know, when I got married, I thought, everything's gonna be like a fairy tale now." He shook his head. "I couldn't have been more wrong."

"You were hoping for a traditional kind of marriage, you mean?" she asked. Tori was anything but traditional. Not that it mattered for their fling.

"Well, I don't mean wife in the kitchen and husband taking out the trash or changing the car oil kind of stuff," he explained. "I mean, the *relationship*. The closeness. Us against the world. Her and me, me and her. A unit never to be torn asunder. All that jazz."

"Ah," she said. That she understood. "I wanted that too until I realized I couldn't have everything. Sad as that sounds. And since the rodeo didn't give me any grief and relationships *did*, I decided to focus my life on the rodeo and forget about 'all that jazz.'"

"We're two peas in a pod," he said with a nod, his gaze warm on her as he ate a bite of the pasta salad. "A pair, just like I said yesterday."

Are we? she wondered. Tori wouldn't say she was closed off to anything. She might not believe in love and romance anymore or think she'd ever get married and have a child, whether biological or adopted, but she knew there was a door half open in her heart for the right guy to step through. Bobby's door, on the other hand, seemed open enough for a two-week fling and nothing more.

Then again, he sure was putting a lot into the start of that fling. Romantic picnic by the overlook at sunset? A stashed-away basket thoughtfully filled? She wouldn't have been surprised if he'd hired a jazz trio to ride out and serenade them.

No one is just one thing, she reminded herself. People were multifaceted. Bobby might be protective of his past and limiting his future, but his true colors were what you saw. What he was showing her. And those colors were sparkling and bright.

He poured them two glasses of cider and handed her one. "Did you get your interview?" he asked. "With Kacey Karrow?"

She was glad he'd changed the subject. His romantic side was both welcome *and* throwing her off. If she was "two peas" or a pair with anyone, it was Kacey. Rodeo background. Never married. No kids. But then again, Tori had a big family, and Kacey didn't seem to have *anyone*.

She took a bite of the delicious fried chicken. "I tried—hard." She explained about showing up with the cupcakes, the three dogs, the greeting by rifle and then the unexpected but too-short chat on the swing. "She never married or had kids. She's been living in that remote house for decades on her own."

"That suits some people," he said, scooping more pesto pasta salad on his plate.

Tori glanced out at the overlook for a moment. "I can't stop wondering what drove her from the rodeo. All those fans. Burgeoning fame. One of the first women in rodeo. I saw some footage of her and she was mesmerizing. She did say it wasn't sexism that drove her away."

"Maybe she got her heart broken, her dreams crushed and nothing else mattered," he said. "After all, love is the great destroyer."

Tori frowned. "Bobby Stone, you can't mean that. Love doesn't destroy anything. *Lack* of love does."

"Well, doesn't it always turn to that? First there's love and then there's a lack. A big nothing where there was once something."

"People get hurt all the time," she said. "First thing I learned in rodeo class as a four-year-old was to get myself back up if I fell down. That's my life's motto. It has to be. Every time I got my heart broken, I licked my wounds till they healed and tried again. I mean, here I am, right?"

"Well, come on now," he said. "This—" he wagged a finger between them "—is temporary."

She bit her lip. "But I'm here. And so are you. A fling or not, we're both here, giving this a real go. For two weeks."

That meant something. It was big for her and it had to be huge for him. She was here because she couldn't keep away. It was that simple. The man intrigued her on every level.

"Some people are just loners," he said. "They don't need love. Flings, maybe. Now and again."

Didn't everyone need love, though? Maybe she'd been okay on her own between relationships because she had the love and support of her family. The rodeo. Her side job at the magazine. She felt fulfilled. Sort of. She'd always been aware that there was something missing. But something she wasn't willing to chase after anymore.

Had she given up? Sure sounded like Bobby had.

But there was nothing wrong with wanting to be on your own, she amended. People didn't have to be paired up to be happy.

"Take Kacey Karrow," he said. "If she's lived out on

a remote piece of land for decades, she must like it that way. Doesn't mean she's lonely or miserable. She really just might be a loner. In fact, maybe she couldn't stand the limelight. Maybe she just wanted to be alone—like Greta Garbo."

Tori considered that, the iconic photo of the beautiful forties movie star coming to mind. "Maybe so. But she does have three cute dogs for company. Not that they can have a conversation beyond barking."

"I'm glad she has the dogs," he said, finishing his pasta salad. "Pooches are great company."

She gave a nod, going over in her head everything Kacey had said, which hadn't added up to all that much, but there was a story in that prickly woman. "You know, she started to say something—I thought maybe about a sister, but I did a little research when I got back to the cabin and I couldn't find a record of any siblings. I just want to know *everything* about her. Maybe her parents got sick and she left the rodeo to nurse them." She shrugged. "I'm just speculating."

"I like that, actually," he said, taking a bite of the drumstick. "Speculation. I always find it interesting to wonder about something, the different possibilities for why something is. A few of the cowboys here at the Grange once told me all the scenarios they'd come up with for why I suddenly left town three years ago."

She tilted her head. "Oh yeah? Tell me some of their theories," she said, noting that he brought the subject up. He had to be feeling more and more comfortable around her. To seem like she wasn't hanging on his next words, she took a bite of the creamy pesto pasta.

"The favorite among the ranch hands was that I was

on the lam—running from a crime the police hadn't even realized I'd committed. Murder. Double homicide, in fact."

"Yikes," she said, almost choking. "Please tell me they were far off."

He raised an eyebrow. "I assure you."

"Phew," she said with a smile, taking a sip of her cider.

"Another is that I slipped off the cliff and knocked my head on a rock and got amnesia," he said. "For three years. Until I happened to read that piece from Sullivan on social media about searching for his long-lost twin brother and it was so emotionally powerful that it knocked my memories back in my brain."

She grinned. "I prefer that to you being a killer."

He nodded. "Me too. But nope, no amnesia. I didn't forget why I left town. Not for a minute. It's what kept me away. And it's not like one big terrible thing happened, Tori. It was just…me."

She sucked in a breath, his words echoing in her head. She hoped he'd elaborate, but he didn't. "Can I ask you one question about that night?"

"Sure," he said in kind of a hesitant way.

That was promising. That he wasn't completely closed to questions. "If you hadn't discovered you had a twin brother—and one who'd come to town looking for you—would you ever have come back?"

He glanced at her for a moment, then out at the view. "I honestly don't know, Tori. But finding out about Sullivan got me back overnight. The brother I'd wished I had my entire childhood. Someone to go through all that stuff with, to talk to about it."

All that stuff… She wanted to know all about his

childhood. What his mother had been like when she had been around. How he'd felt when she'd left for good, though Tori could imagine, of course. What life was like with his grandparents after that. If he had cousins, aunts and uncles. If he even knew his birth story, how he and Sullivan had gotten separated and why...

She gave his hand a squeeze, keeping her questions to herself. "I know what you mean. Anytime I was upset about something, I went to one of my sisters. I didn't realize how lucky I was to have four siblings while growing up, but I sure know it now."

"How do you do this?" he asked, his brown eyes soft on her. "How do you get me talking? It's like some secret superpower you have. Sometimes I think I need to be careful around you and then a second later, I'm spilling my guts." He squeezed her hand back and didn't let go.

Then he leaned forward and kissed her, and she closed her eyes, savoring the moment, the setting sun warm on her face, his lips red-hot on her mouth. A moment later, he pulled his handsome face away, his eyes lingering on hers.

Now she leaned forward and cupped both hands around his jaw, lifting up on her knees to kiss him. He pulled her tight against him, deepening the kiss, then laid her down on the side of the blanket, his hands moving into her hair, his lips down to her neck, her collarbone.

"I could get used to this," she murmured, running her own hands along his strong back, wishing she could tear off his dark green Henley shirt and feel his bare skin, the rippling muscles.

"Me too," he whispered, then leaned a bit to the right and plucked a strawberry from its little container. He dangled it over her mouth and she lifted up and slowly sank her teeth into it.

"I like this picnic," she whispered back.

Suddenly, a few raindrops landed on her forehead and neck. "Uh-oh," she said. *You have crappy timing, rain,* she silently yelled at the sky. *Things were just getting started.*

She could still feel the imprint of his lips on hers. Of his body pressed against hers on the blanket.

Bobby held out a palm, a fat raindrop falling in. "There was no rain in the forecast. I checked."

The sky turned misty and the barest of drizzles began, the drops actually feeling good on her overheated skin because of how attracted she was to Bobby—and because of that incredible long and hot kiss. They both sat up and quickly put everything back in the picnic basket. "See that overhang there," he said, pointing to the right. "Beyond it is a small cave we can dash to. The horses will be protected by the overhang."

A cave in the rain on a summer evening? Oh, she was there.

Bobby led the horses over to the covering, tall trees at the cave entrance indeed providing extra blockage from the rain for them. He tied their reins around the tree, then they headed into the cave with the picnic basket just as a light rain came down. "I'll spread out the blanket," he said.

They had to hunch over in the cave, but it was a good size for their blanket, and once they were sitting, there was enough clearance even above Bobby's head.

He took out the goblets. "Sparkling cider or wine?" he asked.

"A little wine this time," she said.

He poured for them, then held up his glass. "To this," he said. "To now. And tomorrow."

Her heart gave a happy little leap at the toast. At the inclusion of tomorrow. Even if soon there wouldn't be a tomorrow for them.

She clinked. "To us," she added.

They sipped and held each other's gazes, then sipped again, finishing the bit of wine quickly. Bobby took her glass and set it on the side of the blanket with his own.

He looked at her for a long moment, his hand reaching for the side of her face. The tenderness in his eyes, in his expression almost undid her. This wasn't just about sex for him. She could *see* that.

It wasn't for her either.

This was a big step for both of them. Temporary affair or not.

She waited, anticipating his kiss, his touch.

Wanting him.

And then he reached for the first button on her Western-style pale pink shirt. She sucked in a breath, glad she'd put on her lacy white bra that always made her feel sexy. And the matching undies. She hadn't been sure they'd move so fast, but she'd figured she'd be ready in case they did. As the first button came undone, she could smell the dab of sandalwood perfume she'd dotted on her cleavage.

He was staring at that cleavage, giving his lips a lick. Another button opened, then another. Then he sucked in a breath.

"You're so beautiful," he said, his voice gruff as her shirt fell open.

Holding his gaze, she slowly took off the shirt and tossed it aside, then reached for the buttons on his own shirt. One, two, three, four, five, six. He'd groaned at the third. She could see him pulsating at the fifth. And when her hands touched his bare chest to spread apart the shirt, he groaned again, and laid her down, lifting up to take in her bra before his mouth trailed kisses along the tops of her breasts. His hand snaked under her back to unclasp the bra, and then his hands and lips were all over her.

Tori arched her back, kissing him, her arms wrapped around him. As he pressed into her, her nails dug into his back and he moaned. His fingers reached for the snap of her riding pants. She slid away, stood up and gave her hips a wiggle before sliding down the pants and stepping out of them and kicking them aside. She moved on top of him, inching down with kisses along his chest and the line of hair that disappeared into the waistband of his jeans. She unsnapped those and he moaned again, shrugging out of them.

And finally they were naked, the *tat-tat* of the rain the only sound other than their breathing and beating hearts.

He reached back into his jeans for his wallet and pulled out a condom, which she took, eliciting a low groan and the closing of his eyes as he lay back. She straddled him, her hand tight around his manhood, up and down, up and down, his sharp intakes of breath and deep-throated moans delighting her, sending hot pulses all over her body. She rolled the condom on him, and then holding her tightly he flipped her over.

"Tori," he whispered before he thrust into her, his mouth claiming hers so possessively she gasped. She met him thrust for thrust, arching her back, scraping her nails down his back, kissing his neck, his mouth.

"Oh, Bobby," she moaned. They both opened their eyes at the same time, the desire in the dark depths driving her wild before she exploded in waves of pleasure that obliterated all thought from her head.

Bobby lay on his back on the blanket in the cave, eyes closed, both he and Tori breathing hard just moments after the most incredible sex of his life, when he felt her slip her warm hand into his.

He froze. Except for his eyes, which popped open, and his hand, which went kind of…limp.

Intimacy during sex was easy. Intimacy after? Different story. For him, anyway. His throat was now tight, his head feeling both empty and stuffed with cotton. Was the cave suddenly smaller, the rough gray walls closing in on him?

Tori must have been well aware that he didn't tighten his hand around hers and move even closer to her as would naturally follow such great sex, though they were already right next to each other, their shoulders and hips and thighs touching. His body was so still, as though he were holding his breath.

She quickly pulled her hand away and turned on her side, facing him, propped up on an elbow. "That. Was. Amazing. *Amazing.*"

She's trying here, despite whatever the hell you're doing. Don't shut her out. Try back, he ordered himself.

"It was," he agreed, turning his head slightly toward her in acknowledgement, but then looking up at the roof of the cave again, as if the most beautiful woman on earth wasn't next to him. Naked. "Rain let up," he added, glancing toward the opening of the cave.

That was the opposite of trying. That was pure distance from everything they'd just shared.

Now he felt *her* freeze, her body stiffening before she lay back down, then sat up. There was a sudden chill in the air, despite the warm temperature and humidity.

Tori grabbed her shirt, turning away from him. "Is it me or did things just get awkward?" she asked while she put on her shirt and buttoned it.

Dammit, he thought, sitting up too and reaching for his boxer briefs, which he pulled on, followed by his jeans. He was going to screw this up. Already had. Despite being aware of that, despite caring that she was clearly hurt, Bobby's head was full of static, his chest was seized up, and he felt the urgent need to sprint out of the cave and gulp in some air.

Because a woman he'd just made love to reached for his hand afterward?

Get a damned grip, Bobby, he ordered himself. *She didn't propose marriage. She just held your hand.*

This was supposed to be a fling, though, he thought in self-defense. Hot and light, no strings, no expectations, just two people enjoying each other. But that hand slipping into his felt like she'd been staking some kind of claim or asking for something without saying a word.

Which was ridiculous.

Fix this, he told himself. *Now.*

Yet instead of turning to her and telling her he was sorry and trying to make sense of how he was acting, he said, "We should probably get the horses back."

He mentally shook his head at himself. A half hour ago, he'd told her she got him to spill his guts. Now he couldn't say anything that wasn't impersonal. Rain. Horses. *Back.*

As in away from here.

Her heard her sigh.

The sigh of disappointment.

"I'll be honest with you, Bobby," she said, turning to face him, now fully dressed. "I thought we'd cuddle and feed each other grapes and strawberries and swap stories about this and that. All fling-appropriate. Now, yeah, things are awkward."

Where words should be forming in his head, coming out of his mouth, there was just more static. He wanted to take her in his arms and apologize for being so bad at this *and* race away on Bucky. Back to his cabin.

What the hell was going on with him? Why had he closed up so suddenly? The past three years, he'd been with a few women. No commitments, no strings. He'd made that clear from the get-go. He could recall a sweet, sexy blonde resting her head on his shoulder after sex and holding his hand—tightly—and he didn't react in the slightest.

It was different with Tori.

And he knew why. He knew exactly why.

Because he felt something for Tori Hawkins, something that had him turned around and had him tied up in knots.

"I think I can find my way back to the stables," she said. "So, I'm just gonna head out. I'm, uh, meeting my sisters in a little while, so I'm kind of in a rush anyway."

He nodded.

As she started to duck out of the cave, he could feel her waiting for him to say something, anything. But he couldn't even get out an apology. He could barely accept that what he felt for this woman went beyond what flings were made of. And a fling was the deal they'd made, sealed with a kiss in Kendra's Cupcakes.

But Bobby had been undone by her hand in his.

Dammit.

Chapter Eight

Fool! Tori chastised herself as she rode fast to the stables and led Bluebell to her stall. *This is a casual two-week summer romp and you went and got emotional and Bobby wasn't having it.*

Was reaching for his hand some huge emotional commitment, though? Come on. They'd just had sex. Great sex. And she'd felt close to him. Connected. And since they weren't physically one anymore, she'd wanted to hold his hand.

She sighed again, shaking her head. Maybe she couldn't do this—have a lighthearted fling. This was supposed to be no strings. No expectations. And here she was, derailed by his…awkwardness. Well, really by his complete emotional withdrawal from her.

You're human. Don't be so hard on yourself.

But she told herself not to expect anything from Bobby, either. She got a little zapped, a little cor-

rected. This was a fling. Not a relationship. Nothing was
building.

No hand holding.

No looking to him to feel close.

Just fun. Picnics. And great sex.

As she slipped Bluebell an apple slice from the little
baggie in her jacket pocket, she glanced around, looking out the side window of the stable toward the pas-
ture Bobby would likely emerge from, but there was
no sign of him. He was probably still at the cave. Giving her the long head start. *He's making sure you have
time to get Bluebell settled and to leave the stables so
he doesn't have to make more awkward after-sex chitchat with you.*

"Well, hello," came a flirtatious, slightly creepy
voice. A familiar voice.

Tori turned and there was the man who'd warned
her from Bobby the other day. He was heading her way
with two other men, who turned for the next aisle where
a stable hand waited to take their horses. With a smug
smile he approached her, peeling off his riding gloves.

"Will Kennely," he said with a smile, his ice-blue
eyes running a quick glance over her form. "I'm glad I
ran into you, Miss Hawkins."

Ugh, *Ms.* Hawkins if he had to call her anything.

"I'll cut right to the chase," he said, running a hand
through his thick blond hair. "I find you utterly enchant-
ing and I'd like to get to know you better. Dinner tomorrow night? Anywhere you'd like. As a rodeo queen, I'll
bet your favorite place is DJ's Deluxe for their excellent
ribs." His gaze dropped to her chest for a moment like
the last time, then went up to her face.

She'd had dinner at DJ's with her sisters and cousins the first night she'd arrived in Bronco, and the food— yes, she'd had the ribs—was amazing. Still, a big *thanks but no thanks, mister* to this guy. "I'm flattered," she lied, "but to be honest, I'm seeing someone, so…"

Disappointment crossed his face. "Not that Stone character, I hope."

How dare he? "Well, actually yes," she said, lifting her chin.

He snorted. "You've got to be kidding me. A ranch hand who fell off a cliff in the woods at night, then faked his own death? What could *possibly* be the draw?"

"I have to be somewhere," she said. She waved over the stable manager and nodded that he should get Blue-bell settled for the night.

"When you come to your senses, let me know," Will Kennely called as he walked away.

Jerk. Tori hurried out of the stables and dashed over to her car, her heart racing. *Shake it off*, she told herself, taking a deep breath. He was just a big jerk.

You know what the draw is to Bobby Stone.

Chemistry. Attraction. A friend and a lover in one.

But not a "morning after" guy, as she'd learned a little while ago. Expecting him to be had been her mistake.

This is a two-week hot fling, Tori. That's what you said yes to. If that's what you want and need, maybe as prep for opening your life to the man you're meant to be with, or maybe to learn that you were right all along and you're supposed to be on your own, then keep your head straight and enjoy Bobby for now.

Yes. That. She would enjoy him. Their fling. She'd

find out what she truly wanted. Might hurt some, maybe even a lot since she was rubbed a bit raw from what happened in the cave. But she'd find out, right? Their fling would be a learning experience. *This is good for you*, she told herself.

Feeling a little better, she drove back to her cabin, unable to stop thinking about why she was so out of sorts about how he'd acted.

Because you like him more than you realized. Or more than you're supposed to.

So much for feeling better.

As she pulled into the parking area for the cabins near the arena, she noticed her cousin Audrey Hawkins, the bride-to-be, leaving big sparkly silver bags hanging from her sisters' cabin doorknobs. She had one more in her hand. Tori got out of her car and headed over. "Hey, Audrey," she called.

Her petite cousin smiled, pushing her long dark hair behind her shoulder. "Oh, good, Tori, you're here—I was just about to knock on your door. Faith and Amy aren't home. I wanted to drop off a gift from the rodeo promotors that they'd like us all to wear around town for the next two weeks. Honestly, you don't have to. Tell your sisters too."

"Should I be afraid to look?" Tori asked, taking the bag from Audrey and peering inside. She pulled out a pale pink cowboy hat with dark pink stitching that read *Jack Burris & Audrey Hawkins, lassoed for life! Don't miss the Bronco Summer Family Rodeo!* Two hearts bracketed the embroidery. Tori smiled and put on the hat.

"Sorry," Audrey said, rolling her brown eyes.

Tori laughed. "I think it's adorable."

And then Tori did something out of character. Her eyes got all misty and she could feel her face kind of crumple.

"Honey?" Audrey said, peering at her with concern.

"I haven't been in town very long and managed to meet someone I actually like," Tori said. "We're sort of dating but we both know it's temporary since I'm leaving right after the rodeo."

"And the tears…?" Audrey prompted, wrapping her arm around Tori's and leading her over to the picnic table a few feet from the cabins. They sat down on the same bench.

"He's somehow got me all turned around. You think you know yourself and then wham, some guy gets in there in two seconds and has you thinking too hard and questioning yourself."

Audrey gave a gentle smile. "Well, if it helps, you could be describing me when I first met Jack last summer. We instantly clashed. I should have kept my distance—I told myself to run anytime I bumped into the guy, which was often since we're both rodeo performers. Now we're gonna be 'lassoed for life,'" she said, upping her chin at the hat Tori wore.

Audrey reached up and gently took the hat off Tori's head, placing it on the tabletop. Tori stared at it, the hearts, the words *lassoed for life*.

Why was just liking a man always so damned confusing?

"Sometimes the right man comes in the strangest form," Audrey added. "He can seem like Mr. Very Wrong. But when you get right down to it, to yourself at the core, he can be very right. That's how it was for me. Maybe you'll find that with your guy too."

"It's just seems so…complicated," Tori said.

"Oh, I know all about that too," Audrey said. "I've realized that when it's the real thing, it just comes for you. Nothing you can do about it."

It just comes for you. "That actually makes me feel better. Like I just have go with it."

Her cousin nodded. "Yup. And then all of a sudden, you're handing out these ridiculous hats to family and friends and total strangers on the street."

They both grinned, Tori actually feeling better now.

Audrey's phone buzzed and she grabbed it, eyeing the screen. "Oh gosh, I've gotta go. Tori, you ever need to talk, just call me, okay?"

"I will. And thanks. For the hat too."

Audrey smiled and hurried to her car.

As she watched her bride-to-be cousin drive off, Tori stared at the hat on the table some more. *Lassoed for life.*

Would be nice, she vaguely thought, surprised she'd apply those forever-sounding words to herself. Hadn't she given up on that? Wasn't that really why she'd agreed to the fling with Bobby? Because she didn't think forever with the right guy was ever going to happen for her anyway?

And because Bobby was full of secrets and closed off and looking for a two-week romance and nothing more. That had allowed her to say yes to the fling. No strings, no expectations.

But here she was, eyes misty, chest tight, a silly tagline for a rodeo-promoted wedding suddenly undoing everything she knew about herself.

The man couldn't even hold her hand after incredible sex in a cave during a romantic sunset rain shower, she reminded herself.

He's not your real thing. Nothing's coming for you with Bobby Stone. So if you're going to have this fling, have it right. Light and fun and no expectations.

Why did she have to keep repeating that to herself?

Tori sighed. Maybe what she'd learn from her fling with Bobby was that she *did* want more. That she *did* want to lasso the heart of the man she loved and pull him in tight and never let him go.

That was what she was afraid of.

Nothing like mucking out a stall on the overnight shift to distract yourself from thinking too much, Bobby thought as he raked the straw on the floor. He and two other cowboys were working tonight, though Bobby hadn't even been on the schedule. He'd made sure he was free the entire night in case his date with Tori went overtime.

Instead, it had ended with a spectacular flop. He'd gone back to his cabin after she'd ridden off and paced for a good twenty minutes. Then paced out back another twenty minutes. Then went to the barn and stables and saw someone had called in sick, so he'd added himself to the roster and gotten busy. He'd been at it for four hours, trying to keep up with the conversation around him, his fellow cowboys' jokes and talk of the women in their lives—one had had a date go south last night.

Between the talk and the hard physical labor, Bobby

had been plenty distracted. Until he'd look over at Bluebell in her stall and be right back to remembering what happened earlier.

You blew it. Tori will be dropping by tomorrow—no, correction, she'll be texting *tomorrow—to dump you and tell you the fling is over.*

"She wants to know if we're boyfriend-girlfriend," Jimbo was saying, straightening up from where he'd been hunched over with his rake two stalls to the right from Bobby. He was tall and lanky with a mop of dark blond hair. "I mean, do things have to be so *defined*? I really like Maya. We were having a great time talking over dinner at DJ's last night, and then whammo, she wants me to meet her whole family at her dad's birthday party this weekend. Um, kind of early for that! We've only been dating for like a month."

"I thought you really liked her," dark-haired PJ, in his signature straw cowboy hat, called out from two stalls over on Bobby's left.

Jimbo let out a sigh. "I do but…" He stopped talking and rested his chin on the handle of the rake.

"But what?" Bobby asked. Both ranch hands were young, early twenties, and good guys. They often came to Bobby for advice and thought he was the "wise old dude" of the cowboys. Little did they know.

"My last girlfriend's parents didn't like me even before they met me," Jimbo said, frowning. "Once they heard I'm a cowboy they wrote me off as not good enough. I got dumped the next day."

"Not good enough? Why?" PJ asked, looking worried.

"They told her that cowboys were hard-living players

who couldn't be trusted and that I'd likely never have my own ranch," Jimbo said.

Bobby raised an eyebrow. "Well, none of that is true. Some of the best people I know are cowboys—and cowgirls. And who's to say you won't have a ranch of your own if that's what you want? Put your mind to it, you'll make it happen."

Jimbo brightened, then his face fell. "Well, now Maya's not talking to me. I texted her a little while ago to ask if we were good, and she said, 'no, we're not' with a mad face emoji. Now she won't answer my calls."

"Just because your last girlfriend's parents had a thing against cowboys doesn't mean Maya's will," Bobby pointed out.

"Yeah," PJ said, lifting his hat to run a hand through his hair. "You can't give up on something before you even give it a shot, you know? But you should probably know if you want to be exclusive."

Bobby stared at PJ. Dammit, if the kid wasn't dead on.

And it suddenly occurred to Bobby that a fling, a no-strings hot summer romance was as labeled and defined as Jimbo's gal wanting to know if they were a couple. Maybe that was the issue. No strings meant no labels, but came with its own definitions. Such as: *Don't expect anything from me. I like you, but...* But, but, but. What stood in the way of anything more than the word *but*?

Maybe if they just went with what they were *feeling*, they could both relax a bit more.

Or was he trying to rationalize how he'd acted earlier? Tori had gone with what she was feeling and reached for his hand, then got hurt when he'd gone with what *he* was feeling and retreated. The two had not meshed. *That* was the only problem.

And *that* could be worked out. Talked out. Talked about.

"You know what, dudes?" Jimbo said. "I'm gonna go over to Maya's place right now and tell her I'm sorry, I was a fool and yes, we *are* boyfriend-girlfriend, and that I'm excited to meet her family. I'll even ask what I should bring." He hurried over to the equipment locker and stashed his rake, then jogged out of the stables.

If only Bobby could fix his love life so easily.

Then again, maybe he could.

"Well, shift's over," PJ said to Bobby. "Want to hit up Doug's for a beer and wings?"

PJ had no idea how much Bobby appreciated the invitation. It would almost feel like old times, going to the dive bar after work, playing darts, enjoying a plate of buffalo wings. "You know, I would but I have a lady to apologize to myself," Bobby said.

"Good luck," PJ said. "I was hoping to meet someone at Doug's but maybe all this apologizing means I'm lucky I'm single."

"You're right and wrong at the same time," Bobby said as he clapped the kid on the shoulder and headed toward the lockers.

Twenty minutes later, with a bouquet of wildflowers he'd plucked near his cabin using the flashlight feature on his phone to make sure he wasn't grabbing weeds, Bobby arrived at Tori's cabin. It was just after midnight.

He stepped onto the porch and knocked, hoping he wasn't waking her. The door opened and there was the face he'd been thinking about all night. She wore a white T-shirt, gray yoga pants and fuzzy pink slippers with cat ears poking out the sides on her feet. Her long dark hair was loose around her shoulders. He held out the flowers, which she took and brought to her nose. "I'm sorry that I'm knocking so late. I wake you?"

"Nope," she said. "I was about to head to bed. But I'm glad you're here." She looked at the bouquet. "I love wildflowers—thank you. Come on in," she added, backing up and holding the door for him. He followed her to the kitchen, where she found a vase and filled it with water, then plunked in the flowers and set it on the counter.

"Here's the thing, Tori," he began, digging his hands into his pockets. "I'm doing this fling thing all wrong."

She tilted her head, a smile forming. "Me too. Obviously."

He appreciated the smile, that she was willing to talk. That he hadn't completely blown it. "It occurred to me while talking to two very young, smart cowboys at Dalton's Grange a little while ago, that calling what's between us a fling is asking for trouble. I think we should just go with the flow."

"The flow?" she asked.

"Let's just see each other and go from there. No labels."

"Ah," she said, the sparkle back in her eyes. "Huh. Maybe you have a point, Bobby. Maybe it *is* the labels that bring the trouble. Supposed to feel this or not. Supposed to be this or not."

"Exactly."

"We know only one concrete thing," she said. "That in two weeks, I'm leaving town, leaving the *country*.

So yes, let's just see each other. And yes, go from there, knowing what we know."

He stepped closer and held out his arms and she walked into them. "I do know one more thing about us," he said. "That I want this."

"Me too," she whispered.

"So tomorrow night, if you're free, I'd like to make you dinner—maybe that childhood mac and cheese I was telling you about since it's all I've really mastered."

Whoa. Why had he offered to cook *that* of all things? Was he asking to be hit with who-knew-what kind of memories while he was with Tori? Granted, it was just boxed mac and cheese, and he'd been making it for himself for decades now. The orange processed goodness didn't often make him think of anything but how much the stuff hit the spot.

"I'd like that, Bobby."

"It's a date then. Seven o'clock? My stove top is on the blink, which I discovered this morning while trying to fry up some bacon. I'll bring the fixings here, if that's all right?"

She nodded. "Can't wait."

"Same," he said, a warmth spreading through his chest.

And then he was heading back to his pickup, all too aware that he felt more for Tori Hawkins than he could process.

Maybe that would work with their no-labels romance, if he was allowed to call it even that. As he started the truck, he realized with a tiny bolt of lightning that he and Tori were simply *dating*. An innocuous enough term. Dating with an expiration. All he had to do was remember that important detail and he should be absolutely fine with holding hands after sex. Cuddling. Or whatever else added up to intimacy. Because it would all come to a bittersweet end and that would be that.

Chapter Nine

The next afternoon, Tori was on her way to Kacey Karrow's house with another box of cupcakes, including two pumpkin spice. She'd spent a few hours at the arena this morning, practicing with her sisters and cousins, her times consistently three seconds slower than yesterday's practice and almost five seconds slower than her best. Not good. At all. The local coach she and her sisters had hired for the lead-up to the rodeo had shaken her head more than once, yelling at Tori to "get her head in the game." Which of course had elicited a few stares from her sisters, who seemed more concerned about Tori than about her times.

Time, speed in barrel racing was everything.

Usually Tori could block out anything going on in her life when she was in the arena, when it was her and Bluebell doing their clover-leaf pattern, speeding around the three barrels like one unit. Not today. Which was strange, she thought, as she approached the turn for Kacey's house. It wasn't as if she and Bobby were still in the awkward aftermath of their rendezvous in the cave. He'd come over with wildflowers last night, they'd made up quite beautifully and they had a date tonight, one that she was very much looking forward to. So why had she been so distracted in the arena all morning?

Maybe Kacey could help her figure it out.

As Tori headed up the long drive to the house, she could see Kacey standing on the porch at an easel, a paintbrush in her hand. When she parked, the dogs that had been on the porch swing jumped off and dashed over to her car, and Kacey scowled at her.

Uh-oh. Tori got out of her car with the box of cupcakes, hoping the offering would turn that frown of Kacey's upside down.

"They were napping and being perfectly still models until you showed up," Kacey said, but her tone was light, a chuckle in her voice. She set down the paintbrush on the rim of the easel and took off the smock she was wearing, hanging it on the back of the easel. Her long silver hair was in a braid down her back, and she wore a plaid Western shirt and blue jeans.

"Sorry," Tori said, walking up the steps, dogs at her feet.

"Did I introduce them last time?" Kacey asked. "The mostly brown one is Pumpkin, the lightest one is Taffy and the black-and-white is Cutie."

Tori laughed. "I love their names." The woman was a constant surprise. Tori hadn't taken Kacey for someone who'd call her dog Cutie. "And speaking of pumpkin, there are two pumpkin spice in here. Plus three others."

"Wonderful. I'm about ready for a break anyway," Kacey said. "Come on in and I'll make us a pot of coffee."

Tori's heart lit up. Yes! An invitation *inside*. And coffee too.

Kacey held the door open, and Tori stepped in, amazed at how warm and cozy the small house was. The walls were a soft white, paintings on almost every available space.

"Wow," Tori said. "Did you do all of these?" She went up to the long wall in the living room, where at least ten paintings hung above the ecru-colored sofa. Most were of a similar style that immediately spoke to Tori, a sort of abstract, whimsical quality to people and boats and bodies of water, the colors soft and hazy.

Kacey nodded. "Many of the paintings hung up are mine, but I've bought quite a few over the years. I have my favorite local artists and like to support them. I paint under a pseudonym so that there are no ties to my former life, no preconceived notions, no interest in the works just because I used to be a rodeo queen. I do pretty well even though I keep my favorites."

Wow, Kacey was also an artist—and a very good one. No wonder she was able to live here all these decades on her own. She had her art, which had to be very fulfilling, and which brought in money. "I have to admit, Kacey, I want to know everything about you. You've lived such a fascinating life and have such an interesting perspective."

"Eh," Kacey said. "I'm just me. Come into the kitchen.

I'll put on the coffee. And you can tell me what's wrong." She paused when Tori stopped in her tracks, surprised it showed. "I can see you're tense."

Tori let out a sigh. "I am. My times were bad this morning at the arena. I'm distracted and that's unusual for me."

Kacey gestured at the round table by the window, and Tori sat, admiring the paintings along the wall, many of them still lifes in that same appealing style. As Kacey made coffee and got out mugs and plates, Tori got up and looked closely at the art, admiring Kacey's work.

"I never thought I'd do anything other than perform in rodeos," Tori said, moving over to a beautiful still life of three pears, the final one on its side, a sliver of sunlight hitting it. "I mean, I've been involved in the rodeo since I was four, taking classes, competing in the pee wee groups. And I love it and don't plan to retire anytime soon. But when I started writing for *Rodeo Weekly*, I realized how fulfilling I actually find it. I really enjoy interviewing people, learning what makes them tick, their processes, their hopes and dreams. And then with all that swirling in my head and heart, I sit down and start writing and it just seems to flow out of me. I really love it. And then to see my work in print— that never gets old. It's so thrilling every time a new issue of the magazine comes out or the online edition is updated with new content that I've contributed to."

Kacey came over with a tray holding coffee and fixings and plates, then sat down across from Tori. "I know just what you mean," she said. "You won't be writing about me, though. I mean, you *could*, of course. I wouldn't be able to stop you, but I won't be granting an interview."

She sounded pretty set on that. "If you prefer I don't write about you at all, I won't," Tori said. "You have my word."

Kacey held her gaze. "I do prefer it."

Drat. Tori took a sip of her coffee, disappointment jabbing her in the stomach. She'd been so hoping Kacey would grant her the interview, open up to her, share her story with not just Tori but all the people out there who'd never forgotten her. The refusal made Tori all the more curious about what went on all these years ago that had led to Kacey leaving the rodeo for good. Why, why, why?

Tori decided right then she'd better just accept it instead of keep hoping Kacey would change her mind; Tori didn't think she would. "Well, then everything is off the record. That's a promise."

Kacey nodded and took a pumpkin cupcake from the box. "So what has you all distracted? The man you're having the fling with? The one who seems different?"

Tori tilted her head. Interesting that Kacey remembered everything Tori had said about Bobby. "Yup. Well, we decided to take all the labels of what we are off the table. We're just…going with the flow."

"And that messed with your times this morning?" Kacey asked, her eyebrow raised as she took a sip of her coffee.

"I just can't stop thinking about him. Everything about him. And how we relate to each other, our chemistry. We had the most incredible date last night and then it got very awkward and then it was all better and

now we're having a date tonight. I'm a mix of butterflies and excitement and anticipation and flat-out fear."

"Because you like him so much?" Kacey asked, biting into her cupcake.

Tori nodded. "I'm not supposed to. Though even that
isn't really a rule anymore since we're no longer necessarily having a fling, just a romance until I leave. Which
I suppose is still a fling." No wonder this was confusing.

Kacey was regarding her, and Tori wondered what
she was thinking. She wanted to know about *Kacey*'s
romances—if there were any. "What about this guy is
so worthy of your attention? What makes him different, as you said he was?"

"Do you read local news?" Tori asked.

"Sure. I get the paper delivered every morning, actually."

"Do you recall reading about a man named Bobby
Stone, who supposedly died in a fall off a cliff in the
woods but who actually faked his death for three years
and only came back to Bronco because he'd learned that
he had a twin brother he never knew existed?"

"I was mesmerized by that story," Kacey said, taking
another sip of her coffee. "I still remember the headline:
Bobby Stone, Not Dead, Returns to Bronco."

"Well, that's my guy."

Kacey's eyes widened. "Is he tightlipped about his
past?"

"Very. He says he won't answer questions about what
happened the night he walked away from Bronco and
let everyone think he was dead."

"Is that what has you distracted?" Kacey asked.

"That you're so smitten with someone who won't open up to you about who he is?"

"Well, that's the thing. I'm not sure I have to know. What matters is who he is now, right? The man he is now. He's very honest when he does share something with me. But whatever made him give up on himself, walk away from Bobby Stone and his former life—that seems to still have a hold on him."

"I'm sure it does," Kacey said. "You know, when I walked away from the rodeo, I didn't talk about it, either. I said goodbye to that life, to the woman I'd been, and I moved back to Bronco and took up painting, and adopted a few dogs, who make wonderful companions. In fifty years, I've never talked about why I left the circuit."

Tori bit her lip. "Because it was too painful?"

"It was just complicated. Very complicated. Much like Bobby's past is to him."

Tell me about the complications, Tori wanted to shout. At both Kacey *and* Bobby even though he was miles away from here. *Tell me how. What was complicated? What happened?* But she knew if Kacey Karrow hadn't talked about why in fifty years, she certainly wouldn't start now.

Bobby might be more likely to come around with his past.

"I did date a little," Kacey said. "A few times a year, maybe for a few years when I moved back here. But they all said the same thing. That I was hard to get to know. That I was secretive. That if I couldn't open up about my past I must not trust them or love them. Blah, blah, blah."

No, not blah, blah, blah, Tori thought. She could imagine how frustrated the men in Kacey's life must have been when she wouldn't open up to them. How could you have a relationship that way? A whole world hidden inside Kacey, off-limits.

Huh. Maybe it was important to her that Bobby share the fundamental things about himself. Who he was had everything to do with who he was now.

Kacey sipped her coffee. "But I suppose you and Bobby won't run into those problems because, as you said, you both know it's ending soon. You're leaving and that'll be that."

Tori bit her lip and took a long drink of her coffee too. "We already have those problems," she admitted.

"Ah," Kacey said. "Maybe he will open up. Anything's possible, after all."

"You haven't in fifty years and have no plans to," Tori reminded her.

Kacey had been about to pop the last piece of cupcake in her mouth but put it down on the plate. "I'm just saying you never know, Tori."

"Bobby seems resolute on that subject," she said. "He almost didn't want anything to do with me after finding out I'm a journalist on the side."

"Seems *wanting* a lot to do with you has more weight. That's a good sign."

Tori brightened at that. "Then there's the matter of me liking him a bit too much for my own good."

"If you want my advice, and it's as clichéd as they come—follow your heart. I did."

Tori felt her eyes widen. "You did?" Her heart led her back home? To an empty house? No rodeo? She'd said she'd dated unsuccessfully so it definitely wasn't a big romance that made her quit the circuit.

"Yup." Kacey picked up her mug and took a sip, then ate the last piece of cupcake.

Elaborate. Explain yourself. Tell me everything!

"Well, all done with my break," Kacey said. "Time to get back to painting. I'm calling this piece 'Three Napping Mutts.'"

Tori grinned. "Can I come back soon?" *Please say yes. Make my day.*

Kacey reached over and very briefly covered Tori's hand with her own. "Sure."

"I'm so glad to hear that. Because Bobby's making me his signature dish tonight and I have a feeling things are going to get—to use your word— *complicated.* I'm gonna need more advice, I'm sure."

"My advice will always be to follow your heart, Tori."

But what about when your head is telling you something entirely different?

Bobby had everything for tonight's date with Tori on the kitchen table in his cabin. Two boxes of macaroni and cheese, plus the add-ins, a small container of milk and a stick of butter. Also, a bottle of white wine. A green salad he'd picked up at the gourmet takeout that had opened while he'd been gone. A sourdough boule. And a small raspberry cheesecake. He grabbed one of his reusable grocery store bags and was about to pack everything when a telltale knock on the door sounded—to the beat of some song he never remembered the name of. No one knocked like that but Sullivan.

Bobby opened the door and there was his twin, holding his own reusable grocery bag. "Sadie and I had lasagna tonight and she made one for you—said you deserved it for buying the most expensive picnic basket Holiday House sells. I said, 'Bobby doesn't go on picnics' and she said you do now that you're dating Tori Hawkins. I have to hear this secondhand from my fiancée?" he asked with a grin, giving Bobby a faux punch in the arm. "Good for you, bro."

Bobby smiled. "Tell her thanks for the lasagna," he said, taking the bag from Sullivan.

Sullivan eyed the makings of a dinner on the table. "Looks like someone has a date tonight. I'd switch out the boxed mac and cheese for the lasagna, though."

"Actually, the boxed stuff is the star of the show. I promised Tori I'd make her my specialty. What my grandmother taught—" He paused, always tripping over the *my* and *our* when it came to relatives they only shared through DNA. "Our grandmother taught me how to make it so I wouldn't starve when Aubrey took off for days at a time."

Bobby had started referring to his mother as Aubrey to avoid the *my* and *our*. Sullivan hadn't known he was adopted until just last year, which had led him to the genealogy site that had uncovered a twin. Sullivan had told Bobby how angry he'd been at his parents for withholding that, and for a while, the word *mother* had been loaded.

"You know, when I found out that Aubrey kept you and gave me up for adoption," Sullivan said, "I was pretty shaken. Jealous, I guess. But once I really started thinking about how you were raised, what you went through, making your own dinner at age five, finding your only parent passed out drunk on the porch of your rundown house…" Sullivan exhaled and ran a hand through his hair.

You didn't miss anything was on the tip of Bobby's tongue, but he didn't say it because of course it wasn't true. Sullivan *had* missed something, cruddy upbringing or not. Twins had been separated, secrets buried.

Sullivan had told him all the details he'd learned from their estranged aunt—whom neither had known about until Sullivan had found her last year—that first night he'd returned to Bronco. The reason he and Sullivan had been separated. Why Aubrey had taken Bobby home, while Sullivan had been adopted. Bobby had listened, his stomach twisting, bile rising, and he'd excused himself outside because the truth of their birth story had made him so damned sick. And sad.

"Whenever Sadie and I talk about this, why we were separated, neither of us can actually believe it all happened," Sullivan said.

How had they gotten on this subject? Neither of them liked talking about it. Bobby glanced at the boxes of mac and cheese on the table. Right—that was how. Maybe he shouldn't make Tori his "signature dish."

"I hate thinking about it," Bobby said. "I hate the whole story. When I do think about it, when I talk about it, it makes me wonder about what people are capable of. The lies, the omissions, the secrets—about the fundamental things. Shakes what little trust I have, you know?"

Sullivan put a hand on Bobby's shoulder. "Yeah, I know."

"Maybe I *will* bring the lasagna instead of those

boxes of mac and cheese," Bobby said. "Making that for her will just bring it all up and she's so skilled at reading people because of her reporting job that she'll lure it all out of me."

"Does she know the story?" Sullivan asked.

He shook his head. "She knows a fair bit, actually." Because he'd opened up to her. Surprising himself yet again.

"Good. Because I'll tell you one thing I learned about relationships, Bobby. Clamming up about who you are, where you come from, what keeps you up at night isn't the way forward. Talking things out makes things better, not worse."

Bobby did *not* agree. Yes, he'd told Tori a lot about his past. But hardly *everything*. "Except once you say something, once it's out there, you can't unsay it, and then you feel like hell. Exposed."

"All I know is that, for me, doing all that talking, all that exposing, got me Sadie. And I don't have to tell you how great she is."

Bobby smiled. "She's pretty great."

"Leave the lasagna in the fridge," Sullivan said. "Make the boxed stuff. And try to remind yourself what's riding on everything."

"What is riding on everything?" Bobby asked.

"Tori," Sullivan said. "It was Sadie for me and it's Tori for you."

Bobby shook his head. "We're just casually dating until she leaves Bronco."

Sullivan raised an eyebrow. "If you say so. But I think you and I will both look back on this part of the conversation and laugh."

"She *is* leaving," Bobby said. "That's a fact."

"She might be leaving, you might be casually dating, but that doesn't mean you're having a meaningless fling. Meaningless flings don't involve everything on that table," he said, upping his chin.

Ugh. This was the thing about twin brothers. They butted right into your business, said whatever they wanted. "You should probably be getting back," Bobby said but with a smile. Talking about all this—the mac and cheese, their history, Tori—had made him feel both seriously heavyhearted and lighter at the same time. He had no idea how.

"Should I take the lasagna with me?" Sullivan asked. "Once I tell Sadie why, she'll be glad I grabbed it away from you."

Bobby stared at the blue and yellow tall, narrow boxes of macaroni and cheese on the table. At the fancy bread and raspberry cheesecake. At how for a two-week romance that would end with August, he sure was putting a lot of thought into their dates.

He inwardly sighed. "Yeah," Bobby said. "Take it."

"Good."

As Sullivan left, Bobby wasn't sure it *was* good. Tori was already too easy to talk to. But there were some things in his past better kept there. He felt exposed just being back in Bronco, a feeling that hadn't gone away in six months. He'd keep the hard stories to himself.

Because Tori *would* be leaving. That was a fact. And therefore there was no reason to talk about the stuff that kept him up at night.

Chapter Ten

"Tori Hawkins, this is an intervention," Faith said.

"And we hereby declare this cabin a man-free zone," Amy added.

Tori raised an eyebrow at her sisters, who were standing on the porch of her cabin, looking a little too serious. Maybe she wouldn't mention a man would be coming over in about fifteen minutes to make her dinner.

Tori had just gotten out of the shower after spending the past two hours at the arena, where she'd worked on her times, her sisters and a couple of her cousins also taking the extra afternoon practice. She'd done better than she had this morning, but she was still three seconds off.

"Well, you are forty…" the coach had said, and Tori wanted to pinch her.

"I had some of my best times a few months ago," Tori had clapped back. "So don't give me that hooey!"

Faith and Amy pushed past Tori into the cabin, both their arms crossed as they stood right in the middle of the small entryway. Tori sighed and took the towel off her head, using it to pat dry her long hair.

"We thought you seeing Bobby Stone would be a good thing, honey," Faith said, tucking a swath of hair behind her ear.

Amy was right beside her. "But we've discussed it and we're worried he's distracting you to the point that you're going to come in *last* at the Bronco Summer Family Rodeo. You can't let Callie Dennis beat your times, Tori!"

Callie Dennis was a smug, entitled barrel racer who ran her mouth at all her competitors, and she had a special distaste for anyone with the last name Hawkins because of their popularity with fans—and how good they were.

"According to Coach Tamara, it's my creaky old bones at age forty," Tori said, trying to lighten the mood. Her cousin Brynn had done a lot of coaching for the family but with so many Hawkins sisters in town now, Brynn had suggested some of the cousins work with Tamara Beauchamp, a trusted former rodeo champ, so that all the sisters would have the benefit of a dedicated coach. Tamara had been joking about her creaky bones; Tori and her sisters—who joked among themselves about their own repetitive injuries from the sport—liked their new coach a lot.

She eyed the round clock on the living room wall. Bobby would be here in fifteen minutes with the makings of his signature dish, and she'd prefer this time to get ready and anticipate their date—not have this conversation with her sisters. Even if they were right.

"Our Bronco coach doesn't know you've been distracted by a hot mysterious guy," Faith said.

Amy nodded. "And we do. Look, Tori, we want you to be happy. Of course we do. But we've never seen you fall behind like this. Either this guy is good for you because you've found someone special you like to the point he has your total attention—or he's bad for you because he has your total attention."

"Maybe you should stop seeing him till after the rodeo," Amy put in.

"But after the rodeo, I'll be gone," Tori pointed out. "We only have till the rodeo!"

"Then just put blinders on when you get on Bluebell, hon," Faith said. "At practice tomorrow, make that commitment. Honestly, I'm afraid you're going to get hurt."

"I just pointed out that I'm leaving in a couple weeks," Tori said. "I doubt either of us will get hurt." Although she knew that wasn't true. Far from it.

"I'm not talking *emotionally*," Faith countered.

"She's right," Amy said. "One off-veer around a barrel and you could get thrown at really fast speed."

Tori inwardly sighed. "I appreciate that you care about me. And I hear you. I'll put the blinders on tomorrow morning. Okay?"

Her sisters seemed slightly appeased. Maybe Tori should shoo them away before the doorbell rang.

"He's coming over tonight?" Faith asked.

Tori nodded, a smile breaking through despite her trying to hold back how excited she was about seeing him. She'd liked last night, liked how he'd come over to apologize and change tactics for their romance. She'd liked the wildflowers.

Amy rolled her eyes but there was a twinkle there. "Enjoy him tonight, sister dear. Then tomorrow, *blinders*!"

"Blinders," Tori repeated. "I promise." She bit her lip as an unease slid inside her. Here she was, the eldest of her four siblings, and she was being schooled by her sisters on priorities. Over the years, Tori had been in their position a time or two; they'd all had to remind one another that once they were in the arena, only their horse and their events mattered. They were the Hawkins Sisters—individuals yes, but a group. They represented one another.

Tori would not let them down.

Once they left, she went to the bathroom and stared at herself in the mirror above the sink. A forty-year-old face might be staring back at her, but Tori could well remember being five and meeting her new sister for the first time. Then another, then another, then another. With each subsequent adoption in the family, Tori's heart had swelled to accommodate all the fierce, protective love she'd felt for her sisters.

No, she would not let them down.

But as she swept on a little mascara and dabbed a bit of bronzer to her cheeks, and then slicked on her favorite lip stain, she knew that something was going on inside her, something was changing.

What exactly, she wasn't sure. But it had to do with accepting that she was falling for Bobby Stone.

Bobby stood at the stove in Tori's tiny kitchen, stirring milk into the pot of macaroni and cheese, his attention more on Tori, who seemed lost in thought. She sat at the breakfast bar, facing him yet staring down at the piece of sourdough bread she was dragging back and forth in a small bowl of infused olive oil.

"I think that piece of bread soaked up *all* the oil," he said, raising an eyebrow. "You okay?" Something was definitely on her mind. Him? Their…whatever this was?

"Just thinking about my times at practice today," she said, hopping up and grabbing the bottle of olive oil he'd brought over. She poured more in the bowl, dipped a new piece of bread into it and quickly gobbled it up. "I'm off by a few seconds."

"What do you make of that?"

"My sisters think I'm distracted by the new man in my life," she said, pouring two glasses of iced tea from the pitcher she'd set on the bar.

"Well, if it's any help to know, twice today I lost count of the herd I was tracking. And I was in the hundreds when I had to start over."

She smiled at that. "Stop making me think about you when you're not around."

"I just told you I'm bad at that when it comes to you, so…" He grinned and spooned the creamy, fragrant orange pasta into two bowls and brought them over to the bar. But his smile faded. "I definitely don't want you to be distracted over us when you're in the ring, Tori. That could be dangerous."

"I know. I promised my sisters I'd be fully focused tomorrow morning and I intend to be." She sniffed the air. "Okay, enough about me. Let's talk about how good dinner smells and looks."

"Ladies first," he said, gesturing at her bowl as he sat beside her. "Tell me how it is."

She dug in. "Yum. Really good." When he took a bite, she added, "Is it the same as you remember as a kid?"

What was interesting was that while he was making it, pouring the macaroni into the pot, adding the milk and butter, stirring in the orange cheese powder goodness, he hadn't really been thinking about his childhood. Maybe because Tori had been close by. He'd been thinking about her. "Every bit as delicious," he said.

She grinned. "My dad loves mac and cheese and made a huge potful with like five different cheeses every Sunday when my sisters and I were growing up. But when I lived with my aunt Gertie when I was very little, I remember she made this kind. Honestly, that blue and yellow box is one of my earliest memories."

He tilted his head. "Aunt Gertie?"

"My biological parents died when I was a baby," she said. "A car accident. My aunt Gertie—my birth dad's older sister—was babysitting me at the time and she was my only family. But she died of cancer when I was four. I don't remember her well, but I have a few memories—her sweet blue eyes, the mac and cheese box, the yellow walls of the kitchen." She smiled and seemed lost in thought again.

Bobby paused, fork midair. "I had no idea, Tori. I thought you had this big happy family, four sisters, all close. I didn't know you had this in your history. How did you become a Hawkins?"

"It's an amazing story, actually. My aunt Gertie was a huge fan of the Hawkins Sisters, the second generation. When she started losing her hair to chemo, she wore a pink cap every day with the Hawkins Sisters logo. Turns out the hospice nurse was a neighbor of a

Hawkins Sister—Suzie—and asked Suzie if she'd come visit, say a quick hi and sign her cap. Well, Suzie spent two hours with my aunt and when she found out a little girl was being left behind, living in a group foster home, Suzie said she'd recently completed the steps to become a foster parent with the goal of adopting like her mother had. She took me in and adopted me later that year. That's how I became a Hawkins. My four sisters came along a bit later. They're all adopted too."

"Wow," he said, shaking his head in wonder. "That *is* an amazing story, Tori."

She smiled around a bite of mac and cheese. "My mom—Suzie—is a really lovely person. My aunt was too. And from the stories she shared with Suzie in hospice about my birth parents, they were too. My mom plunked me on a horse the first week I moved in with her. The rest is history. I wrote all about that for an essay contest I entered for *Rodeo Weekly*—it's how I got my start in reporting for them. I only got third place, but it might as well have been first, that's how thrilled I was."

He turned toward her and put both hands on either side of her face. "I have so much to learn about you."

"Same," she said, her brown eyes thoughtful. "You know, Bobby, I don't often talk about my origins, even though it's as nice a story as can be from tragedy and loss. And whenever I do talk about it, it sticks with me for a while and I usually need to take a long walk or a long ride, let it settle back into those nooks and crannies. But right now, I feel…comfortable. I'm not itching to get away with my thoughts and memories. I don't know if it's because you're so easy to talk to or if it's because I figure you understand."

He reached for her hand and gave it a squeeze, then sat back, his appetite seriously waning. "I was talking to my brother about this very subject before I came over. He thinks talking about my past, my family history, will help me deal with it instead of just the thought of it burning a hole in my stomach."

"And what do you think?"

He shrugged. "Sometimes I think, tell her everything, get it all off your chest, open up already. Because she's leaving. Come end of August, she's gone with all your secrets. So you might as well talk to her."

From the look on Tori's face, maybe he shouldn't have said that.

"I don't want you to open up to me because you're never going to see me again, Bobby Stone. Open up to me because you can talk to me. Because you want me to know you."

"It's a rough story, Tori. That's why I don't want to tell you. Or think about it."

"I understand," she said.

He glanced at Tori as she pushed around his signature mac and cheese, her expression strained. If he wasn't mistaken, her eyes were a little misty.

Last night, he'd told her they should forget labels and just be. Right now, maybe he had to forget that she was leaving—and just feel. And what he *felt* was close to her. As always.

He wanted to tell her, wanted to open up. But then afterward—what? He'd feel like hell and what would he do with everything that had come out of him?

You'll be here. With Tori.

But what he'd said a little while ago, about sharing who he was with her because she was leaving and would take his secrets, all he'd exposed of himself, the vulnerability he hated… Well, now that didn't seem completely true.

He wanted to tell her the terrible story because, as she'd put it, he wanted her to know him.

He let out a hard exhale and put down his fork. "I told you that Sullivan tracked down an estranged aunt—my mother's sister, who I didn't even know existed. Apparently, she moved away after Sullivan and I were born, and both sides wrote each other off. Well, the aunt told Sullivan the basics, and he told me. I think we'd both have been better off not knowing, Tori. It's ugly and why I don't talk about my past at all."

"Wouldn't you always want the truth, though?"

He gave something of a shrug because he honestly wasn't sure. "If you had a choice of not knowing something awful about your past or finding out because it's the truth, would you necessarily want to know? I'm not saying ignorance is bliss, but learning about my past didn't do a damned thing for me. In fact, it made things worse."

"How?" she whispered.

"It made me lose my faith in people all the more. People who were supposed to care about me. My story is riddled with secrets, lies, omissions, abandonment."

Tori bit her lip and looked so fraught that he felt like a jerk for saying all that—or saying it the way he had.

"I want you to tell me so it's not all bottled up in here," she said, putting a hand to his chest. "You can trust me. Trust me not to judge or ask probing questions. Just to listen. Just to be here for you."

Oh, Tori. She was both *too* much and everything he needed in one.

Talk to her. Tell her. Just get it out.

He put his hand over hers, then held her hand for a moment before letting go. But he found himself not saying anything. Unable.

Until he looked at Tori and saw the interest in her eyes, the compassion—and eyes, and yes, the lack of any judgment.

Would it feel good to talk about all this? Or he would just feel…exposed?

He was used to not talking. Not sharing. And he was supposed to be changing. *Trying* to change.

"My mother, Aubrey, was sixteen when she got pregnant," he blurted out before he could clam up. "Her parents, my grandparents, convinced her to give the baby up for adoption."

Tori's eyes widened and she held his gaze, the interest and compassion even more so in her expression.

"She didn't want to," he continued, "but they told her they wouldn't help her with the baby, financially or otherwise, that she'd be on her own. The baby's father was twenty and he ended up in jail after he ran away and abandoned my mother once he heard she was pregnant."

"That's a lot on a sixteen-year-old," she said.

He nodded. The times he'd think about exactly that, he'd feel more compassion for his mother. "Her parents got her to agree to give the baby up. When she went into labor, they took her to a clinic in Bronco Valley, near where they lived. The clinic burned down like fifteen years ago and good riddance."

Tears misted Tori's eyes.

"I told you, it's a rough story. And it gets really bad right about now."

She bit her lip and squeezed his hand.

Part of him wanted to stand up and run.

But another part wanted to keep going. To talk. To share. With her. With *Tori*.

"Sullivan was born and the adoptive parents were in the waiting room, ready to take him home. But Aubrey refused to sign the papers. She wanted to keep him. Apparently, she was sobbing. Then, she screamed in pain—*another* baby was coming. No one knew she was pregnant with twins. I was born two minutes later, sickly, small, and the doctor said he was sorry but he didn't think I'd make it beyond a day or two."

Tori gasped, her hand flying to her mouth.

"My grandparents told Aubrey that if she signed the paperwork to give up her parental rights to the first baby, she could keep me until the sad end. Apparently, it was enough to get her to sign—and my twin went home with his new family, never to be seen or heard from again—well, until recently."

"But you clearly survived," Tori whispered.

He nodded. "Against all odds, I thrived and caught up with milestones by my first birthday. Turned out my grandparents were right, that Aubrey was too young to be a mother. She went out all the time, leaving my grandparents frustrated. She started drinking so she wouldn't have to deal with anything, like hearing me cry or having to take care of me. My grandparents ended up raising me most of the time, after all."

"Were they resentful?" she asked.

"Hard to say since I didn't know any of this growing up. My grandfather was short-tempered with me. He was a long-haul trucker and rarely home. My grandmother loved me but she was in her fifties and tired. And I was *a lot*. Like most kids."

"Oh, Bobby," she said, reaching a hand to his face. She stood up and wrapped her arms around him, burying her face in his shoulder.

He stood too and pulled her against him. "Turns out it doesn't feel good to have told you. I feel like hell. I mean, I'm glad you know. But putting it all out there? Why would that feel good? And now I feel close to you and want to run out of here at the same time."

She pulled away and gave him a gentle smile. "I want you to stay, Bobby. But I know telling me probably took a lot out of you. You do what you need to, okay?"

Her words shot inside him. No judgments. No expectations. *You do what you need to.*

Yeah, he felt exposed. And his least favorite emotion—vulnerable.

But what he needed, right then, was to hold her tight. And never let go.

Something hard gave a little inside his chest. "Remind me never to make this mac and cheese for you again. Who knows what I'll tell you next?"

She smiled, then laughed. "How about a drink? I have that bottle of wine. And beer. Or we could just have coffee."

He felt his shoulders relaxing, something in him unwinding. She clearly knew that he needed a break from all this. "Coffee. Strong and sweet."

"Coming right up. And we can have cheesecake. I also have a box of cupcakes. Extra benefit of visiting

Kacey Karrow today. Got one box of six for her and one for me and you."

"The more sweets, the merrier," he said. "Did she suddenly tell you her story?"

Tori shook her head. "Nope. In fact, she doubled down on the assurance that she won't. But I go see her because I want to be in her presence. I want to know her. Not for the story—even off the record."

He pulled her into his arms again. "You're all right, Tori Hawkins."

"Yeah?" she whispered, her voice a bit wobbly. "I think you're all right too."

He tightened his hold, taking in the light scent of her perfume, loving the feel of her silky long hair falling over his arms. He could stay like this forever. But a heartbeat later, he needed a breather again. Needed to get ahold of himself. And she probably did too. "Got a pistachio cupcake?"

She looked up at him and smiled. "You know it."

While she went to start the coffee, he cleared their plates, cleaning up the breakfast bar and stacking the dishes and pots and utensils in the tiny dishwasher. He got the chance to let everything settle, catch his breath—both from opening up to Tori and holding her so closely, feeling her against him.

Just as she reached for two mugs from the cabinet, the doorbell rang. Dammit. The last thing they needed was someone else and whatever they had to say getting between them. Or inside them. Right now, things were fine and good. And he wanted them to stay that way.

Tori shrugged. "I'll pretend I'm not here," she whispered, holding a finger to her lips.

He smiled. Once again, they were in sync.

But peering in at them through the window— curtains pulled open, unfortunately—was a woman with a big smile and a clipboard, waving at the two of them.

Who was this?

So much for pretending no one was home.

Dammit.

Chapter Eleven

Drat. Tori gave the stranger with terrible timing a little of wave of her fingers and headed to the door. She didn't recognize the woman, who wore a Bronco 7-12 PTA T-shirt and jeans.

"Evening!" the petite redhead said. She looked at Tori, then at Bobby, who was leaning against the bar, and if Tori wasn't mistaken, she was practically beaming. "Two in one visit! This is great!"

Tori eyed Bobby, who had the same question in his eyes. Who was this woman and what was this about? Bobby came over and stood beside her.

"I'm Regina Pearl, the committee chair to sign up volunteers from the community to speak to Bronco middle and high school students at our annual Career Day this fall. Tori, I've signed up your cousin Brynn to speak on rodeo riding, but I'm hoping you'll discuss magazine journalism. Things like interviewing, writing, how you got started, what's involved."

Tori could not have been more surprised, her heart giving a little happy flip in her chest. "Huh. Well, that sounds like something I'd like to do."

"And, Bobby," Regina continued, "you saved me a trip back out to Dalton's Grange. I was just over there and spoke to Dale Dalton, and he recommended you as a great choice to talk to the students about a career as a ranch hand."

Bobby looked shocked. "He recommended *me*?" He looked at Tori in confusion, then back at Regina. Tori knew that Dale Dalton was a son of the owners of Dalton's Grange.

The woman nodded. "Yesiree. Dale said you were one of the best ranch hands he'd ever had the pleasure of working with and that you knew the ranching industry inside out."

"Well, I'm flattered as hell," Bobby said. He flinched, then added, "Sorry, I know I probably have to watch my language around the students. But obviously, I'm not much of a public speaker."

Regina grinned. "That's fine. Giving a short presentation—like fifteen, twenty minutes on what it's like and what's required for the cowboy life—means talking from the heart. Most of our participants find themselves going way over their time allotment. You want to be sure you leave room for the Q and A."

Bobby glanced at Tori and she could see he really was "flattered as hell." He gave something of a happy shrug. "Sign me up."

"Ditto," Tori said. "When is Career Day?"

Regina was beaming. "Mid-September. Wednesday the 17th. Eight a.m. to noon with each participant taking four sessions so that the kids can sign up for all their top choices."

Tori's face fell. She'd always known she was leaving, of course. That her time in Bronco was limited. But suddenly, that she wouldn't be here the second week of September hit her hard. "Oh, I'll be long gone by then. I leave Bronco to rejoin a tour in Australia right after the Bronco Summer Family Rodeo."

"Oh darn," Regina said. "What a treat it would be for our students interested in magazine journalism to have Tori Hawkins speak to them."

Tori bit her lip. Would have been a treat for her too. Double darn.

Regina turned to Bobby. "Well, I'll sign you up for sure. I really appreciate it."

Bobby smiled. "Thanks for asking."

Regina left and Tori closed the door behind her. "Aw, I would have loved to do that," she said.

"Guess you'll just have to stay in Bronco," he said. Then froze and coughed as though he definitely hadn't meant to say that. She was sure he didn't in any read-between-the-lines kind of way. "But when you leave," he added fast, "you'll always know that you got Bobby Stone to give a talk to students about being a cowboy."

"Me? I didn't have anything to do with that. You came highly recommended by Dale Dalton."

"Trust me, you had everything to do with it, Tori. You've changed me since I met you. I probably would have quickly said no had Regina asked me last month. I kept my head down, lay low, avoided people. I mean, me? A question and answer session?" He shook his head with a wondrous smile. "Sullivan and Sadie won't believe it. You'll have to confirm I really said yes."

She grinned, but could feel it fading fast. "I'll go get the coffee."

But he grabbed her hand. "Hey," he said gently. "What's wrong? Is it the disappointment about not being able to give the talk?"

"Well, that and…the thought of leaving Bronco in less than two weeks. Leaving you." She could feel her cheeks flame a bit. "Oh God, did I say that out loud?"

"I think about it too, Tori. But I guess we know that we're doing each other good while we're together."

She sucked in a quick breath and hurried over to the kitchen to grab the mugs. She'd almost said something she would have regretted. Something she wasn't supposed to say. Or feel, for that matter.

Like the fact that it's getting clearer and clearer that you do want more than a casual romance? That he's reminding you that you can feel something so deep and special for a man, after all?

Thing was, she wasn't sure she did want to explore any of that. Her feelings for Bobby were strong, yes. And she was wildly attracted to him as she'd never been to any other guy. But let herself go with what she felt for him? Why? To tear herself apart? Break her own heart? She was forty and had never had a successful relationship. How could she trust in this one, with this complicated man?

She mentally shook her head. Like she'd told her sisters, she'd put on her blinders tomorrow morning. When it came to the rodeo, she'd focus on her passion, her livelihood, her family. And then come the end of August, she'd ride out of town, Bobby Stone a lovely memory.

But as she poured the coffee, she knew she was trying to talk herself into something. Trying to get control of something *out* of control. Bobby Stone a lovely memory? *Come on, Tori. The man is etched in your heart.*

Little late for keeping that heart out of the supposed fling. She laughed to herself. *Fling.* This wasn't even that anymore. Even if Bobby hadn't said what he had about labels last night. That there was something serious here was undeniable.

At least there was something Tori could always count on—that caring about a man was confusing as ever.

They'd had their coffee and dessert in the living room, keeping the conversation light and planning on finding a movie to watch. Bobby had his arm around Tori, who sat snuggled beside him on the sofa, her feet up on the coffee table next to his.

"The rodeo promoters gave all the participants a welcome basket when we arrived in town," Tori said. "I have really good caramel popcorn but I'm too stuffed to have any."

"Can't watch a movie without popcorn," he said. "I'll eat it all. I love that sticky stuff. My grandfather might not have been around much when I was young, but when he was, he'd take me to the college baseball games and we'd always get the caramel popcorn."

"I'm glad you have some nice memories too," she said.

Huh. He supposed he did. "I guess I do."

"Tell me another one," she said.

He thought for a second. "My mother loved Halloween. Went all out decorating inside and outside the house. The years she was working, she'd take me to buy any costume I wanted. I always went for the scary ones. She let me eat all the candy I got trick-or-treating too."

He hadn't thought about those times in a while. Sullivan had asked if Aubrey had any good points, and he'd told his twin that she definitely did. The bad had outweighed the good, though. A few fun times, once or twice a year, which had still always annoyed his grandmother, hadn't been enough to blot out the fact that he hadn't been able to count on his mother. That she'd split on him. That she'd left her parents, who'd raised their kids, with a ten-year-old.

But it was nice to think of the good times. How she'd taken so many photos of him in his ghoulish costumes. How when she wasn't drunk or out with her friends or a boyfriend, she'd teach him how to play card games and they'd watch kiddie movies. She liked all the modern classics, like *Toy Story* and *Toy Story 2*.

She smiled. "My mother and father always let us have a bunch of our Halloween candy every day until we were sick of it."

"Your parents sound great. What are they like?"

Tori smiled. "My mom is just the best—in a million ways for a million reasons. My dad too—Arthur. He used to be a rodeo star until an injury sidelined him. He never stopped being my mom's—my whole family's—biggest champion."

"You got very lucky there," he said with a smile.

"I definitely did."

"So what's your favorite candy?" he asked.

"Anything chocolate. Yours?"

"I like sour lemon drops," he said. "Sadie's Holiday House has great candy at the register. I get my fill for free for having an in with the owner."

"Favorite food?" she asked.

"A good cheeseburger. Even a bad fast-food cheeseburger is always still good."

"Yeah, I agree. Favorite movie?"

"Original *Star Wars* trio. My grandmother liked those movies too." Huh. Another nice memory. When he was a teenager and he got in the mood to watch all the movies again, she'd sometimes watch with him. His late ex-wife had also loved *Star Wars*.

Nothing is really ever black and white, Bobby, Dana had said to him a time or two, when he'd talk to her about his childhood. Sometimes he wished things *were* black and white. No gray areas. Because it would be easier to know how to feel.

He supposed that was true. His relationship with Tori certainly wasn't just one-way. It went off in a lot of different directions. And like he'd said last night, he was just going to go with it.

Till she had to leave Bronco, anyway.

"Mine is *When Harry Met Sally*," Tori said. "I can watch it over and over and it never gets old."

"Maybe we should watch that tonight, then."

She grinned and stood up. "I'll get the caramel popcorn."

Bobby was about to turn on the TV and do a search for the movie on the pay channels when Tori sat back down.

"You know, I have a better idea of what we can do right now," she said with a very sexy smile.

He liked the sound of *that*.

"I'm in," he said. "Whatever you have in mind, I'm definitely in."

She leaned over to kiss his cheek, then took his hand and led him into the bathroom.

Um, interesting.

She kneeled down beside the bathtub and turned on the water, then poured in some fragrant bubbles.

Oh yeah, he definitely liked this.

Tori stood and faced him, holding his gaze as she unsnapped the buttons of his Western-style shirt. Her tongue slipped out of her mouth and licked at her lips as the shirt parted and she took it off him, flinging it to the side. Then she knelt again, but this time right in front of him, and he sucked in a breath and closed his eyes, anticipation building to the point that he had to grip the towel holder lest he completely lose control. And no way did he want to do that at this point.

She unzipped his jeans, tugging them down his hips and thighs until he stepped out of them. And then she reached inside his black boxer briefs and wrapped her hand around his manhood. He groaned and looked right at her, and the desire in her eyes almost undid him again.

She peeled down the boxer briefs just as he lifted off her tank top, a white lacy bra taking his breath. He unclasped it, grabbing it before it could fall in the half-filled tub.

"Great reflexes," she said, standing and wrapping her arms around his neck.

He groaned again and pulled off her flouncy cotton skirt, then dipped a hand down her lacy white underwear. Now she groaned, arching her back, and he inched down the undies.

Both of them buck naked, he picked her up and she wrapped her legs around his waist. He grabbed hold of the towel bar with one hand and used every abdominal muscle to lower them both to the floor, on the plush bath mat. He was sitting up, leaning against the tub, Tori straddling him, kissing him, now trailing her lips across his collarbone. She reached behind him to turn off the water to the bath.

He grabbed his jeans and found his wallet, taking out the condom he kept there, and she took it from him and tore it open, rolling it on. He closed his eyes again, barely able to contain himself.

And then she sank onto him, her lush breasts crushed against his chest, her nails slightly digging into the back of his shoulders. She rocked against him, her breathy moans and his groans driving him wild. And when she stared climaxing, he focused every bit of his attention on her pleasure while holding back his own until it was his turn.

And then he exploded, her mouth on his, and he couldn't get enough of her, never wanted this to end.

This time, as she collapsed against him, reaching for both hands with hers, he didn't freeze, or hesitate or run out of the room. Instead, he kissed her, tenderly.

"Bath is ready," she whispered.

He picked her up and then carefully reclined in the tub with her back against his chest. He wrapped his arms around her.

"This is heaven," she said.

"Agreed." It absolutely was.

They stayed in the tub, soaping each other, shampooing each other's hair, pouring fresh water over their heads, and when the tub water got too cool, they grabbed towels and dried each other.

Bobby was sure he was dreaming. Towels wrapped around them, Tori drained the water, then took his hand and led him to her bedroom. They both let the towels drop and then crawled under the blanket and Tori put her head on his chest, her eyes fluttering closed, just as his were.

Next thing he knew it was very dark inside and out the window, the alarm clock on the bedside table indicating it was 1:13 a.m. He couldn't be more relaxed, more sated, more at peace. His chest wasn't tight, nor was his throat. He didn't need air. Or space. He just wanted to stay there, Tori curled up beside him, forever.

Chapter Twelve

"Fourteen twenty-two!" Tori's coach yelled the next morning. "Excellent, Tori!"

Yes! she thought, nudging Bluebell over to the side of the arena in the convention center where her coach and sisters were waiting. In Tori's competitive world, completing the pattern in anything under fifteen seconds was solid. Both her sisters high-fived her. She'd been practicing since 8:00 a.m. and it was now just past eight thirty. Which didn't sound like a long time, but for barrel racing, practicing the patterns in fifteen-second intervals or so added up to a lot. Bluebell would need a good rest, and Tori could use another coffee. *And* a chance to finally let herself think about last night... and Bobby.

She'd thought about nothing else but him when he'd left early this morning around five thirty, since he had to be at work at the ranch at six. She'd taken a long hot shower, remembering every moment of their evening together. Then she'd gotten dressed for practice, had her coffee, some hearty oatmeal with bananas—and prepared herself for her sisters' knock at seven thirty. With that knock, she'd put the blinders on. There was no Bobby; there was only barrel racing. Only the Hawkins Sisters. Only the rodeo.

"We'll ask you about your hot date after practice," Faith had said as they got into Tori's car.

Amy had nodded. "Believe me, we want to know, but right now, blinders!"

Tori had laughed. And she'd forced any stray thought of her hot cowboy from her mind, and had gone over her strategy instead.

But what a night it had been. They'd spooned and snuggled and had made love again when they'd both woken up in the middle of the night, thanks to a brief thunderstorm. Being in bed with Bobby with the rain coming down against the roof and windows had been so cozy and romantic. They'd made plans to go riding again early this evening and have another picnic and hit up the cave, rain or shine. She smiled at the thought, happy goose bumps running up her spine.

"You're definitely back in the game this morning," the coach said.

No need to mention that she'd just this very second been lost in memories of her night and the delicious morning-after with the man in her life. It was post-practice and fully allowed, she thought as she recalled how Bobby had trailed kisses from her lips past her chin and neck to her breasts to her stomach until he got all the way to her toes.

Toes that were curling now just thinking about it.

"Go, blinders!" Amy said with a grin.

"Great job," Faith added.

Tori shook off her very private thoughts and focused on where she was.

"Bluebell, you're the best," she told her horse. "Okay, one more time, then we'll take a breather."

Blinders, she reminded herself. But just thinking about being in the cave with Bobby tonight, his too-sexy black boxer briefs, the long, passionate kisses and the way he looked at her as if she were the most beautiful woman on earth, the delicious thought of him dangling grapes over her mouth… Mmmm, she didn't want to think of anything else.

"And go!" Coach called.

Tori was momentarily startled but quickly got her head where it belonged. She raced for the first barrel, but Bluebell nicked the side of it, which would have been a penalty in an actual race. The fact that she'd let herself be distracted and that her horse might have gotten injured because of her messed with her even more, and when she approached the second barrel she veered Bluebell too sharply and got thrown, hitting the ground hard on her left shoulder.

"Tori!" her sisters called out.

Oh hell, she thought, trying to get up—and clearly nothing was broken—but she felt dizzy and sank back down.

"What happened?" Faith asked, rushing over, Amy right beside her.

"I had Bluebell angled too far," Tori said, tears filling her eyes. "Is she okay?"

The arena vet had already rushed over and was examining Bluebell. "She's fine," he called out.

The coach was shaking her head, which had become her specialty. She pulled out her cell phone and called the arena's medical team over. Two EMTs were hovering over Tori in a flash.

"You didn't hit your head?" one asked.

"No. Just my shoulder."

"Let's get you to Bronco Valley Hospital for X-rays just in case," the other said.

Tori shook her head, the movement not hurting in the slightest. "I'm sure I don't need all that. I'm fine," she added, but she had to admit her shoulder was throbbing.

"We insist," Amy said—firmly.

"Yup," Faith added. "You're going, end of story."

Fifteen minutes later, Tori was in the ER and luckily, it wasn't very crowded. She was in an exam room right away, grateful that the nurse had a bigger mouth than her sisters and had made it clear they would wait in the waiting room or she'd have them escorted out of the hospital. Tori appreciated their concern but she was a weepy mess and wanted to be alone.

She could have gotten really hurt. Bluebell could have gotten really hurt.

And now she'd taken practice time not only away from herself, but from her sisters because they'd want to be here with her. No way would they leave and they'd insist on hovering over her at the cabin once she was released. They'd lose the whole day due to her thinking about her love life instead of her job.

Dammit.

* * *

"I really appreciate that you recommended me to the PTA chair for Career Day," Bobby said to Dale Dalton in the barn at Dalton's Grange. Bobby had been about to lead two mares out for transport to the rodeo arena when he noticed the tall, tanned rancher returning a horse to the stable manager. He was very glad about the assignment to bring the horses to the convention center; he could watch Tori practice. It was nine thirty now, and she'd likely still be there. Leaving her bed this morning, particularly before the crack of dawn, hadn't been easy. He'd be happy with just a quick glimpse of her to get him through the long day until their date tonight.

Dale took off his Stetson and ran a hand through his dark hair, dabbing at his forehead with a bandanna. Bobby respected him for the way he worked so hard—just like his father and brothers, even though they were millionaires who could leave the manual labor to cowboys like Bobby. Patriarch Neal Dalton had struck it rich gambling and had bought the ranch, and it had become a family affair with the five Dalton sons and their mother, Deborah, running the place.

"You're a great cowboy, Bobby," Dale said. "You have an extensive knowledge of how a big ranch operates. You're hardworking, fast thinking and great with the young hands. The way you gently correct them, with just the right words, so that they don't get defensive and huff off, how you are with the horses and cattle, even the working dogs. I can always count on you to know how to handle any issue. Since you came to work for us six months ago, the whole family has noticed."

Most of him heartily appreciated that Dale had said

all that. Another small part was aware that it meant the family *talked* about him. He wasn't sure he liked that. But then again, Bobby had applied for a bunch of ranch jobs when he'd come back from the dead, and Dalton's Grange had been the only operation to take him on. That was likely because the Daltons had once been quite rough around the edges themselves, back before Neal had struck it rich, and they were all believers in redemption. Six months ago, Bobby hadn't been sure he was capable of redeeming himself, that anyone except his brother and Sadie would give him the chance to try. But he supposed his work at the ranch had spoken for itself.

He was about to tell Dale that he'd never imagined himself doing any public speaking, especially in a school setting, when a couple walked by with their horses, and Bobby heard the words *Hawkins Sister*. Naturally, his ears perked right up.

"I heard she got thrown really hard and got knocked out," the woman said.

"Really?" the man with her asked. "I thought someone said she broke her collarbone or something."

Bobby froze. *Knocked out? Broke her collarbone?* "Which Hawkins Sister are you talking about?" he called to them.

The couple stopped and turned, both shrugging. "I'm not sure—the one with the long dark hair," the woman said. "I don't know her name. But I did hear she was taken to the hospital," she added before they resumed walking.

Faith and Tori both had long dark hair. Not that he in any way wanted it to be Faith who'd been thrown. He didn't want either of them to be hurt.

"Most likely Bronco Valley Hospital," Dale said. "Go," he added. "Take the day if you need." Bobby realized then that Dale must have seen them riding together on the property the day of their romantic picnic.

"Thanks, man," Bobby said and rushed over to his truck.

Was Tori unconscious in a hospital bed? How injured was she?

As he pulled out of the parking area, he snapped on Bluetooth and asked his phone to call Tori's cell. No answer.

Damn.

His phone rang as he was on the service road toward Bronco Valley. It was Sadie.

"Bobby, I thought you'd want to know… I heard that Tori Hawkins was taken to the hospital a little while ago. Apparently she got thrown at practice in the arena. I don't know anything else."

His heart was pounding now. "I'm actually on my way to the hospital. I heard it was a Hawkins Sister but I didn't know it was Tori."

"I don't want to distract you from driving by talking, so I'm gonna let you go. Let me know how she is, okay?"

"K," he said and disconnected. He could see the hospital in the distance.

Distract you… Sadie's words echoed in his head.

Had Tori been thinking about him—and all he'd laid on her last night? They'd talked about some very heavy stuff. Had she been distracted by that and gotten hurt? Tori had never said anything about getting hurt or being thrown before, though she must have in her long career as a rodeo performer. Still, he felt like this was his fault. Hadn't she told him last night that her sisters were worried about her head not being where it needed to be?

Their romance was supposed to be light and fun and hot and sexy. It was hot and sexy, and there were elements of fun, but *light* it was not.

He pulled into the parking lot and raced out of his truck and into the hospital, only pausing to get Tori's room number. She was still in the ER. When he got to "curtain 7" he found Tori lying on a cot, her sisters in chairs on opposite sides. They both popped up when they saw him, their expressions not exactly welcoming.

He nodded at them, but his focus was on the woman in the cot in the flowered blue hospital johnny, a thin cotton blanket pulled up to her chest. With her fresh-scrubbed face and high ponytail, she looked so young. Maybe for the first time since he'd known her, she seemed vulnerable to him. Tori Hawkins was so independent, so accomplished, so assured of who she was, that she'd seemed impervious. But he knew now that wasn't the case—physically *and* emotionally.

"Tori, are you all right? Are you injured? I heard you might have broken your collarbone?"

"I'm fine," she said, reaching out a hand toward him. He took it and she squeezed, then let go. "Definitely no broken bones. I'm just waiting for the doctor to come talk to me about my X-rays—but the radiologist assured me nothing was broken, so that's a relief."

"You're damned lucky, Tori," Faith said, barely looking at him.

"Damned lucky," Amy repeated, narrowing her gaze at Bobby.

He frowned. Her sisters hated his guts.

"Look," Faith said to him, "we're glad that Tori is happily dating someone special to her. But she needs blinders in the arena!"

Amy nodded. "So stop making her so happy, okay?" At the look on Bobby's face, which had to be misery and shock, she added, "I'm kidding. A little."

"Oh God," Tori said. "Leave the man alone. My being here isn't his fault. It's mine."

"We'll give you guys some privacy," Faith said.

"Sorry for getting on your case, Bobby," Amy said. "I know it's not your fault."

Looking at him a bit more compassionately than when he'd arrived, the protective sisters slipped through the curtain. Bobby moved over to the seat Amy had vacated.

"You're okay?" he asked, his heart racing. She looked so slight in the cot, which wasn't very big to begin with.

"I'm fine. I promise. I bumped my shoulder when I fell, but like I said, nothing's broken. I just got a little bruised. Shoulder and ego. Falling is rare and embarrassing."

He could feel his heart sinking lower and lower. Maybe he needed to step away—from *them*. Let her do her thing while she was here in Bronco. She was leaving anyway.

And he'd be here, carrying on as usual, working, brooding, hanging out with his brother and Sadie, talking to the young hands. It was a good, decent life now as long as he didn't think too hard about his recent past— the divorce, that fateful walk in the damned woods, the escape from Bronco but not his memories, which were always there, poking at him just beneath the surface.

A decision slammed into his head.

"We shouldn't date anymore, Tori," he said. "It's bad for you in more ways than one. And when you leave, it'll probably be bad for me. So let's cut our losses," he added without emotion, his stomach twisting.

"Cut our losses?" she repeated, her brown eyes glinting. "After last night? Are you kidding me?"

"No, I'm dead serious. You got hurt because of me. Your sisters are upset because of me. We were supposed to have some fun fling and instead it became... something that feels out of control. I like control. So I'm stepping out."

"Stepping out," she repeated through gritted teeth. "No, you will not, Bobby Stone. You will face the issues that get thrown at you. That's what life is about. I fell—I got up."

"No, apparently you were lifted onto a stretcher and taken to the hospital by ambulance. Because of me, because of our relationship distracting you from the most important thing in your world. Your great passion as a barrel racer. Your role as a Hawkins Sister."

"So you're going to tell me how to live my life?" she said, shaking her head. "We're both forty years old, Bobby. Trust that I know who I am."

"Do you?" he asked. "You said you were done with romance. Yet here you are, fully in it."

"Maybe because there's something very special between us, Bobby. Something that feels once in a lifetime. And when you also feel like you've lived a lifetime already, that becomes even more special. Is this making any sense to you?"

"I just know I'm not good for you right now, Tori. I'm going to let you go so you can concentrate. My whole life seems to be about bad timing. This is no different."

Her eyes were glinting again—with sadness, with anger, with determination. "You're a lot of things, Bobby, but cold has never been one of them. This isn't you—you're forcing all this. You don't mean any of it."

"I care about you, Tori. So I have to back off."

She sighed, shaking her head.

He couldn't possibly feel worse.

"You heal up and get back in the ring," he said, forcing a neutral expression. "I refuse to stand in your way."

With that, he turned and rushed out, almost bumping into Faith and Amy, who were staring at him with what looked like absolute horror on their faces.

He closed his eyes for a second and then practically ran down the hall and out the door and into his truck. For a moment, he just sat there, trying to catch his breath, trying to forget the look on Tori's beautiful face as he'd said all he'd had.

But the fact that his heart was breaking in two? *That* he didn't want to forget because he deserved it. He'd hurt her. Literally and figuratively.

Then he drove off, sure he was doing the right thing by her.

And yes, himself too.

That it hurt so damned bad was just how it had to be.

Chapter Thirteen

Tori lay in the hospital cot, half spitting mad, half heartbroken. But she wasn't done with Bobby Stone. If she were in a position to run after him and give him a piece of her outraged, upset mind, she would. But her shoulder ached despite the pain tablets she'd taken. And Bobby was no doubt long gone.

"Um, we might have overheard all that," Faith called from just outside the curtain around her cot.

Her sisters burst through and sat down in the chairs on either side of her bed. "I almost cried and I'm not even you," Amy said.

Faith's eyes were misty. "Me too. Is this our fault? Did we get in your business too much?"

"No way," Tori assured them. "This is Bobby finding an excuse not to keep this great thing going. I'm gonna get him back."

Amy smiled gently. "He sounded pretty resolute, Tori. Just how are you planning on changing a stubborn cowboy's mind?"

"I've got my tricks," Tori said. "First of all, no one dumps me for my sake. That is a load of BS. Either he admits he's walking away to protect himself or I'm going to have to insist we continue our romance."

Faith laughed. "You are something else, Tori. I wish I had your confidence."

"Comes with age, dear sister," she said. "You know what, I sure could use a cup of coffee. Mind getting me one?" she asked, looking between Faith and Amy. "But not hospital cafeteria coffee. I need the good stuff. A large, light and sweet, maybe a swirl of something fun, like caramel. From Kendra's or Bean & Biscotti."

"We're on it!" Amy said, and they both popped up.

"Back in about twenty," Faith added and they headed out.

Tori felt herself relax a bit. She did need some caffeine. But even more, she needed time to herself, to let all that bravado she'd just let loose gel inside her. She'd said it, now she had to do it. Get Bobby back, get him to see they were too good for each other to possibly be bad.

But he was one of the most stubborn people she'd ever met. The good news was that a plan was forming.

Tori smiled. She always went after what she wanted. And she wanted Bobby Stone in her life.

Her smile faded. She was used to running that life. Being in control. But this wasn't solely about her. Just like she'd told him he couldn't make decisions for her, she couldn't make decisions for him. And here she was, bossily insisting he was going to date her whether he thought they should or not.

She felt herself deflate, all that confidence whooshing out of her.

Her phone rang; it was actually a video call from her mom. Tori instantly brightened. Her mom always made her feel better. Tori hit Accept and there was her mother's beautiful face.

"Hey, sweetheart," Suzi Hawkins said. "How are you?"

Instead of saying fine, which her mother would clearly see was not the case, Tori burst into tears.

And told her mom everything.

"Aww," Suzi said. "That sounds hard, honey. But that Bobby cares about you is obvious. He'll be back."

"I don't know," Tori said. And she really didn't.

All of a sudden she felt very tired. And like she was a million years old.

"Sweetie, rest up. I'll call you later, okay? Your dad sends his love."

"Love you both too," she said and clicked off.

She thought about what her mom had said. That Bobby would be back.

Tori sure hoped so.

"Tori?" called a voice from beyond the curtain.

Tori sat up. Was that who she thought it was?

"Kacey? That you? Come on in."

It *was* Kacey. She stepped through the curtain, big black sunglasses on, her long signature braid clearly twirled up under a straw cowboy hat. She took off the shades and tucked them in the pocket of her shirt.

"Brought you a cupcake," she said with a smile, her green eyes tinged with concern.

"I'm so touched. You have no idea. Thank you for coming. And for the treat. My sisters just went to get me coffee, so this is great timing."

"Well, I won't stay long," Kacey said. "I happened to be in town buying dog food when I heard you got thrown. You look okay—anything broken?"

"Nah. Just a bruised shoulder. I'm sure I'll be told to rest for a day and then I can get right back in the saddle."

Kacey smiled. "I got thrown twice when I used to do barrel racing. A zillion times when I started bronc riding. But that comes with the territory."

"Bobby thinks I got hurt because I'm distracted by us," Tori said. "In fact, he dumped me about five minutes ago."

"Sorry," Kacey said with a hand atop hers. "But what do *you* think?"

"I think that if I got distracted because I'm in love, it's a good thing," Tori said, her entire body freezing. "Oh God, Kacey. What did I just say?"

Kacey smiled. "I saw it in your eyes and face and voice last time you were over. And about the distraction? I don't disagree. It's not ideal when you're supposed to stay on the horse. But the love part? Grab it and don't let go unless you really have no choice."

Was Kacey speaking from experience? Had love been the reason she left the rodeo all those decades ago?

Kacey sat down in the chair Faith had vacated. "I had no choice to let go. But for me, that was the right decision on a few levels."

"There was a man?" Tori asked, trying not to look like she was on the edge of her seat, which she was.

"Well, the man was kind of secondary. But I did have feelings for him. I had stronger feelings for someone else, though."

Someone else? Tori held her breath and hoped Kacey would continue, that she wouldn't suddenly clam up.

"Do you want to know how I got into bronc riding?" Kacey asked. "For the cold hard cash and no other reason. No love of the sport, the horses, the ring. Just money. My dad left me and my mom when I was young. He moved from mistress to mistress, and I lost track of him. He didn't pay a penny in child support, so to help my mom, who was sick and unable to work, I started working young, at twelve, on a ranch as a hand. I didn't love the work, but it was a job I could get on the sly and it paid well, even for a kid."

She looked away for a moment as though she was lost in thought.

"My mom's illness got worse when I was sixteen," Kacey continued, eyes on her lap, "but she couldn't afford a doctor and the free clinic was no help, and I was so scared for her. So scared to lose her."

Tori felt her eyes mist over—for the girl Kacey was and for the barely there memories of her aunt Gertie, Tori being told she was sick and would go to heaven soon.

"One day," Kacey continued, "I saw a poster for a rodeo tryout for 'healthy, attractive young women looking to become stars.' Under that was a lasso around a lot of cash. I thought the rodeo could be my ticket to a good doctor for my mom. I could ride and it turned out

I was pretty good at a few different events. A manager took me on and I quickly fell for him. He helped me become a star. I was more passionate about him than the rodeo, but I was making good money and could take care of my mother."

Tori could barely keep up with everything she'd just heard.

"Well, about a few years into it, when I'd made a name for myself, guess who turned up out of the clear blue sky? A half sister who I'd never known about."

Tori gasped. "A half sister?"

So she'd been right that day at Kacey's house, when Tori had been sure Kacey had been about to mention something about a sister.

Kacey nodded. "Iris. She was just eighteen and running from an abusive boyfriend. We got very close very fast. Turned out she hadn't seen our mutual father in years and since her mom hadn't married him, she didn't have the Karrow name. But she had the telltale Karrow green eyes, and wow, were we similar. I taught her how to ride a bronc, and she was pretty good and a stunner, so I convinced my manager to take her on."

Tori bit her lip. She was pretty sure she knew where this was going. Then again, with Kacey, you never really knew till she told you outright.

"Well, my manager—my beau—he worked with Iris, but I kept overshadowing her. And then I could see that the two were falling for each other, which hurt, even though Iris was clearly fighting against it. But I knew he wasn't the one, and Iris seemed to truly be in love. I decided to take a step back and let her soar in both departments. My mother was gone by then and

I'd socked away a lot of money, plus I had the house. So I let my sister take my place, with no one knowing we were related."

Tori's mouth had long dropped open. Iris Johannsen. Tori knew the name from having researched women in rodeo. Now she *did* know where this was going, and her heart broke for Kacey.

"But just when Iris started making a name for herself, she was killed in a car accident—nothing to do with riding. I was so grief-stricken over losing her. And her manager—my former beau—barely shed a tear. He found another beauty to turn into a product and I was so disgusted that I guess I turned inward and put my heart into painting and my dogs and my land. I became something of a recluse."

Tears slipped down Tori's cheeks. "I'm so sorry you lost your sister."

Kacey squeezed her hand. "I really loved that gal, despite not knowing her very long. She was such a spitfire, full of passion and drive. She had a real love for the rodeo and bronc riding. Not like me. I know you understand what it is to love a sister. Maybe that's why I felt comfortable telling you, Tori."

Now Tori's tears were coming fast and furious. "Oh, Kacey. I can see why you never wanted to talk about why you left."

"I was wrong to give up on love and people, though," she said. "But I was bitter then. I blamed my former manager for using my sister and then not caring that she was gone. And having lost my mother and my father being a philandering louse who only came to see me when I was a star…well, give me a dog and a paint-brush for the rest of my life."

Tori managed a smile. "And some pumpkin spice cupcakes."

That got a smile out of Kacey too. "You know what, though? I realized too late that I should have fought for myself. Instead of letting bitter experience turn me into Miss Havisham, I should have turned my back on louses and creeps and kept my faith in humanity and the good folks out there. But I didn't realize that for a long time. And an old lady gets set in her ways."

"And now that you know it?" Tori asked gently.

Kacey rolled her eyes with a smile. "Honey, I'm seventy-five. I don't think Tinder is for me. Sometimes, sure, I think it'd be nice to sit on my porch and paint a man I'm smitten with, share a steak dinner and a good cupcake."

Tori brightened with an idea. "You could come to the Bronco Summer Family Rodeo. And attend my cousin's wedding. You'll meet a handsome cowboy in no time. He'll look just like Sam Elliott."

Kacey laughed. "I don't think so, Tori. But it's nice to fantasize about such things every now and then. Now as for you, my dear, don't give up *your* faith in your own heart."

Now she understood why Kacey had told her to always follow her heart. Kacey hadn't until she'd actually quit the rodeo.

But Tori found herself giving a little shrug, her shoulder aching a bit. "I'm leaving for Australia in a week. Day after the rodeo. I'll be leaving my heart behind."

"So invite him with you," Kacey said. "Take your young Sam Elliott on the road with you."

Tori blinked. What? No way. "Bobby just found his way back to his life here. He has his twin and soon-to-be sister-in-law. And a great job that he loves." She envisioned him standing in front of a classroom of middle and high school students, talking about the cowboy life, answering their questions. Bobby had signed up for all that. "He has a real future here. Bronco feels like home to him finally. I won't ask him to give that up. I can't."

Kacey slowly nodded. "And he won't ask you to give up the rodeo and life on the road for him. But if you two want to be together, you'll have to figure out a way."

Tori let out a hard sigh. "Maybe we're just meant to have this, now, and then go our separate ways. I always thought that no matter what, we'd each learn something important from this supposed casual romance. And I guess we have."

"I don't know, honey. That doesn't sound like a plan to me."

"To me either," Tori said with a frown.

"You two are here now. You have a week. Forget getting ahead of yourself with what comes after you leave. Focus on now and the next several days. You're gonna let him go when you're together *now*?"

"He was pretty resolute about us breaking up," Tori said.

"So you be too."

Tori stared at Kacey, a strength flowing back in her veins. She sat up, that old determination back. "You know what, yes. I *am* going to fight for us. We have a whole week." He wasn't going to ask her to stay and she wasn't going to ask him to join her. But they did have *now*. She just had to make him see that.

"That spirit is why we're friends," Kacey said. "I admire you, Tori."

Tori gasped, her heart swelling. "That means the world to me."

Two familiar female voices could be heard coming up the hall, so Kacey smiled at her and said she'd slip out now and to take care.

Tori's swagger was back a bit. Enough that she'd not let Bobby go without speaking her mind. She'd give him some time—not that they had much to spare—to miss her, to come to his senses, and then she'd lasso him right back over to her.

"Bobby Stone," a male voice called out, heels clicking on the floor of the stables at Dalton's Grange as a man headed Bobby's way.

Bobby was mucking out a stall, the physical labor as good as putting on some boxing gloves and getting his bad energy out on a punching bag. He didn't recognize the voice of the man who'd called his name and he didn't want to talk to anyone, so he ignored whoever it was. He'd left Tori's hospital room barely two hours ago, and he still couldn't get their conversation out of his head. Every rake of the straw, something he'd said, something she'd said back would echo in his ears.

"Stone," the voice said again. With a bit more edge this time too.

He sighed and turned. A tall blond guy, maybe late-thirties, stood there in fancy riding attire. Will Kennely was his name. He boarded his pricey stallion at Dalton's Grange and was rude to the cowboys, who he clearly thought were beneath him.

"What can I do for you?" Bobby asked, eyeing the guy.

"You can stay away from Tori Hawkins," Kennely said.

Bobby's moment of shock was replaced by anger. "Why would I do that?" He was *already* doing that, but he didn't need this jerk to know his business. Or Tori's.

"Because you're clearly bad news, Stone. And now she's in the hospital. I'm sure the two have something to do with each other."

Bobby clenched his fist.

"Go ahead," Kennely said, glancing at Bobby's balled-up hand. "I'll have you in jail in five seconds and my lawyer will make sure you stay there a looong time. That'll easily get you out of my way."

Out of his way. So the jerk was interested in Tori. He'd probably already asked her out and gotten turned down.

Footsteps were approaching, and they both turned. Dale Dalton was coming their way.

"Mr. Kennely, as of right now, you'll need to find another stable for your horse. You're no longer welcome at Dalton's Grange. Apparently, this is your second strike in antagonizing Bobby, a valued staff member, and your unacceptable lack of manners with the stable manager and the hands add up to the third. You'll be issued a full refund. Take your horse and go."

"You've got to be kidding me," Kennely practically spat, his ice-blue eyes glinting. "You're defending what he did?" he added, jabbing a thumb in Bobby's direction. "Faking his death? Most likely to hide from some criminal activity."

Dale stared down the guy with steely blue eyes. "Take your horse and get off my property."

"With pleasure," Kennely said, spitting on the floor and huffing down the aisle toward his horse's stall.

They both watched him go, Kennely yelling into his cell phone about booking a trailer to transport his horse to another ranch.

"Damn," Bobby said to Dale. "It's not easy to shock me, but you just did."

"We should have tossed that jerk out a while ago." Dale shook his head. "Who does he think he is trying to come between you and Tori Hawkins?"

"You heard that part?" Bobby asked.

"Yup. I was in the next aisle over. Look, I'm the last guy who believes in happy-ever-after. But don't mess with a man's romance. Cowboy code 101."

"I'm with you on the fairy-tale nonsense. No such thing as happily-ever-after. My divorce taught me that. But there's no romance to mess with anyway—Tori and I aren't dating anymore. Not that I'd give Kennely the satisfaction of knowing it."

"Well, that's a real shame about you and Tori," Dale said. "My brothers and I saw you two out riding last week, and I thought, 'Good for him. When you get a second chance at life, you have to run with it.' No one knows that better than the Daltons."

He knew what Dale was talking about. Their own second chance, their own redemption. A few years ago, the five Dalton brothers had joined their parents in Bronco on their new venture with Dalton's Grange and had changed their lives, their attitudes and the state of their family. All through time and hard work. Yeah, patriarch Neal Dalton had hit it big gambling and won a fortune, but it was what he'd done with it that counted. Now the Daltons were millionaire ranchers with the hard-won respect of everyone in Bronco.

Bobby let out a hard sigh. "I tried. Everything in me said to stay away from dating when I came back. And for the past six months I did. Until I met Tori. But she's only here temporarily, and I'm meant to be on my own, anyway. And like you said, there's no happy-ever-after, so what's the point?"

Dale adjusted his Stetson. "I'm hardly the guy to give advice on the subject, Bobby. Marriage, family life—nope, not for me. But three of my brothers are married and I've never seen them so damned happy." He gave something of a smile and shrugged. "They tell me when it gets you, it gets you. But I'll tell you, it's not getting *me*."

Bobby grinned. "You're a lone wolf. Like I am. Or was." He sighed hard. "People tell me to do what feels right."

"That's solid advice," Dale said with a nod.

Except *nothing* felt right. Walking away from Tori. Being with her when he knew he was bad for her. Just like that assclown Kennely had said.

You can stay away from Tori Hawkins. Because you're clearly bad news...

He was going to let Kennely dictate his life? Somehow it was different when Bobby called *himself* bad for her. Hearing it out of that jerk's mouth was a whole 'nother thing.

And when Dale got called away and Bobby went back to mucking out the stall, he stewed over it all for a good long while.

Chapter Fourteen

On Sunday afternoon, three days since she'd been in that hospital cot getting dumped by Bobby Stone, three days of him obviously not missing her, obviously not coming to his senses, Tori was forcing herself to be fully present at her cousin Audrey's bridal shower. They were in a lovely private room at The Library, a restaurant in Bronco Valley that her cousins and the groom's mother and both grandmothers loved. This was where Audrey and Jack had their impromptu engagement party for their family and friends.

After an amazing lunch—Tori had been surprised she'd had an appetite for the array of delicious tapas that had been served—Audrey was now opening gifts.

She'd gotten a lot of lingerie. Brynn, one of Audrey's sisters, sat beside the bride, dutifully sticking each bow from the gaily wrapped gifts onto a lasso instead of the usual boring paper plate. Tori had given Audrey a bottle of her favorite perfume, along with body lotion and powder.

"Oooh, sex-y!" Audrey said with a grin, holding up the black lace teddy from the box on her lap. When her soon-to-be mother-in-law covered her eyes with an ever bigger grin as she'd done quite a few times already, everyone broke into laughter.

"It's from my aunt Suzie," Audrey said, reading the little gift card. "I'm so glad she'll be here for the wedding."

"Go, Mom," Faith said, wiggling her eyebrows.

Amy let out a low wolf whistle.

What Tori would give for her mother to be beside her right now, but her parents were enjoying a long-dreamed-about vacation in Australia while Tori's other two sisters and a few cousins were there on an extended rodeo tour. Hopefully everyone would be in Bronco for the wedding, at least. Tori had loved seeing her mom's face when she'd video-called her in the hospital after she'd gotten thrown. It had felt so good to tell her mom everything, to get Suzi's support about Bobby. Tori had explained how she'd fallen for someone against her better judgment—not because he wasn't a good guy but because it was just complicated, and her mom had said that most things *were*.

He'll be back, her mom her said.

Tori just needed to believe it.

She eyed the sexy nightie that her cousin was folding back up in its box on her lap. Tori had bought herself a black lace teddy similar to that one and had even brought it to Bronco "just in case she met someone."

Well, she had met someone. And she hadn't gotten a chance to wear it before he put the kibosh on their romance. She'd been feeling so confident about them getting back together, at least for the final week of her time in Bronco, but her plan to give him time to miss her didn't seem to be having an effect on him.

It had been three days since he'd walked out of her life. She hadn't heard from him at all, which wasn't like him, either. The Bobby she knew would have texted to ask how her shoulder was. That meant he was working hard at the no-contact thing. She knew he had to be missing her. Tori had no doubt that Bobby Stone had strong feelings for her.

Stubborn man.

Another of Audrey's sisters, Remi, in charge of handing each gift to the bride-to-be from the big pile stacked at her feet, gave a card-sized box a gentle shake. "Hmm, not big enough for lingerie. Maybe a sex toy?"

Brynn gave Remi a mock scowl. The eldest, happily engaged since last year, and a mother hen to the others, Brynn was a source of comfort to Tori. She could always be counted on for a good answer, but her cousin had been so busy with the shower the past few days that Tori hadn't had the opportunity to knock on her door. Next to Brynn was the fourth of that set of Hawkins Sisters, Corinne. Like Tori and her siblings, Remi and Corinne were adopted and biological sisters. Tori adored her cousins and knew that despite their happiness for Audrey and her upcoming big day, they were all worried about their parents, Tori's aunt Josie and uncle Steve, who were currently separated.

Bobby would say it figured. That love didn't last and they were an example.

Audrey opened the little box. It was an IOU for a weekend stay at any romantic B and B, anywhere in the world, from her mom, Josie.

Tori took a sip of her sweet iced tea and eyed her phone for the umpteenth time. An hour to go of the bridal shower. Not that she wasn't having a good time. But she just wanted to flop on her bed and let herself feel what she was feeling so she could deal with it—unlike how Bobby handled his less-than-ideal emotions. She also wanted to work on Plan B—exactly how she was going to convince Bobby they should be together, at least until she had to leave.

Then what, she had no idea. But being apart? It was the pits. It had to be for him too.

A half hour later, Audrey was passing her phone around with photos of her dress, and when the phone got to Tori, she felt an immediate lump in her throat at the sight of her cousin, so beautiful in her fairy-tale wedding gown with a cathedral veil. The dress was so elegant—a mermaid style, Tori thought it was called—strapless with a deep sweetheart neckline, and a long elaborately beaded bodice with tulle flaring down from the thighs.

Did she feel that lump of pure emotion because Tori wanted that for herself? She certainly hadn't been interested in marriage in her twenties. She would have jumped into Mr. Right's arms if he'd come along, but he hadn't, at least not one who'd allow rodeo to be important in her life, be a priority. But she certainly wasn't going to be barrel racing forever and the idea of sitting on the porch, drinking sweet tea and sharing a pistachio cupcake with the man she loved sounded as good to her as it did to Kacey.

Did she want to get married? At forty?

And was this about wanting to marry Bobby Stone?

No, no, no, she told herself. *You just* like *the man—a heck of a lot—and want to enjoy the time you have with him while in Bronco.*

You more than like him, Tori Hawkins. Admit it.

She bit her lip and passed the phone on as if it was suddenly a hot potato, her sisters oohing and aahing before it went to the next attendee.

"You okay?" Faith whispered to Tori.

Tori gave a small, pathetic shrug. No. Not really.

Amy had taken a trip to the dessert buffet and returned with a plate of the most delicious-looking confections for them to share but Tori had zero appetite now. The lump had taken care of that.

"I miss him," Tori admitted. "I don't know how long to give it before I go tell him how wrong he is. I mean, we don't have much more time together. I really wanted *him* to come to *me*."

"Go see him tonight," Faith said.

"As long as you keep those blinders on when you get in the ring," Amy added with narrowed eyes. "You did so well at practice yesterday and today."

That was true. She'd worked hard to clear her mind before she got on Bluebell. For her horse, for her sisters and cousins, for the rodeo. But the turmoil in her head and gut had come blazing back the minute she'd hopped off Bluebell.

"I promise," Tori said. And the only way to ensure

that was to go see him, get an answer to her burning question: Can we just keep enjoying each other until I have to leave?

Enough with it being up in the air.

I'm coming for you, Bobby Stone.

"What do you think, Bobby? Bolo or bow tie?"

On Sunday afternoon, Sullivan was very seriously looking through the tie display on a wall in The Dashing Cattleman, a men's formal wear shop in Bronco Heights. There had to be hundreds of ties: long and skinny, traditional, bow ties and the Western bolos. Bobby had come here to get outfitted for his own wedding years ago. Another lifetime ago.

Sullivan held a bow tie up to his neck and eyed himself in the full length mirror. "Is it me?" he asked with a grin. "Oh hey, what about this one?" he added, putting back the bow tie and grabbing a skinny long white tie with tiny red hearts. "I'm kidding, I'm kidding." He replaced that one and grabbed a bolo.

"I really don't know," Bobby said, dropping down on a velvet bench and staring off into space. Like he'd been doing the past three days. Since he'd last seen Tori. In that hospital cot. Since they'd had that awful conversation.

It had taken every bit of his self-control not to text her later that day to ask how she was, how her shoulder was faring. He knew anyway, of course, because Bronco was a small town and everyone else had asked and he'd heard secondhand. She'd been fine enough by the next morning to be cleared to get back to practicing; he'd heard that when she did her first pattern, a crowd watching broke into cheers and claps. He wished he could have been there. To cheer her on, to support her, to catch her if she went flying. That last part she wouldn't allow, but he'd try anyway. She wasn't his anymore and he had to stop thinking of her.

"God, Bobby, just *call* her already," Sullivan said, eyeing him sitting there like a mopey lump. "Tell her you were wrong. Make plans for tonight to at least *talk*."

"What's the point? I'm bad for her. And she's bad for me, Sull. She's leaving very soon. Headed to Australia to continue a rodeo there with some of her sisters and cousins. She'll be gone anyway."

"She's here *now*. In Bronco."

"Sullivan, you of all people know I should stay away from her. With my past? Come on. She got hurt because of me. And she has a lot of people counting on her. Her family. Her fans."

"Bobby, you're my brother and I'm gonna give it to you straight because you missed out on getting my words of wisdom for the past forty years."

Even Bobby had to smile at that.

"I think that you think you're cursed. Like that haunted barstool in Doug's. You sat on it for some reason, and then three days later, you supposedly died. Everyone kept a serious distance from that stool before, as you know, but they really avoided it *after*. Even now that you're back, very much alive and well, no one will risk it. Because they figure sitting on that stool is just plain bad luck. You sat on it and you're still waiting for the other shoe to drop."

"Are you close to the wisdom part?" Bobby asked. He got what his brother was saying—sort of—but it wasn't the dumb haunted barstool, symbolically or otherwise, assuring Bobby that he had bad luck. The one woman he was interested in since his divorce was leaving town. The country. *Him.* That was bad luck. And the story of his life.

Sullivan took a deep breath and was looking at him thoughtfully, which meant something was coming. A speech Bobby probably didn't want to hear. "You took off your wedding ring that night in the woods—by that cliff," his twin said. "And you either meant to throw it or you dropped it, I don't know. But the day Sadie and I went to the spot where your backpack was and we found your ring in the leaves, Sadie said you always said you'd never take it off. And you didn't, even after the divorce. The fact that you did take it off that night tells me…something."

Bobby leaned his head back against the wall, not the least bit interested in this conversation. "Tells you what?"

"I thought it meant you had to really be gone, Bobby. I didn't want to believe it. But when we found the ring, I thought you must have taken it off because you'd given up on life. I don't know if you got too close to the edge of the cliff or what…"

Bobby's stomach twisted. "God, Sullivan, this is a little heavy. We're in a tux shop. For your wedding. Your Christmas wedding. Deck the halls with boughs of holly," he sang, trying—desperately—to not let what Sullivan had said get in his head. He was done thinking of that night in the woods. He'd been done since he'd walked out of Bronco three years ago.

"Bobby, you have to deal with this."

"I don't. I'm back, right? I'm here. Things are good right now. Let it be, Sullivan."

"Things are good? You broke up with a woman I think you're in love with."

Bobby felt the jab in his chest. "Can you not tell me how I feel? You've been conjecturing a lot since we've arrived in this shop five minutes ago."

"Well, then *tell* me. How do you feel about Tori Hawkins?"

Bobby stood up. He had to get some air. Fast.

"I like you better when you don't push, Sullivan."

"I like you better when you let yourself be happy," he countered.

Bobby let out a hard sigh. Looking at Sullivan was like looking in a damned mirror, which was a problem when his twin was throwing truths—or what Sullivan *believed* was the truth—at him.

"Go for the bow tie," Bobby said. "It's a classic." He made a show of pulling out his phone. "Uh, text from Dalton's Grange," he flat out lied. "I've gotta go."

"Yeah, right," Sullivan said, raising an eyebrow with a good-natured shake of his head. "Before you go, let me suggest something."

Oh Lord, what now? "If you have to."

"I think you should go pay our aunt Michelle a visit. Talk to her about Aubrey and her parents. About what happened the day we were born."

"What the hell for?" Bobby asked, truly having no clue why Sullivan would think that was a good idea. The woman was his biological aunt, his mother's older sister, and had never once reached out to him. She'd estranged herself from the family.

"I didn't know anything about my birth family until Sadie told me what she knew from you and being your sister-in-law. Just basics. Michelle filled in a lot of details."

"Which you already shared with me. I know the story, Sullivan. I don't need details."

"Maybe you do, Bobby. Maybe you need to just meet her, talk to her, get some closure about that part of your past. I think everything's connected and it all starts with that."

Dammit to hell. Something about what Sullivan was saying sounded…reasonable.

Sullivan put a hand on Bobby's shoulder. "Okay, I'm gonna put this in very simple terms because our past is complicated. Ready?"

"I guess," Bobby said.

"If you want Tori Hawkins, little brother, you'll deal with your past. That simple."

Sullivan was two minutes older. Where did he get off acting like the wise old brother? "You keep forgetting that Tori is *leaving* in a few days. Gone with the wind."

"She's not disappearing in a tornado, Bobby. She's just going to Australia for a tour. She'll exist in the world after that. You know that, right?"

Bobby hadn't really thought past her leaving. He'd always been an out-of-sight, out-of-mind person, which was how he'd dealt with his anonymous existence the three years he'd been out of Bronco.

Bobby crossed his arms over his chest. "You said your solution was simple."

"Well, it is. Do this, have that."

Bobby had to smile.

"Just call her," Sullivan said. "Go do it now so I can focus on picking out my bow tie."

For a moment, Bobby had to admit that he was kind of overwhelmed with affection for his twin brother. Something that after six months still hadn't ceased to amaze him whenever he'd be struck with a blast of it. That he loved this busybody, insightful dude who looked just like him. That he had a brother at all. And how lucky he was that it was Sullivan.

So maybe take his advice, Bobby heard a low voice whisper deep inside him.

Chapter Fifteen

Channeling all her courage, confidence and the words of her sisters and Kacey Karrow, Tori got in her car and drove over to Bobby's cabin. By the time she got there, the sun was beginning to set and casting a beautiful glow over the property.

He was sitting on the porch, on the top step, his phone in hand. When she got out of her car, he stood up, looking quite surprised.

"I was just about to call you," he said. "Well, I pulled up your number like five times and then swiped out. But the sixth time was gonna be the charm."

She'd missed him so much. How she wanted to just rush at him, arms open, feel his strong ones around her.

But now that she was here, looking at him, an unexpected blast of fear hit her in the stomach. All her bravado—gone. This man had hurt her. He'd walked away, out of her life, and here she was, about to tell him he should walk back in.

That was a fool's errand.

Turn around. Leave, a little voice said.

But as Tori looked at Bobby, this man she loved so much, she knew she wouldn't leave. She'd come for a reason. Because she fought for what she wanted. What she *believed* in.

And Tori believed in Bobby. She believed in *them*.

She lifted her chin.

He'd said he was just about to call her, which had hope flaring just a bit. Maybe he'd been about to call to ask how she was feeling, doing.

"I thought you were done with us," she said. "What were you going to say when you called?" She held her breath. *Please say you realized you were wrong and that we should just see this through.*

"That I miss you like hell, Tori. That the past three days have been torture. That I didn't expect any of this and don't know where to go from here."

She let out the breath, relief flooding her, her heart giving a happy little flip.

This, she could work with.

You called it, Mom, she thought. *Just as Suzi Hawkins always did.*

"What brings you here?" he asked, and she could see the flare of hope in his eyes. That she wasn't here to say she agreed with what he'd said in the hospital, after all.

Tori didn't know what was going to happen between them. She only knew she had to be with this man, had to give it everything she had and was. "I know where to go from here, Bobby. Let's just take each day as it comes. And we'll cross the last day when we get to it."

"I like that idea, Tori. I really do. But I also really don't think I should get in your way. With practice and your sisters and the upcoming rodeo."

That was called life. And what Tori did understand about Bobby is that he was really just coming *back* to life. It was like he'd been reborn and he didn't really know it. It was hard to see the forest when when you were pushing through the trees, finding your way.

She was about to tell him just that, or something like it, when he walked toward her.

He stood just inches from her now, his brown-green eyes intense on her.

"Thing is, being apart is worse than anything," he added, stepping closer still. He put the phone in his back pocket. "So I think we need to go with your idea instead of mine. And that we both think less, kiss more."

Oh, the relief. A burst of happiness exploded in her heart.

She laughed. "*That* is a plan." And now, she did rush at him. He opened up those arms and held her tight.

"All I know is that right this minute, Bobby Stone, I belong here. Right here."

"Same," he said.

She lifted her chin and he kissed her. Passionately. Tenderly. With so much feeling, her knees felt wobbly in the best way.

"How about I make you dinner?" he asked. "I have steaks and potatoes. Sadie gave me her recipe and the ingredients for peppercorn sauce the last time she invited me for dinner because I raved about it. I could make that too."

"That sounds very, very good."

Her toes tingled. Goose bumps flew up her spine and across her neck in joyful anticipation of a very good night ahead.

For how complicated it all seemed, getting back together had been remarkably simple.

A half hour later, they were sitting on the back patio at the table, enjoying dinner and the warm summer night air. They kept the conversation light, Tori telling him how well practice at the arena was going and sharing some cute stories from her cousin's bridal shower, how Audrey got at least ten black negligees, and Bobby told her about the wall of ties in The Dashing Cattleman.

"So did he go with the bow tie?" she asked, adding a little sour cream to her baked potato.

"I actually don't know," Bobby said. "I had to get out of there. We'd been in the place for like five minutes when the conversation turned deadly."

"Uh-oh. About family stuff?"

"Well, more about the fact that I'm not dealing with my past," he said. "Any of it. And how it's holding me back."

"From what?" she asked, all the air in her lungs stilling.

"From you. From a real relationship. From happiness."

There he went being all honest again, something she could always count on with Bobby.

"What does he think you should be doing?" she asked. "Opening up more about the night you left Bronco?"

He nodded. "He also thinks I should talk to my aunt—my estranged aunt who I never even knew existed because no one ever talked about her. She washed her hands of her sister, her parents—and me—and moved over five hours away to Rust Creek Falls right after we were born, according to Sullivan."

Tori paused her fork. "And what do you think?"

He shrugged. "What could she possibly have to say that would change anything? She wasn't interested in knowing me as a kid. Apparently, she came back to Bronco for my grandmother's funeral and I didn't even know it. I didn't recognize my own aunt. She didn't introduce herself, either."

"Well, she must have had her reasons, right?" Tori asked gently.

"I suppose. But I don't want to know those reasons. My grandmother kept vital information from me, Tori. That messed with how I felt about her. I hate to admit that, but it did. She knew I had a twin brother out there and took it to her grave. And my mother? I know enough about her. So what's the point in meeting my aunt or even talking to her on the phone?"

She could understood both his and his brother's points of view. "Sounds like Sullivan thinks it would offer you some closure. Because an aunt *is* out there and it's like a lost piece of the family puzzle."

Bobby poked at his steak. He gave another shrug and then sat back, clearly thinking things over.

"Have you ever visited the house you grew up in since you've been back in Bronco?" she asked, taking a sip of her iced tea.

"No. My childhood home is long gone. Once I started

working full-time, I renovated the house for my grand-mother, half myself, half with help. When she passed away, I sold it. Sullivan said he visited once, just drove past it, but I told him it looked nothing like the home he would have grown up in in a parallel life."

"Wow. That's pretty intense to think about." She rarely let herself think about what her life would have been like had things been different in her own past. If she hadn't become a Hawkins. It was very hard to imagine.

"He dodged a bullet by getting adopted. I told him so. Not being raised in that rundown house. Not finding his mother passed out drunk on the floor, sometimes with a strange guy beside her. Getting abandoned by that mother. Never knowing his dad. Being thought of as a pain in the neck by tired grandparents who thought they'd done their job of rearing children."

Tori bit her lip, her heart going out to him. "It's a very emotional, complicated subject. If he'd been raised in that house, he would have had his twin brother."

He seemed lost in thought for a few moments. "Yeah. We've talked about it. Sullivan's at peace. I think Sadie has a lot to do with that. I know it's why he's so damned pushy about me getting you back. So I'll be at peace—or go after it."

She smiled at that. "Which entails possibly getting closure by talking to your aunt."

He sighed. "It's just gonna dredge up all those thoughts I'd rather forget. My birth story is pretty awful, Tori. And like I said, my grandmother kept the knowl-edge of my brother from me. So did my mother, of course, but I didn't expect anything of her. I trusted my gran—so I'd rather not delve too deeply into her thought process on the day we were born and all the years after."

She could understand that. She dabbed a bite of steak in the peppercorn sauce.

"How'd we get on this topic, anyway?" he asked, eating the last of his potato. "I'd rather talk about how beautiful you look tonight."

She laughed. "In my jeans and flip-flops?"

"You're very sexy in those jeans and flip-flops. I like your sparkly green toes."

She wiggled her feet.

"And the way that silky shirt drapes over your curves," he said. "Very, very sexy."

"I find you pretty hot yourself, Bobby Stone."

"Oh yeah?" he asked, standing up and moving his chair right beside hers. He leaned over and tipped up her chin. "I'm so glad you're here. I'm so glad we're back together."

"Me too," she whispered.

And then he scooped her up, the plates and cups and dishes and cleanup be damned, and carried her to his bedroom.

Bobby woke up to a dog barking and he bolted straight up in bed. It was still light out, barely nine o'clock. He glanced wildly around—no dog. He'd been dreaming. Of Sarge, his mother's German shepherd mix. Sarge had looked just like the purebred except he was half the size and not all that furry. Bobby had adored him. But when his mother left when he was ten, she took the dog with her. He'd slept with one of Sarge's old stuffed toys under his pillow for a couple years, hoping his mother and the dog would come back one day, but they never did.

He sighed and leaned back against the headboard, glancing over at Tori, so beautiful and sleeping peacefully. They'd both dozed off after a round of incredible sex and a shower for two. His chest, his throat had that tight feeling, and he wondered if it was the dream about Sarge or that here he was with Tori again when she was leaving in days. Or maybe it had been the conversation with Sullivan in the tux shop, then with Tori over dinner, about his aunt.

Sounds like Sullivan thinks it would offer you some closure. Because an aunt is *out there and it's like a lost piece of the family puzzle.*

Would it? Was it the key to letting go of all that?

Maybe it was the start, like Sullivan thought. Deal with that part of his past, his family, and maybe he could start letting go of the other stuff.

Such as how he'd failed as a son and a grandkid. And then failed as a husband. How he'd hit rock bottom three years ago in the woods.

Call her, he vaguely thought, trying out the idea in his head. *It's not like she could make things worse. There is no worse.*

He looked at Tori again, his beautiful Tori, and got out of bed and slipped on his boxer briefs and a pair of sweatpants, then grabbed his phone from the bedside table and headed into the living room.

Just do it, he told himself. *Call her.*

He knew her name—Sullivan had told him. A quick Google of that name and Rust Creek Falls, Montana, brought up her telephone number.

He glanced at the time on his phone. 9:06 p.m. Late-ish. But hell, if he was going to do this he was going to do this now.

He pressed in the numbers. A man answered.

"My name is Bobby Stone," he said. "I'm—"

"Oh gosh," the man responded. "I know who you are. I'll go get Michelle. Just hang on for a moment."

Sullivan sucked in a breath. He could hear muffled voices, as if a hand was over the mouthpiece. Then a woman's voice.

"Bobby?" she asked.

"I hope it's all right that I'm calling. And so late. I had it in my head to do it, to just talk to you. If Rust Creek Falls wasn't five hours away, I might have just gotten in my truck and driven to see you. Talk to you in person."

"I understand, and it's fine. I met your brother. Last December."

"I know. We're very close now."

"I'm glad to hear that, Bobby. What happened when you two were born was terrible. But no one can change that—you've only got now and the future. So I'm really glad to hear you and Sullivan found your way back together."

"I'm wondering if you have anything to add to what you told Sullivan when he came out to see you."

"I really don't," she said. "I estranged myself from my parents and sister because I fell in love with a wonderful guy who made me realize I didn't need to be around toxic people, and back then, when I was eighteen, my parents and sister were toxic for me. We had big problems, constant fights. Aubrey and I never got along. We certainly weren't close. And granted, she was kind of wild and sixteen is way too young to be a mother, but the way my parents treated her when she told them she was pregnant was one of the last straws for me."

He was nodding inwardly. Everything she was saying sounded like the Stone household. Rough, not a real happy place.

"And then when Aubrey brought you home from the hospital and everyone was just waiting for you to die, I couldn't take it," she said. "Aubrey wailing. Our mother in constant tears. Our father not knowing how to deal with any of it. I was very young myself and couldn't handle it either, I suppose. I moved to Rust Creek Falls, found a job, fell in love and that was that. I'd heard through the grapevine that you'd survived and thrived, and I was very glad. But I was done with that part of my past and cut all ties. I'm very sorry I wasn't there for you."

All the air in Bobby's lungs whooshed out of him. Huh. Of all the things she might have said, he hadn't considered how things had been for his mother or grandparents and now her. They'd all been waiting for him to die, like the doctor had told them he would.

How awful and stressful that must have been. How harrowing. It had to have affected them all, maybe more than his grandparents had ever counted on. Especially because he kept *not* dying. Month after month, the tiny, sickly baby they hadn't planned to hold in their hearts longer than a day or two had lived and then started thriving. His mother had probably been scared to love him.

"I guess maybe you didn't need to know that," Michelle said suddenly. "About how hard it was on everyone, how painful. Gosh, it's impossible to know how much of the truth is helpful."

"No, I'm grateful you told me." Her words were knocking around in his head, but instead of feeling worse, he felt…better. Why, he wasn't yet sure.

"Oh, good," she said. "And I'm glad you called, Bobby."

He was too. Unexpectedly. "Well, maybe sometime we can all get together."

"I'd like that," she said, her voice emotional. He had a feeling getting together would do her a world of good too. Even if it was just a one-time thing.

And then they said their goodbyes and Bobby sat in the living room chair for a good long while, just letting things settle.

Somehow, what his aunt Michelle had said did give him closure, did fill in a missing piece. He couldn't be sure of anything since his mother and grandparents were all gone. But based on what Michelle revealed, he felt like he finally understood his family, the choices they'd made, who'd they been. He might not like it, but he had a better understanding of the whys and the whats.

The longer he sat there, thinking it all over, not wondering about anything but simply *accepting*, the more he felt something like forgiveness unfurl deep inside him.

The past was complicated. But letting go was easier than he'd thought.

Well, damn.

Bobby got up and went back into the bedroom, slipping into bed beside Tori and resuming the position he'd woken up in, spooned around her.

"I've been awake since you sat up an hour ago," she whispered, holding on to his hand.

He kissed the back of her head, resting his cheek against it. "So you heard me on the phone with my aunt?"

"Just your side of the conversation. Given how the call ended with you suggesting getting together some day, I'd say the talk went well."

"It did," he said. And he told her all about it. "You wouldn't think her sharing something so harrowing with me would have helped, but it did."

Tori turned around and took his face in both her hands. "I'm very glad, Bobby."

She kissed him, and he couldn't remember feeling so at peace.

Chapter Sixteen

The morning of the Bronco Summer Family Rodeo dawned sunny and cool, the forecast calling for perfect temperatures—for a rodeo and a wedding. Tori was three minutes away from her first competition, waiting on the sidelines atop Bluebell, her coach yammering at her to keep her blinders on. Tori had discovered that thinking about Bobby actually revved her up, and that setting her focus squarely on the ring with a minute's countdown seemed to do wonders for her performance.

She had two minutes to let herself remember every delicious detail of their past few nights together.

Just an hour ago, Bobby had kissed her goodbye after yet another great evening spent together. Eating, talking, laughing, taking bubble baths, making love. True to their word, they'd enjoyed each other to the fullest for the remaining time as a couple. They'd finally watched *Star Wars: A New Hope* and *When Harry Met Sally*, and last night, when they'd lain in bed wrapped in each other's arms after more incredible sex, he'd told her that he was thinking of a getting a dog. A German shepherd mix like he'd had when he was young until his mother had taken off with Sarge.

Tori's heart had swelled. If Bobby was thinking of adopting a dog, it meant he was allowing permanence in his life. It meant that Bronco truly felt like home to him.

She was glad for him. But what did it mean for *them*?

What Tori had said to Kacey was one hundred percent right—she couldn't ask Bobby to join her just as he wouldn't ask her to stay.

So this was it. They'd have tonight, then an hour or two tomorrow morning to say their goodbyes, and then she'd fly off to Australia—Bobby Stone a beautiful memory.

She wasn't sure how that would go. Would her heart be aching with longing for him? Would she spend her evenings off-center, missing him like crazy, not wanting to go out with her sisters and cousins? Would she mope around, feeling like something just wasn't right?

She could come always come back to see him, and maybe they could pick up where they'd left off until she'd have to leave again for another tour. But how? Weeks or even months would have gone by. They'd have missed out on the daily comings and goings of each other's worlds. They wouldn't be close anymore. Things would just be…different.

Now, as she watched the big clock in the arena, nearing the countdown to a minute to go, Tori turned off all thought to everything but Bluebell, to what they needed to accomplish in the ring.

"And now, competing in the barrel racing event, here's one of the famed Hawkins Sisters, Tori Hawkins!" the announcer called, and the crowds in the wraparound stands at the arena went wild, cheering and clapping. All of it went right to Tori's heart. She *did* love the rodeo.

Tori rode Bluebell around the barrels, shaving three seconds off her best time, which had the crowd in a happy frenzy. As she trotted off toward the sidelines and her snooty competitor, she could see Bobby, Sullivan and Sadie in the front row, in their finest Western wear and Stetsons. Bobby was on his feet, clapping and wolf whistling.

The rodeo is my home. But so are you, she thought. *I love you, Bobby Stone.*

There. She'd admitted it. Finally.

Just in time to say goodbye. Just in time for a wedding tonight to remind her in excruciating romantic detail how much she loved him, how much she wished they could be together.

Put your head where it needs to be, she told herself. For the next hour, she kept her attention on the competitors, focusing on why she was here.

"One minute to go, Tori," her coach said.

Tori nodded, glad she'd blinked away her love life and put on the blinders. "We've got this, Bluebell," she whispered to her horse.

Her least favorite competitor had had a bad turn and then two more barrel racers had been slow. If Tori could keep her pace like her last pattern, she could win the event. And she intended to.

Her love for Bobby sending her adrenaline soaring, Tori went out and beat her last time by just over a second. She'd won first place.

She could see Bobby, Sullivan and Sadie on their feet, clapping and cheering. Two rows over, her parents were screaming and hugging along with her grandmother Hattie. Her aunts were waving Hawkins Sisters flags with huge smiles on their faces.

Her mom, dad, and Hattie were running over to her, pushing past the crowd and down the steps to get to her. She hurried over to them, each wrapping her into a warm hug.

"Wow, Tori!" Hattie Hawkins said, tipping her silver Stetson at her. "Great racing! I'm so proud of you!"

"Aww," Tori said, squeezing her grandmother, this trailblazing legend, into another hug.

"We're so proud of you," her dad, Arthur, said, clapping her on the back at least ten times. There were tears misting his eyes, and Tori knew he was feeling all the fatherly feels—his daughter had been injured, his daughter had gotten her heart bruised too, and his daughter had had a very good day in the ring.

She hugged her father, her mom wiping under her eyes.

"Okay, I'm emotional!" Suzie said with a grin.

Coach Tamara was calling Tori over for a quick meeting, so she had to say goodbye to her family for now. She loved this crew so much—and was constantly reminded how truly lucky she was to have them.

The rest of the day passed in an excited blur of activity, lots of wins or near wins for her, her sisters, and cousins, a family lunch in a private room at DJ's Deluxe, more competing, a brief tribute to the second generation of Hawkins Sisters, which had Tori and her sisters crying and wolf whistling. She must have signed hundreds of autographs at the arena, said *sure thing* with a smile to hundreds of selfies with fans. She'd been able to see Bobby for only a minute or two here and there as the hours had worn on; he'd find her on the sidelines for a quick congratulations and a hug that always ended way too soon.

She'd whispered in his ear that she couldn't wait for tonight. The wedding reception might be public but tonight, at either her cabin or his, would be very private. At least they'd have that.

Now the time was nearing 3:00 p.m., the end of the Bronco Summer Family Rodeo. Tori was both tired and amped up. It had been a truly great day and she'd loved every minute of it.

"The clock is winding down," the announcer called out over the loudspeaker. "But it's just beginning for our happy couple, who'll be getting lassoed for life in a private ceremony right here at the rodeo! Everyone, put your hands together to welcome Audrey Hawkins and Jack Burris!"

The crowd jumped to their feet, cheering and clapping.

Just then, Audrey and Jack came riding out, holding hands, in fancy white Western wear, waving at the crowd.

"Their wedding reception is open to anyone with a ticket to the rodeo, so come celebrate true love at 7:00 p.m.!" the announcer added.

Tori and her sisters and cousins watched Audrey and

her groom lean toward each other for a kiss, which had the crowd going even more wild.

"Let's get back to the cabins to rest up before we have to get dolled up," Faith said. "I'm so excited for the wedding."

Amy patted her heart. "I'm already crying, I'm so happy for Audrey."

Tori grinned. "Let's go," she said, catching Audrey and Jack riding off into the chute that would lead to a back entrance. Jack carried his bride off her horse and gave her one heck of a kiss.

Tori's knees gave a wobble at how in love they were, how romantic this all was, huge crowd and everything. Her cousin was marrying the man she loved. That was what mattered.

And tomorrow, Tori would be saying goodbye to the man *she* loved.

They'd just have to make tonight one for the record books because no matter how Tori looked at it, she didn't see how they could stay together.

Despite the public spectacle and hoopla surrounding the wedding, the ceremony itself was an intimate affair, held in a beautifully decorated private ballroom inside the convention center, family and friends of Audrey and Jack *only*. The promoters had gone all out for their rodeo stars. The room had been transformed into fairy-tale elegance with a breathtaking crystal chandelier, white flowers everywhere, a stage with marble vases of white and pink roses behind the minister's lectern, the white chairs padded in satin and draped in garlands of pink roses. A white carpet had taken Audrey down the aisle to her waiting groom, and Tori could swear she saw tears misting the eyes of the handsome groom.

There were a few photographers, of course, but Audrey and Jack had hired their own, a professional who was a family friend, in addition to the promoter's photographer and videographer so they could be assured of great candids. Tori had gotten Audrey's okay on writing a feature for *Rodeo Weekly* on what the entire experience was like, preparing for her big day in the lead-up to the rodeo itself, and the magazine's photographer had snapped quite a few pics. Tori had let her editor know that Kacey Karrow had not and would not grant an interview, and when she suggested a feature on the rodeo wedding, her editor had been thrilled since Tori had a "special in," which she would not take advantage of.

"I'm not crying, you're crying," Faith said, dabbing under her eyes as the minister began the vows.

"Oh, I'm crying," Amy said through a grin, tears slipping down her cheeks. "I'm so happy for Audrey."

"Me too," Tori said, her heart full. She glanced at her handsome date, sitting beside her in his suit, and boy, had she been right that first day she'd met Bobby—he *did* clean up well.

"Wow," he'd whispered reverently when he'd picked her up at the cabin just a half hour ago, not hiding the appreciative sweep of his eyes as he took in her pale pink ankle-length silk dress with its delicate off-the-shoulder straps and beading. Tori Hawkins rarely felt like a princess—had no interest in ever feeling like a princess—but tonight, in this dress, with her prince in his pristine charcoal suit, she couldn't help herself. She thought she'd be immune to the wedding, but she wasn't. Far from it. The romance in the air. The love. The flowers and beautiful dresses, the suits and ties and Stetsons, the vows.

Now, as it was Audrey's turn to recite those vows, Tori glanced over at Bobby beside her, wondering if he was thinking about his own wedding, since previous wedding talk seemed to affect him. But he didn't look the least bit uncomfortable—or bored. What *was* he thinking?

The bride and groom were exchanging rings. More tears prickled Tori's eyes. She looked down at her left hand, the empty ring finger, her heart giving a little squeeze.

Was all this unusual emotional response to the wedding trying to tell her something? Tori had never been overly emotional, didn't cry easily, so these tears and chest squeezings were new.

"I can't believe this is our last night," Bobby leaned in close to whisper. "These two weeks went by way too fast."

Suddenly she could feel her lower lip trembling. What the heck was this? She managed a small smile, but this time, she couldn't blame the tears pricking her eyes on the ceremony.

"Way too fast," she whispered back, almost unable to look at him. She'd lose it. She was barely hanging on to control of herself.

Take a breath. Look around. Focus on the cute flower girls. Do not burst into tears at the happy part when the bride and groom are about to kiss!

She let her eyes wander to keep them from sliding over to her hot date. Across the aisle, in the Burris family section, she noticed Jack's brother Mike staring longingly ahead and she followed his gaze to her cousin Corinne, one of Audrey's bridesmaids. Oooh, interesting. Tori had heard Corinne and Mike had something of on an on-again, off-again relationship. When she saw Corinne looking straight at Mike and then quickly shifting her gaze away as if caught, she knew something was up with those two.

"You may now kiss your bride," the minister said, and Audrey and Jack planted one hell of a romantic, passionate whopper on each other.

Everyone jumped to their feet, clapping and cheering and wolf whistling as they had not too long ago at the rodeo.

As the bride and groom and their wedding party passed by up the aisle, Tori watched seven-year-old Mila, Kendra Humphrey's little girl, dash out from her seat to pick up rose petals strewn on the white carpet.

"I can't wait till my mommy is a bride again," Mila said to no one in particular, putting the rose petals in the pockets of her pretty yellow dress.

"I didn't realize your mom was getting married," Tori said, confused and trying not to show it. She turned a bit and could see Kendra sitting two rows behind her own, chatting with the woman beside her. No engagement ring. And no date, apparently.

"Not yet!" Mila said with a grin. "But I'm working on it!"

Tori laughed and watched Mila scamper back over to her mother.

"Uh-oh," Bobby whispered. "Kendra had better watch out."

Was that Tori's heart deflating second by second until it was like a pancake?

"Watch out for what?" she asked before she could grab the words from her mouth. Ugh. She really hadn't meant to say that aloud.

Bobby shot a glance at her. "I just mean that all this eventually leads to *this*—" he said, taking his double fists and jabbing them in his heart as if stabbing himself with a dagger.

Oh Bobby, she thought, unable to help the frown on her face.

He might have strong feelings for her, but maybe she finally had to accept that those feelings only went so far. That dagger wasn't about them, she knew. It was about his divorce, which had done a number on him. He didn't believe in love and forever anymore. If he ever really had.

And Tori Hawkins, surprise-surprise, *did*.

This *was* their last night. And she needed to keep that in mind *and* forget it so that she wouldn't ruin it by feeling that imaginary dagger jab her in the heart.

Chapter Seventeen

The reception was being held in a section of the arena that had been transformed by the convention center crew into another beautiful space. Tori could barely believe that just several hours ago, the arena had been full of grass and horses and barrels and courses, and now, it was a fairy-tale setting. What seemed to be hundreds of round tables of all sizes were on one side, a large dance floor set up on another, white muslin tents festooned with sparkling lights where multiple bars were located, and countless huge vases of flowers.

The party was crowded. The reception was open to anyone with a ticket to the rodeo, which had ensured huge sales. Bronco residents had jumped on that, so the party was full of familiar faces, hometown folks and of course, the bride's and groom's families and friends. But there had to be at least three hundred people milling about with glasses of champagne or on the dance floor or under the tents.

Bobby was under one of the tents, chatting with his brother and Sadie, who looked so beautiful in her lemon yellow dress. Tori had been surrounded by her sisters and parents a moment ago, but they'd flitted off, and she was grateful for a few seconds not to have to concentrate on conversation around her. She was seriously preoccupied.

"Well, hello there," said a familiar and very welcome voice.

Tori could feel herself lighting up as she whirled around.

There stood Kacey Karrow.

She wore a silver Stetson, her long gray braid down one shoulder with a sparkly white band, and a salmon-colored satin pantsuit with white cowboy boots. She looked amazing.

"I can't talk long since I told my 'date' I'd be right back with two glasses of wine," she said, gesturing at a table for two across the grass.

Tori's mouth dropped open. Kacey was not only here, she had a date! "Did you say a date?"

"Well, I air quoted it, but kind of," Kacey said with a smile. "He's a former rancher, eighty years young, has three dogs of his own. He's been asking me out for years—whenever I show up in town. Well, I called him up and asked *him* out to the reception. He actually dropped his phone, then picked it up and said yes." She grinned.

"Wow," Tori said. "Wow, wow, wow."

"Yup. I think sharing my story with you unlocked

something in me, Tori. I held on to my past for fifty years. And I'll be honest, I wasn't all that comfortable with it being out there, just in your ears, but still. But as the days went on, I started feeling lighter. And I realized I'd needed to get it out of me to be free."

"Oh, Kacey," Tori said, wrapping her arms around her.

Kacey accepted the hug, warmly embracing her back. "Well, I'd better go get that wine. See you," she said.

Tears pricked Tori's eyes. She'd miss Kacey Karrow. But she was so happy for her.

"So she did open up to you," a familiar and welcome male voice now said. "I happen to know from personal experience that the kind, compassionate, nonjudgmental person you are is no match for secrets."

Tori turned and grinned at Bobby, who was approaching with two glasses of champagne. "You heard that?"

"I didn't mean to eavesdrop, but yes."

"I'm so happy for her," Tori said. "She'll be sitting on her porch in her golden years, painting a man she's smitten with, sharing cupcakes and sweet tea, just like she'd imagined."

Bobby smiled and handed her the champagne. He clinked her glass and they sipped their drinks, holding each other's gazes.

I love you, she wanted to say. *Come with me, ask me to stay…*

But she knew she couldn't ask and neither could he. They were stuck.

Stop it, she told herself. *You have tonight. Make the most of it instead of moping.*

So she did. For the next couple of hours, they talked to a lot of Hawkinses, congratulated both sides of the happy families who were now in-laws, mingled, ate great food and sipped champagne in between dancing a lot. Fast. Slow. A couple of line dances that Bobby was pretty bad at, making her and Sadie hoot with laughter. And he'd showed her a ton of photos and videos he'd taken of her competing. There were also a lot of kisses.

Then suddenly it was close to midnight.

Pumpkin hour. And the day she'd be leaving. Her heart was so heavy she was surprised she was still standing.

"It's the last dance," Bobby said. "Shall we?" He gave a gallant bow, then held out his hand, his smile warm, his brown eyes full of tenderness and desire.

She took his hand and accompanied him to the dance floor, never wanting to let go.

Bobby had been thinking about something all night, something kind of monumental. It involved Tori. And tomorrow. And not letting her get away.

He was going to flat out ask her if he could hit the road with her.

He could be her personal roadie, her horse caretaker, her friend, her lover, her…man. He didn't know what their future held, but he wasn't letting her go without giving *more* a shot.

Right now, as he held her in his arms, slow dancing to the band's pretty good version of a Frank Sinatra song, he knew he was not saying goodbye tomorrow.

The big ask involved going back to his cabin, where they'd get into bed and not emerge for a few hours, then catch some sleep, and wake up for the sunrise. He'd suggest they enjoy it out on the back patio, and then he'd tell her he wanted to come with her, if she'd have him.

Would she say yes? He was seventy-five percent sure she would. He knew she had strong feelings for him, as he did for her. He knew she didn't want to say goodbye, as he didn't.

The other twenty-five percent was worried she'd say he'd always known they had an expiration date, that she was her own woman and rode alone, and that their two-week affair was never supposed to be more.

The way he envisioned it, they'd go to Australia together, then attend whatever rodeos she had on her schedule, then come back to Bronco for Career Day at the middle and high schools unless there was a conflict with that schedule, spend some time with his brother and Sadie, and then go from there.

The band was winding down, and when Bobby glanced around, he realized there were very few people left at the reception. Sullivan and Sadie had left a little while ago, as had Kacey Karrow and her date. The bride and groom had taken off a half hour ago for their honeymoon in Fiji, and most of the bridal party and relatives were gone, including Tori's sisters. There were a few stragglers at one of the bars, but even the bartender was boxing up bottles and glasses, a few members of the catering staff hard at work on packing up.

"We're alone on the dance floor," Bobby whispered, his arms down low around her waist, Tori's wrapped around his neck.

"And I can't wait to be alone at your place in a little

while," she whispered back with a grin, tipping up on her toes to kiss him.

This night could not get better.

"How can you dance with this lying fake nobody?" an angry, slurring voice called out.

Bobby froze. He stepped out of Tori's embrace to find that jerk Will Kennely staggering toward them, a glass of what looked like whiskey in his hand.

"He made his wife so miserable she left him," Kennely spat out, his ice-blue eyes glinting with disgust. "I knew Dana in high school. Nice gal. Till she took up drinking because of her marriage. And then this jerk fakes his own death because his life is obviously falling apart. Lets everyone think he's dead. Including his own family. Who the hell does that? How can you let this lying bastard near you?"

Shock, nausea, anger, pain all mixed in Bobby's chest, burning, aching, stabbing.

He heard Tori's gasp and saw her clench her fists at her sides.

His own were clenched too.

Kennely was staring at those fists. "Yeah, go for it, Stone. You should have stayed dead." He staggered toward Bobby.

Bobby instinctively slipped Tori behind him. Kennely took a drunken swing and then stumbled and fell down, knocking himself out.

"Sorry," called a man rushing over with two members of the catering staff. "They're going to help me get him in my car. He's my friend—I'll get him home."

Bobby glanced at Tori, who closed her eyes for a moment, her face pale. There weren't many people around at this point. But the one he wished hadn't heard any of that diatribe was standing right beside him. It didn't matter what was true and what wasn't.

A lot was true.

Bobby's throat was closing in on itself, his stomach felt full of acid, and he wanted the ground to swallow him up.

He wanted to disappear again.

As the three men dragged an unconscious Kennely out of the arena, Bobby couldn't get out of there fast enough.

"I'll take you home," he said—flatly—to Tori.

"I thought we'd go to your cabin," she said in an encouraging but unsure voice, as if she knew the night was ruined. Over.

Bobby just stood there, staring down at the ground. The night *was* ruined.

"You're gonna let that damn drunk take our last night from us?" she demanded, hands on hips. "Come on, Bobby."

He looked at her, saw the steely determination in her brown eyes. Then the wavering of her chin. "It's not Kennely," he said. "It has nothing to do with him. He just happened to remind me who I am. I forgot these past few days. Tonight, in particular. But I can't run from who I am."

Like to Australia.

Who had he been kidding with that big plan?

"I'll take you home now," he repeated.

He could see her eyes get misty, then turn glinty again. She stalked off to an exit that he knew led to the parking area.

He followed her. She was pacing in a fury by his truck.

When he unlocked it, she got in and so he did he, quickly buckling up and starting the engine.

She put a hand on his arm. "You listen to me, Bobby Stone," she said, her voice trembling. "I know who you are. And I love that man."

He almost gasped. Everything inside him froze and he stared at her, then looked away, slightly shaking his head.

"Tell me you don't love me, Bobby," she said, her eyes so full of hope that he had to look away for a moment. "And I'll let you go. I'll give up on us. Go ahead, tell me."

He closed his eyes for a second, and he was back on that cliff in the woods. Then he was falling, falling, falling, scraped by brush and beaten up by the rocky wall and the hard ground he finally hit. Rock bottom, like his life had been.

"We never said anything about love, Tori. This was just supposed to be a two-week thing. And it's over now. So let's not make it more than it is."

Her eyes narrowed. "I don't think you mean any of that." She grabbed his hand. "Bobby, you have to let go of what led you away from Bronco. You're back. You've *been* back. You have a brother. You have me. You have the next half of your life ahead of you. You're gonna adopt a dog, for Pete's sake."

His head felt like it was about to explode. He put the truck in reverse and backed out of the spot and out of the parking lot, heading toward her cabin, which thankfully was only a few minutes away. He needed to be alone right now.

"Take me to the woods," she said. "To the spot where you were last standing three years ago. Where your brother and Sadie found your wedding ring."

He almost pulled over. "What the hell for?"

"I'm asking you for this one thing, Bobby. I'm leaving tomorrow—today, actually, in just several hours. Do this for me, okay?"

He didn't want to. But he found himself turning the truck around almost as if someone else was guiding his hands on the wheel. He drove in silence to the woods, and parked. Tori got out and started walking toward the trailhead, using the flashlight on her phone to light the way toward the path through the trees.

He hadn't been back since that fateful night.

And he had no idea what being here was going to do to him. It had been three years since he'd been at rock bottom. Seven months of being okay. Two weeks of being happy in a way he'd never expected.

Until rock bottom had come back for him, overtaking him.

"What's the point of this?" he asked as he neared the spot where he'd stood three years ago. He stopped when he recognized the hollowed-out log he'd sat on for a while back then. Right next to it was where he'd stood, staring down over the edge, then up at the night sky, at the stars. Then back down. Thinking, thinking, thinking of all he'd lost…

"The point is to show you that you're not the same guy you were when you were here last," Tori said.

"I am that guy. Here," he said, slapping a hand on his chest.

"Nope. Because I wasn't standing beside you three years ago, Bobby. But I am now."

He froze, her words a shock to the system.

"Tell me about that night," she said. "Please," she added gently.

He dropped his head back and stared up at the stars, then glanced at her. "Let's get away from the edge." He took off his suit jacket and spread it out on half the log so she wouldn't mess up her pretty dress, then he sat and she did too, not crowding him, not looking at him. Just…waiting to finally hear his story.

Maybe it was time to tell it.

Chapter Eighteen

"I was at Doug's bar, a favorite place of mine to go after work," he said, staring out at the night sky. "And I noticed no one was sitting on the supposedly haunted barstool—the one that ensured you'd meet a terrible fate if your butt touched it."

"I guess you don't believe in that stuff, superstitions and all that."

"I kind of do," he said. "I once even got a reading from Winona Cobb—this lady everyone called the town psychic. This was actually in Rust Creek Falls—I'd been sent there to pick up a part for the auto body shop, and I ran into this very old lady with white hair and a purple Stetson. She told me she had something to say to me. I had no idea who she was until later—or I might not have stood there and waited for her to come out with it. She looked at me and shook her head and said: 'It'll be up to you.' I asked her what she meant and she said it was obvious and then stood up and walked away."

"What do you *think* she meant?" Tori asked…hesitantly, he noted.

He shrugged. "I asked a buddy of mine what he thought. The guy called his wife—she was big into all that horoscope, hocus-pocus stuff—and she said it clearly referred to my fate. It would be up to me to decide my fate."

"Huh," Tori said. "I like that. She was probably right. That was probably what Winona Cobb meant."

"Maybe that was in my head the night at Doug's. I had a lot on my mind that night. I kept thinking about Sarge—the dog I told you about. The one my mother took with her when she left for good when I was ten. I kept seeing my grandfather's pissed-off face. My grandmother's coffin at the cemetery. Dana drunk beside me at eleven a.m., barely standing, asking when the funeral would be over. My grandmother hadn't liked her, and Dana knew it."

Tori touched his arm but didn't anything.

"Kennely was wrong about one thing—Dana didn't start drinking during our marriage. She'd had a problem for a long time, but I thought I could help, that together we could do anything, shoot for the moon."

He glanced up at the moon now, not quite a crescent in the sky. He'd been so naive back then. He was still, he supposed.

"And I kept thinking about how I tried to help her," he went on, "but she refused to admit she had a problem. How when I gave her the ultimatum—me or scotch—she chose scotch. Chose the disease over me. And then the marriage was over. I failed her. I failed my vows. I remember being in Doug's and staring at that damn barstool, the only seat available, and I plopped down on it, not caring what happened to me. The place went dead silent, and some women even tried to get me off it, but I stayed put. The next couple of nights I kept waiting for a truck to run me over or to trip into oncoming traffic. But nothing happened. I just felt like hell, which was nothing new."

He looked over at Tori. The compassion in her eyes, on her beautiful face was almost too much.

"And then a few days after I sat on that stool, I went for a walk in here at dusk. I was tired and tormented by my own damned thoughts, and I sat down for a while on this log, and then I just stood up at the edge of the cliff, feeling so alone. Completely alone. I had nothing and no one. 'It'll be up to you,' I heard Winona say." He could feel Tori's entire body seizing up beside him. Tensing. "What if I fell right off the edge of the earth, I recalled wondering. What if?"

"Oh, Bobby," she whispered, and when he glanced at her, her eyes were full of tears.

"But a second later, I was taking a step back. I thought, damn, Bobby, you need to get yourself together. And I looked up at the setting sun and felt this flicker of hope. I yanked off my wedding ring, ready to throw it because I knew that wearing it, the promise I'd made to never take it off, was holding me back, reminding me of how I'd failed. But I let the ring just fall, and I stared at it, half of it glinting in the leaves, and then I slipped."

"You slipped?" she repeated, eyes wide.

"I fell. I got scraped up pretty bad and landed hard. When I woke up, I was at the bottom of a ravine, nothing but dense brush above me, covered in bloody scratches and bruises. It was really dark by then. I realized I'd been unconscious for hours and that there was no one to notice, no one to care. I was all alone and needed something. A change. So I decided to just walk away from Bronco in the dark so that at first light, I'd be somewhere else, my fresh start already happening."

"Wow," Tori whispered, slightly shaking her head in wonder. "Where'd you go?"

"I took a bus to Wyoming and got a job as a ranch hand under a fake name on a big ranch. I worked hard and really loved being a cowboy. I never gave Bronco another thought. There was nothing here for me, no one missing me. I didn't know anyone would assume I was dead, though."

"You didn't?" she asked, sounding surprised. "That wasn't your intention?"

"No, not in the slightest. I forgot that my backpack had been left behind on the edge of the cliff. When I read a news article about myself a few days later, that I was presumed dead after falling hundreds of feet into a dense ravine, I realized I truly *had* fallen off the edge of the earth. Bobby Stone was gone for good. I was staring over. It wasn't my intention to fake my death, but I sure didn't correct anyone about it. Want to know why? Because I figured no one would really care what had happened to me."

A chill ran up his spine as he remembered that moment. The moment he knew no one in this town cared about him, no one on earth. He'd been alone.

Bobby Stone. Lone wolf. Why had he ever thought he could part of this pack of two with Tori Hawkins?

Tori let out an exhale and seemed to relax a bit beside him, her body posture not so tense.

"And then three years later," he continued, "I happened to be on Twitter because a fellow cowboy said there was a good ranching community on there, and I came across a viral post by a man named Sullivan Grainger. He wrote about coming to Bronco, Montana, because he'd discovered he had a twin brother he'd never known about, but that his twin, Bobby Stone, was presumed dead. I was shocked. I couldn't believe what I was reading. I had a brother? The next day, I came home."

He looked at Tori. Tears slipped down her cheeks, her beautiful face.

"And since I've been back, I've felt like a work in progress. Then I met you and got knocked upside the head by attraction and our chemistry and I couldn't ignore it or you if I tried. I definitely think knowing any romance would be temporary made it easier for me to open up to you."

She nodded, wiping under her eyes.

"How do you feel now that you told me, got it all out?" she asked.

He dropped his head back, his chest aching, his head a jumble, everything he'd said echoing. "I feel like I want to get away from this spot," he said.

She gave something of a smile. "I can understand that."

He stood. "I'll take you home now."

She looked at him, and he could tell she wanted to say something but that she was holding back.

Which was good. Because he needed some time alone. To process. To breathe.

"Okay," she said.

And just like that, he knew he'd lost her. And that he had to let go of any foolish dreams he'd dared let himself have in the first place.

Chapter Nineteen

Tori had barely slept. She was up for good at sunrise, sitting on her porch with a strong mug of coffee. In a little while she'd have to pack. She'd miss Bronco. She'd miss Kacey Karrow. She'd miss Bluebell, who'd stay at Dalton's Grange while she was in Australia for two weeks helping to set up a new rodeo, then her dear quarter horse who'd been through so much with her would hit the road with her to the next rodeo in Western Montana in late September.

Tears pricked her eyes as she thought about what Bobby would be doing just before that. Giving that talk to the middle and high schoolers about the cowboy life. Maybe finally sharing his story with her, combined with all the good things he had going on in Bronco, would add up to a Bobby Stone ready to take on love. He wasn't ready now and she had to let him go.

Some other woman sure would be lucky in the future.

The thought only made her heart hurt worse, so she got up and went inside with the idea of packing, but maybe to have a good long cry first.

She got as far as putting her big suitcase on the bed and flipping it open, then she sat down beside it and let the waterworks come. "Okay, Tori Hawkins. You had your cry. Now take a shower and have another cup of coffee and go get your sisters and be on your way. It's time to say goodbye to Bronco."

The shower helped. As did the second cup of coffee and a bowl of oatmeal with bananas. She was still in her fuzzy robe and cat slippers when she heard a car pulling into the parking area. She glanced out the window. Hattie! Exactly who she needed right now.

Tori ran to the door. "I'm so glad to see you. You came to say goodbye?"

"I just had to come tell you how proud I am of you, Tori. Not just as a rodeo rider, not just as a Hawkins sister. As a woman. As a person."

"Oh, Gram," Tori said, wrapping her precious, amazing grandmother in a hug. She knew Hattie was talking about everything; the two of them had spoken last night on the phone, and Tori had her told her all about Kacey Karrow, leaving out the very personal details, all about Bobby, all about how much Tori had changed since arriving in Bronco at the start of August.

Hattie held a box with the Kendra's Cupcakes logo and set it on the counter. "Got you a bunch of assorted cupcakes for the plane ride."

Tori smiled. "Much appreciated. And yes—for *now*. I'll be back to pick up Bluebell before the rodeo near the Idaho border later in September. I'll definitely stop by to see you and the family."

"Good," Hattie said. "So you and Bobby are saying goodbye too?" she asked, peering gently at her.

"I'm trying to think of that old saying, that it's better to have loved and lost than never to have loved at all. But it's not helping."

"It's definitely better to have loved. I think Bobby knows that too."

"He's letting me go, though," Tori said. "Our time together is over, as it was always meant to be."

Hattie opened her arms, and Tori flew into the warm embrace. "You and Bobby Stone aren't over. You don't get to be seventy-five without knowing a thing or two."

She gave Tori another necessary hug and then left Tori with just the slightest bit of hope. Hattie Hawkins was wise, after all. But the chances of Bobby coming through the door next, telling her he *did* love her, that they did belong together, was, to use another of her grandma Hattie's favorite expressions, pie in the sky.

"What the hell is this about some drunken idiot knocking himself out at the wedding reception while talking trash about you?" Sullivan asked, handing Bobby a take-out cup of coffee.

Seeing the logo from Kendra's Cupcakes on the cup instantly reminded him of Tori. Their first kiss. Where they'd kissed again on a deal to date.

He forced her from his mind and looked up at his twin. "Is that already out there?" Bobby asked, taking a much-needed sip of the coffee. "People sure love to gossip." He was in no mood for this. He'd barely slept last night and had gotten up for good at the crack of dawn, sitting outside with a hoodie in the cool early morning air. His head had felt full of static. Maybe from talking too much on that log. Exposing himself. Becoming way too vulnerable. His least favorite thing to be.

"Well, the people who were talking about it at Kendra's were on your side one hundred percent," Sullivan said. "It's this Kennely dude who's persona non grata now."

Bobby definitely liked the sound of that.

"I told Tori everything," he blurted out. "*Everything.* About our family history. And last night, I told her about the night I stood on the edge of the earth."

Sullivan's eyes widened. "And?"

Bobby took a long drink of the strong coffee and then repeated everything he'd said just hours ago while sitting on that log. When he was done, Sullivan put down his cup on the kitchen counter, did the same with Bobby's and pulled him into a bear hug.

He held on to his brother, his twin, grateful as hell.

Sullivan stepped back and picked up his coffee. "Permission to tell Sadie everything?" he asked.

Bobby smiled and took a sip of his own coffee. "Always."

"So let me ask you something very important," Sullivan said. "You didn't go through the hell of opening up to that woman to just let her go, did you?"

Kacey Karrow's wise words at the wedding reception came back to him.

I think sharing my story with you unlocked something in me... I wasn't all that comfortable with it being out

*there, just in your ears, but still... And I realized I'd
needed to get it out of me to be free.*

Bobby felt something inside him give way, shove
open with a creak. "Before that crap with Kennely, I
was going to invite myself along on Tori's tour of Australia. I figured we'd be there a couple of weeks, then
come back to Bronco for a few days before heading out
to her next rodeo in Western Montana."

Sullivan's eyes lit up. "I like knowing you'll be back."

"You can always count on that," Bobby said, his chest
tightening again but this time with good things.

"Well, I'd get packing if I were you," Sullivan added.

"Why are you always right?" Bobby asked. "It's kind
of annoying."

Sullivan grinned. "'Cuz I'm the wiser two minutes
older twin."

Then suddenly they were bear-hugging again.

"Go get her," Sullivan added.

When his twin left, Bobby stood where he was a
while, thinking hard.

Tori had finished packing her suitcase and two duf-
fels and was about to take a bite of one of the cannoli
Kacey had brought her when she heard loud noises near
her cabin. It sounded like a herd of buffalo, but she
reasoned that it was probably something dragging and
bumping on the ground. But what? Her sisters and their
tons of luggage, she realized. It was a bit early for them,
though, just barely after 7:00 a.m. They were probably
eager to get going.

She took a peek out the window and no—it wasn't
the Hawkins Sisters.

It was Bobby Stone, pulling a big wheeled suitcase behind him. Was he leaving Bronco?

Coming to stay goodbye for good?

She wouldn't have thought her heart could ache any more from—and for—this man. But she felt like she'd failed him. Failed to show him what he could have in this amazing thing called life. Failed to show him that love was worth the risk. Failed to show them had he *could* try again—and that this time, there could be a happily ever after. Not that it was about a fairy tale, but about the strength of their feelings, their love, *working at it*. Being there for each other. Commitment.

She'd tried. Hard.

She sucked in a breath to brace herself, then opened the door. Bobby left the suitcase on the ground and walked up the porch steps. "Come on in," she said.

He followed her into the little cabin, closing the door behind him. "You were right, Tori Hawkins. I'm not the guy I was three years ago at that cliff's edge because this time around, you were standing beside me. I think with you beside me, literally and figuratively, I'll be too damned happy to think much about the past. Only the now and the future."

Tori poked her fingernail into her palm to make sure she wasn't dreaming. That Bobby had really just said all that.

"I do love you, Tori. I did when you said those words to me, but I wasn't ready to hear them. Or say them. I am now."

"But you're leaving?" she asked. "That's a mighty big suitcase out there."

"I'm leaving if you'll have me," he said. "I'd like to

join you in Australia and wherever else you're headed on the rodeo circuit. Maybe we could even make Bronco a home base, a place to come back to that's ours, in between going wherever your career takes you. Instead of being a ranch hand, I'll be *your* hand, your personal concierge. Who knows, maybe on the road I'll find my own new thing, like reporting is for you and painting has been for Kacey."

"Oh, Bobby," she said, her heart overflowing. "This is a dream come true. Fairy tales *are* real, sorry."

He smiled. "I might have been wrong about happy-ever-after. Because I'm gonna do what it takes to make sure we both have that. I love you, Tori. That's all I need to know."

"I love you too." She wrapped her arms around him and kissed him, happy chills and goose bumps dancing along her spine.

"So you'll have me?" he asked, holding her gaze, his arms tightening around her waist.

Tori laughed but her eyes misted with tears—from pure happiness. "I will absolutely have you."

He smiled that warm, happy smile that never failed to steal her breath. "Australia, here we come. Sullivan texted me just as I got here that Sadie adores kangaroos and to make sure I get a photo with a kangaroo giving me a good kick in the pants."

Tori grinned. "I don't think you want to get kicked by a kangaroo. They're cute but pack quite a punch."

"Like you," he said. "And thank the good Lord. You knocked me upside the head and changed my life." His brown eyes grew reverent, intense. "Thank you, Tori

Hawkins," he added on a sweet whisper, pulling her closer against him.

"Look at us," she whispered back. "A couple of forty-year-olds actually riding off into the sunset together."

"Except the sun just rose," he pointed out with a grin.

"Even better. Staring off the day together on a whole new life."

"You and me," he said, taking her hand.

And then they walked out into the Montana sunshine for a new beginning.

* * * * *

Look for the next title in the
Montana Mavericks: Lassoing Love continuity
The Maverick's Sweetest Choice
by USA TODAY *bestselling author Stella Bagwell*
On sale September 2023, wherever Harlequin
books and ebooks are sold.

And don't miss
The Maverick's Surprise Son
by New York Times *bestselling author*
Christine Rimmer

Available now!

Chapter One

Grace Hollister was wearily slipping one arm out of her lab coat when a voice called to her from the open doorway of her office.

"I hate to be the messenger to bring you bad news, Doctor, but you have one more patient to see before we shut the doors."

Grace turned a questioning look at Cleo, one of two nurses who assisted her throughout the busy days at Pine Valley Clinic.

"I do? I thought Mr. Daniels was the last one."

Cleo stepped into the small space and Grace shrugged the white garment back onto her shoulder.

"Harper scheduled a last-minute walk-in," the nurse explained. "Guess she was feeling softhearted."

In spite of being bone-tired, Grace managed to chuckle at Cleo's explanation for the clinic's receptionist. "Harper is always softhearted. And her tongue refuses to form the word *no*."

"In this case, I don't think you would've wanted Harper to turn this patient away. She's five years old and as cute as her father."

Sighing, Grace reached for a stethoscope lying on the corner of her desk and motioned for the petite brunette to precede her out of the office. "Since when have you started eyeing married men?"

The two women started down a short hallway to where three separate examining rooms were located. As they walked, Cleo answered in a hushed voice, "If there's a wife, she's not listed on the patient's information sheet."

Grace rolled her eyes. Being twenty-five and single, Cleo was always looking for Mr. Right. So far, she'd not found him. But it wasn't for lack of trying.

"Hmm. I suppose it was necessary for you to take a peek at the parent-guardian information."

The nurse slanted a guilty glance at Grace. "My eyes just happened to land on that part of the paper."

"You're hopeless, Cleo."

"Yes, but this place would be boring without me."

No, without her two nurses, Cleo and Poppy, the flow of patients going in and out of the clinic would be reduced to a crawl, Grace thought.

"Like watching grass grow," Grace joked, then quickly switched to serious mode. "Is the child in room two?"

That particular examining room was referred to by Grace and the staff as the kid-friendly room. The walls were adorned with playful paintings of animals and clowns, while colorful balloons floated from the handles on the cabinets.

"Yes. And her dad is with her." Cleo followed Grace to the next closed door. "If you can handle this patient without me, I'll help Poppy finish tidying up three."

Grace pulled a clipboard from a holder on the wall and began to scan the patient's information. "I'll call—"

Her words broke off abruptly as she stared in disbelief at the signature at the bottom of the paper. The cursive writing was barely legible, yet the name seemed to leap off the page.

Mackenzie Barlow!

"Doc, is anything wrong? You look sick!"

Tearing her gaze off the signature, Grace glanced over at Cleo. The nurse was studying her closely.

"Uh…no. Nothing is wrong." Even though she was trying her best to sound normal, she could hear a tremble in her voice. "I'm tired, that's all. Go help Poppy. If I need you I'll find you."

Cleo cast her a skeptical look before she walked on down the hallway and entered room three. Once the nurse was out of sight, Grace drew in a bracing breath and passed a hand over her forehead.

You're a physician, Grace. A professional. It doesn't matter that you once planned to marry Mack. You've been taught to turn off your emotions. So turn them off and go do your job.

Determined to follow the goading voice going off in her head, Grace straightened her shoulders. Then, after giving the door a cursory knock, she stepped into the room to find a small, dark-haired girl sitting on the edge of the examining table.

Purposely keeping her focus on the patient, Grace smiled at the girl, who was dressed in a fuzzy red sweater and blue jeans that were stuffed into a pair of sparkly pink cowboy boots. A single braid rested on one shoulder, while her arms were hugging protectively against her midsection. The heels of her boots were thumping rhythmically against the vinyl padding on the end of the table.

To her immediate right, Grace sensed Mack rising from a plastic waiting chair, but she didn't acknowledge his presence. Instead, she closed the short distance between her and the patient and introduced herself.

"Hello, young lady." She held her hand out to the girl. "I'm Dr. Grace. And I believe your name is Kitty. Is that right?"

The girl hesitated for only a moment and then with an affirmative nod, she placed her hand in Grace's. "I'm Kitty Barlow. And I'm five years old."

Grace gave the child a reassuring smile. "Five. I'm going to guess you're in kindergarten."

Kitty nodded again, but she didn't look a bit proud of the fact.

A couple of steps behind her, Mack said, "Hello, Grace."

Slowly, she turned and faced the man who'd once held her heart in his hand. As her gaze settled on his face, everything around them turned into a dim haze. "Hello, Mack. How are you?"

Over the years Grace had often imagined how she might react if she ever saw Mackenzie again. But none of those scenarios came close to matching this moment. Pain, joy and longing were flashing through her as though their parting had only happened yesterday.

He offered her his hand, and as she reached to wrap her fingers around his, she hoped he couldn't detect the cataclysmic effect he was having on her.

"Fine, thanks," he replied. "And I want to apologize for showing up at such a late hour. I imagine you normally shut the doors before now."

Her throat was so tight she was surprised her vocal cords could form a sound. "Normally. But not always."

Fourteen years. That's how much time had passed since Grace had seen this man. The long years had changed him, she realized, but only for the better. The nineteen-year-old she'd been so in love with had evolved into a rugged hunk of man with broad shoulders, a lean waist and long sinewy legs. Beneath a battered gray cowboy hat, his dark hair was now long enough to curl over the back of his collar. Yet it was his face that had appeared to change the most, she thought. The youthful features she remembered were now hardened lines and angles carved from a weathered, dark brown skin that matched his deep-set eyes.

He said, "I appreciate you taking the time to see Kitty. My schedule has been pretty hectic here lately. But I'm sure you're accustomed to hectic schedules."

"Doctors are busy people," she said, then cleared her throat, withdrew her hand from his and turned back to his daughter.

"Well now, Kitty, I'd like to hear how you've been feeling. This paper on my clipboard says you've been having tummy aches. Can you tell me how your tummy feels when you get sick?"

Kitty's big brown eyes made an uneasy sweep of Grace's face before she finally nodded. "It hurts a lot— like it squeezes together."

Grace fitted the stethoscope to her ears. "Well, I'm going to do my best to make all the squeezing go away," she said gently. "Can you tell me when your tummy hurts? Before or after you eat? When you go to bed or go to school?"

"In the mornings—when I get ready for school. And it hurts at school. I want to put my head on the desk, but teacher says if I feel bad I need to go home. So Daddy comes and gets me."

Grace turned a questioning look at Mack and she didn't miss the lines of worry on his face.

He said, "I've had to pick her up at school a couple of times in the past two weeks and then again today."

"I see." She turned back to the child. "Okay, Kitty, I want you to lie back on the table for me. I'm going to figure out what's causing these tummy aches."

For the next few minutes Grace gave the girl a slow, methodical examination. Throughout the inspection of Kitty's physical condition, Mack remained standing, but thankfully he didn't interrupt Grace with questions. Even so, with his watchful presence, it was a fight for Grace to remain focused on her job.

"Do you think her appendix needs to come out?" Mack asked. "Or does she have a hernia? I know kids her age can get them and she's always climbing and jumping."

"I don't believe we're dealing with anything along those lines," she told him as she gathered up her clipboard. "Wait here. We'll talk in a minute."

Grace left the room and headed down the hallway in search of Cleo. She found the nurse in the storage room, restocking a cabinet with paper gowns.

"Cleo, I want you to keep our little patient occupied while I talk with her father in my office. I'll try to make the consultation as quick as possible. I realize everyone is waiting to go home for the night."

Cleo joined her in the open doorway. "Quit worrying about your staff staying late. We know the score around here. Are you feeling better?"

The nurse's question caused Grace's eyes to widen. "Better? There wasn't anything wrong with me."

Cleo shook her head. "You could've fooled me."

Grace did her best not to smirk. "Send Mack…uh, Mr. Barlow to my office."

The nurse's eyebrows arched, but she didn't say anything as she took off in long strides toward the examining room.

In her office, Grace took a seat behind a large desk and resisted the urge to run a hand over her hair, or look to see if any of the lipstick she'd applied earlier in the day was still on her lips. How she looked to Mack Barlow hardly mattered. He'd been out of her life for years now. And, anyway, he wasn't here to see her. This was all about his little daughter.

She barely had time to draw in a deep breath, when a knock sounded on the door.

"Come in," she called.

Poppy ushered Mack into the room, then closed the door behind her. Grace forced a smile on her face and gestured for him to take a seat in one of the padded armchairs in front of her desk.

"Please make yourself comfortable, Mack."

He lifted the cowboy hat from his head, then ran a hand over the dark waves before he eased his long, lanky frame into one of the chairs. As he settled back into the seat, she noticed for the first time this evening that his clothing was splotched with dust and manure. Apparently he'd come straight here from the feedlot.

"I'm sure you're wanting to kick me in the shins right about now," he said.

Surely he didn't think she was harboring a grudge about their breakup all those years ago, she thought. Yes, he had stomped on her heart, but she'd survived and moved on. Besides, her parents had always taught her, and her seven siblings, that carrying a grudge wasn't just harmful, it was sinful.

"Oh. Why? For yanking my ponytail in chemistry class?" she asked impishly. "Don't worry. I've forgiven you."

Grinning faintly, he raked a hand over his hair for a second time and Grace couldn't help but notice how a thick dark wave fell onto the right side of his forehead.

"Actually, I was referring to a few minutes ago," he said. "I shouldn't have asked you to explain Kitty's health in front of her. I know better than that—but I've been worried about her. I, uh… It's not always easy trying to be both mother and father. Especially now that I have so many things going on with the ranch and my vet practice. I…don't get to spend as much time with her as I should."

So there wasn't a mother in the picture, Grace thought. What could've have happened? A divorce? His wife died? She could pose the question as a medical one. Kitty's lack of a mother could possibly be affecting her health. But given their past history, Grace doubted Mack would view the question as a professional one.

Instead, she said, "I heard about your father's death. Will was a special man. Everyone in the area thought highly of him."

"Thanks. Losing him—it's still a shock. I have to keep reminding myself that he's really gone. Especially now that I'm living on the Broken B. I expect to look around the house and see him. Or find him down at the barns, or spot him riding across the range."

About two months ago, Mack's father had died unexpectedly from a sudden heart attack. Grace hadn't gone to the funeral. At the time, her appointment book had been crammed full and she'd mentally argued that trying to reschedule patients would've been a nightmare for Harper. Plus, closing the clinic for the day, for any reason, always caused double loads of work for the staff later on. Yet in all honesty, Grace had skipped saying a public farewell to Will because she couldn't summon the courage to face Mack. And she'd regretted it ever since.

"I'm sorry I wasn't at the funeral. But I—"

He interrupted her with a shake of his head. "No need to explain. I'm sure you were busy. And, anyway, your parents and brothers were there. That meant a lot to me."

Grace felt like a bug crawling across the hardwood floor of her office. "My family always thought highly of your parents. As did I."

He gave her a single nod. "I've not forgotten."

No, Grace thought. There'd been too much between

them to forget completely. She cleared her throat, then steered the conversation back to his daughter.

"Well, regarding Kitty, it's perfectly natural for you to be concerned and ask questions. But in your daughter's case, I think you need to quit worrying. She's going to be fine…in time."

His dark eyebrows arched upward. "In time? What does that mean?"

Grace was amazed that she could sit here talking to him in a normal voice, while inside she felt as if a tornado was tearing a path from her head to her feet.

"First off, let me say I'm not detecting anything seriously wrong with Kitty's stomach. There's no bloating, bulges, lumps or bumps or sensitive spots that I could detect, and her digestive sounds are normal. She told me she doesn't throw up. Is that true?"

"No. Her meals stay down. She just holds a hand to her stomach and says it hurts."

Grace thoughtfully tapped the end of a pen against a notepad lying on the desktop. "Hmm. When did these stomachaches start?"

"About two weeks ago—after she started school."

Grace nodded. "Does your daughter like school?"

"When we lived in Nevada, she loved nursery school and all her friends. She adored her teacher. But now that we moved up here everything is different for her. She says the other kids look at her funny and the teacher is always telling her to be quiet. Which is understandable. At times, Kitty can be a chatterbox." Frowning, he leaned forward in his seat. "Do you think my daughter is pretending to be sick so she won't have to go to school?"

"No. I believe she's honestly experiencing stomach pains and I have a notion they're all stemming from the stress of moving to a strange place and leaving her friends behind. Tell me, has Kitty lived in multiple places or is this the first move for her?"

He shook his head. "Ever since she was born, we've lived on the KO Ranch, not far from Reno. That's the only home she's ever known. I was a resident vet there."

Grace couldn't contain her interest. "Oh. Must've been a huge ranch. Stone Creek can't afford a resident vet. Although, Dad often wishes he could."

He shrugged. "It was a good place to live and work. And a nice place to raise Kitty. But with Dad's death… well, I want to keep the Broken B going. And I'm hoping the ranch will come to be a good home for her."

She nodded. "I've not forgotten how hard your parents worked to make the Broken B profitable. I'm sure the ranch is very important to you."

He cleared his throat and glanced to the wall on his right, where a wide window was shuttered with woven blinds. "Mom and Dad wanted that place for me. I guess—" His gaze settled back on her face. "Now that I have Kitty I understand what it actually means to build a legacy."

More than once in their young romance, they'd talked about the children they would have and their plans to build their own ranch, together. Unfortunately, some dreams were meant to die, she thought sadly.

The stinging at the back of her eyes caused her to blink several times before she could focus clearly on the prescription pad lying on the desktop.

"Well, uh, I think the issue with Kitty's stomach

will take a little time. Once she gets more settled she should begin to feel better. In the meantime, I'm going to prescribe something mild to soothe her tummy. And don't worry, it's nothing she can become dependent on."

"So how long does she need to take this medication? And if she doesn't get better soon, how long should I wait to bring her back to see you?"

"Give her two more weeks, at least. And then if you don't see an improvement, bring her back to see me and we'll take things from there. Right now, I'd rather not put her through a bunch of unnecessary testing. It would only put more stress on her."

"Yes, I agree."

"Do you want a paper prescription? Or I can call your pharmacy?"

"You still do the paper thing?"

Even though her nerves were rapidly breaking down, his question put a smile on her face. "I do. Some of my elderly patients feel more at ease when they have a piece of paper in their hand. And anything I can do to make them feel better is my job. I'm sure you feel that way about your patients, too."

He smiled back at her and she thought how different it was from the carefree grins he gave her all those years ago. Now she could see the everyday strains of life etched beneath his eyes and around his lips.

"Only my patients can't talk to me. At least, not in words. A kick, or bite or scratch pretty much tells me what they're thinking about Dr. Barlow."

She chuckled. "Sometimes I wish my patients couldn't talk."

She reached for the prescription pad and hurriedly

scratched out the necessary information. Once she was finished, she stood and rounded the desk. At the same time, Mack rose from the chair.

She handed him the small square of paper. "Here's the prescription. If you have any questions about the dosage, just call the office," she told him. "Now, I'll go say goodbye to Kitty and the two of you will be ready to go."

"Thank you, Grace. I, uh, already feel better about Kitty."

She gave him an encouraging smile. "Have faith. Time heals."

He shot her an odd look and then a stoic expression shuttered his face. "I'll keep that in mind."

As Grace followed him out of the office, she realized her remark had struck some sort of chord with him. Perhaps she should have made it clear that she was referring to Kitty's problem, she thought. He'd lost so much in his life already. His mother and father. And somehow, he'd lost Kitty's mother, too. Maybe he'd considered Grace's comment as being trite or even insulting.

Why should it matter if you've bruised Mack's feelings? Toughen up, Grace. It hadn't bothered him to stomp all over your hopes and dreams.

As the two of them walked down the hallway to the waiting area at the front of the clinic, Grace tried to push away the nagging voice in her head. And for the most part, she succeeded. However, she didn't have any luck at ignoring Mack's tall presence.

The way he walked, the lanky way he moved and the scent of the outdoors drifting from his clothes all reminded her of how much she'd once loved having his arms crushing her close to him, his lips devouring hers.

Oh, Lord, how could those memories still be so vivid in her mind? she wondered. She'd just told Mack that time heals. And yet time had done little to wipe him from her memory bank.

When they reached the waiting room, Cleo was reading a story to Kitty from a children's book, but as soon as the child spotted her father, the story was forgotten. She jumped from the short couch and ran straight to his side.

Grabbing a tight hold on his hand, she asked, "Can we go home now, Daddy?"

"Yes, we're going home. As soon as you thank Dr. Grace for taking care of you."

Grace squatted to put herself on the child's level and as she studied Kitty's sweet face, she could see so very much of Mack in her features. She had his rich brown eyes and dark hair. And her little square chin and the dimple carving her left cheek was a miniature replica of her father's.

"It was nice meeting you, Kitty. And I hope your tummy gets better really soon. I'm giving your daddy some medicine to give you so you won't hurt. Will you take it for me?"

Kitty wrinkled her nose as she contemplated Grace's question. "Does it taste awful?"

Numerous children passed through the clinic on a weekly basis and they all touched Grace's heart in one way or another. But none of them had pulled on her heartstrings the way Kitty was yanking on hers at this very moment.

Smiling, Grace said, "Not at all. It tastes like cherries."

"Oh, I guess it will be okay then."

"That's a good girl. And there's something else I'd like for you to do."

Kitty's eyes narrowed skeptically. "What? Take a shot?"

Grace glanced up to see a look of amusement on Mack's face, and without thinking, she gave him a conspiring wink. He winked back and suddenly the tense knots inside Grace begin to ease.

Turning her attention back to Kitty, she said, "No. You don't need a shot. I want you to promise me that when you go to school tomorrow you won't be afraid that your tummy is going to hurt. And you'll try your best to make friends with your classmates."

As soon as Grace spoke the word *friends*, Kitty's lips pursed into a pout. "But the other kids don't like me," she said with a shake of her head.

"Do they really tell you that they don't like you? Or do you just have a feeling that they don't?"

Kitty glanced up at her father as though she wanted him to rescue her. When he didn't, her chin dropped against her chest. "No. They don't tell me that," she mumbled. "But they won't talk to me—that's how I know."

Grace patted the girl's little shoulder. "Maybe they're waiting on you to talk to them first. Why don't you try it tomorrow? I'll bet you'll find out they'd like to talk to you. Do you have a horse or a dog?"

Her head shot up and she nodded eagerly. "I have both! My horse is Moonpie and my dog is Rusty."

"That's nice. So you can talk to them about Moonpie and Rusty and tell them all the things you and your pets do on the ranch. Do you think you can do that?"

To Grace's relief, Kitty gave her a huge nod.

"Good girl!"

After giving Kitty another encouraging pat, she straightened to her full height and turned to Mack.

"Thank you, Grace."

His gaze was roaming over her face as though he was trying to read her thoughts. The idea caused a ball of emotion to suddenly form in her throat.

"You're welcome," she said, barely managing to get out the words. "And if Kitty has any more problems, let me know."

"I will," he assured her.

Father and daughter started toward the door and as Grace watched them go, she was struck by a sense of loss.

"Goodbye, Kitty."

The girl turned and gave Grace a little wave. "Bye, Dr. Grace. Thank you."

Once the pair had stepped outside and the door closed behind them, Cleo immediately jumped to her feet.

"You knew that man! Why didn't you tell me?"

Grace felt her cheeks growing warm. Which was a ridiculous reaction. She shouldn't feel awkward about being acquainted with Mack.

"I hardly thought it mattered," Grace said.

"Grace! He's hot! Hot! Of course, it matters!"

"To you, maybe. Not to me."

Turning away from the nurse, Grace walked over to a low counter separating the waiting area from Harper's reception desk. The young woman with short, platinum-blond hair was busy typing information into a computer, but glanced up as soon as she noticed Grace's presence.

"Shut everything down, Harper," Grace told her. "I'm sorry you stayed so late. You should've gone home before this last patient."

The young woman shook her head. "No problem, Doctor. I thought I'd stay, just in case you needed to schedule the girl another appointment."

"Thanks for being so thoughtful, Harper, but that won't be necessary. At least, not for now."

A few steps behind her, Cleo let out a wistful sigh. "Grace, I don't understand why you didn't suggest a follow-up. You could have included the cost with this visit."

Rolling her eyes toward the ceiling, Grace turned to the nurse. "Cleo, if you weren't so indispensable, I'd fire you."

Cleo giggled. "Oh, come on! I can't help it. It's not every day we get to see a guy like Mr. Barlow. So where did you know him from?"

Not wanting to overreact and cause the nurse to be suspicious, she answered in the most casual voice she could summon. "He's an old classmate. That's all."

"Oh. I thought—"

"What?"

Grace's one-word question must've sounded sharp because Cleo suddenly looked a bit shamefaced.

"Uh...nothing. If you don't need anything else, I'll go tell Poppy we're closing up."

"I'd appreciate that, Cleo. It's been a long day," Grace told her. "And right now I just want to pick up Ross and go home."

She started down the hallway to her office and Cleo walked briskly at her side.

"Grace, I'm sorry if talking about Mr. Barlow offended you. I never thought it would make you…well, angry with me."

Holding back a sigh, Grace said, "Forget it, Cleo. I'm not angry. And if I sounded cranky, just chalk it up to exhaustion."

"Is Kitty going to be okay, you think?"

"Yes. In time."

"That's good. She's an adorable little girl. Too bad she doesn't have a mother," Cleo said,

"How do you know she doesn't have a mother?"

"Because she told me so. While I was sitting with her in the waiting room."

Pausing in midstride, Grace shot the sassy nurse a look of disbelief. "Oh, Cleo, don't tell me you pumped the child for personal information!"

"No! I promise, Grace, I didn't. She asked me if I had any kids and I told her no. That's when she told me she'd never had a mommy."

Never had a mommy. Grace could only wonder what that possibly meant.

"I see. Well, you know how children are. They say things in different ways. Hopefully she has one somewhere. Because right now she could certainly use one."

Before Cleo could reply, Poppy stepped out of a nearby storage room. As she joined them in the middle of the hallway, she glanced pointedly at her watch. "Should I go ahead and call the Wagon Spoke for four orders of eggs and toast? Someone at the café might take pity on us and deliver it here to the clinic."

Grace released a good-natured groan. "I'm definitely starving. But, no. Let's turn off the lights and get out of here."

Twenty minutes later, Grace picked up her seven-year-old son, Ross, at the babysitter's house, which fortunately was located only two doors down from her own home.

Ross was accustomed to his mother's erratic work hours, but this evening as she unlocked the front door, he was complaining. Grace could hardly blame him. Tonight she was an hour and a half behind schedule.

"Gosh, Mom, I didn't think you were ever going show up! I'm starving!"

"Didn't Birdie make dinner for the twins?"

Besides babysitting Ross after school on weekdays, Birdie held down a computer job that allowed her to work from home. Divorced and in her early thirties, she had twin boys two years older than Ross. Normally, if Grace was working late, Birdie would have Ross eat dinner with them.

"Birdie had a lot of extra work to do. So she's just now cooking dinner," Ross explained. "She gave us cookies and milk when we got home from school, but I'm starving now."

With a hand on his shoulder, Grace guided her son into the house. As they passed through the living room, Ross tossed his schoolbooks into an armchair and Grace placed her purse and briefcase on a wall table.

"I've had a long list of patients today, honey," Grace explained as she tiredly raked a loose strand of blond hair away from her face. "That's why I'm late."

Ross paused to look at her, and as Grace took in his

slim face, blue eyes and wavy blond hair falling across his forehead, Mack's words came back to her.

Now that I have Kitty I understand what it actually means to build a legacy.

Yes, Grace understood, too. She was Ross's sole parent. It was her responsibility and deepest concern to provide her son with a good home and a solid future.

It's not always easy being a mother and father to Kitty.

No, Grace thought, sometimes it was achingly hard to be a single parent. She could've told Mack she knew all about being both father and mother, but she'd kept the personal information to herself. He hadn't brought Kitty to the clinic in order to learn about Grace's private life. In fact, she doubted he cared one whit about her marital status.

"Mom, why are you looking at me so funny?"

Ross's question interrupted her thoughts and she let out a weary breath and patted him on top of the head.

"Sorry, Ross. I was just being a mommy and thinking how much I love you."

He groaned and scuffed the toe of his athletic shoe against the hardwood floor. "Aww, Mom. That's mushy stuff. Boys don't want to hear mushy stuff."

Chuckling now, she playfully scrubbed the top of his head, then shooed him out of the room. "Okay. No more mushy stuff. Go change and wash and I'll see what I can find in the kitchen."

Ross started down the hallway to where the bedrooms were located, then stopped midway to look back at his mother.

"Can we have pizza?" he asked eagerly. "Just for to-night?"

Being a doctor, Grace had tried to instill good eating habits in her son. But that didn't mean she was a strict prude and never allowed him, or herself, to eat something simply because it tasted good.

"Sure we can. As long as you eat some salad with it."

"Okay! Thanks, Mom!"

He raced on down the hallway and as Grace headed to the kitchen, her thoughts unwittingly drifted to Mack and Kitty. The drive from town to the Broken B consisted of more than fifteen miles of rough dirt road. And once they arrived at the big old ranch house, it would be empty. Just like this one.

Maybe he preferred living a solitary life, she thought. But Grace couldn't help but wonder if he might think of her as he went about his nightly chores. Moreover, had she ever crossed his mind since that awful day fourteen years ago when he'd told her their romance was over? Had he ever felt a twinge of regret?

No. Mack wasn't the sort to have regrets, she thought. She remembered him as being the type of guy who, once he made a decision, plowed forward and never looked back. And that was the same way she needed to deal with her own life. Plow forward and forget she ever knew Mack Barlow.

Chapter Two

"Daddy, why don't I have a mommy to braid my hair?"

In Kitty's bedroom, Mack stood behind his daughter, who was sitting on a padded bench in front of the dresser. Braiding her long, dark hair was something he'd done since she was a toddler and the chore came as natural to him as bridling a horse.

"Because you have a daddy to do it for you instead of a mommy," he told her.

From the corner of his eye, he could see her image in the dresser mirror, and the frown on her face said she was far from satisfied with his answer. The fact hardly surprised Mack. The older that Kitty got, the more questions she had. Especially questions concerning her mother.

"But why don't I have a mommy? The kids at school have one."

"All of them?"

"Yes! Every one of them!"

He made a tsking noise with his tongue. "Kitty. I've told you to always tell the truth. Are you telling me the truth now?"

She huffed out a heavy breath. "Oh, Daddy— Okay. I don't know for sure if they *all* have mommies. They say they do."

He fastened the end of the braid with a red scrunchie, then gave her shoulders a pat. "Well, you don't have one because she—"

When he paused, Kitty twisted around on the dressing bench and looked up at him. "'Cause why? 'Cause she don't love me?"

Oh, God, I'm not equipped for this, Mack thought. And he especially didn't need this sort of father-daughter talk this morning. If they didn't leave the house in fifteen minutes, she was going to be late getting to school and Mack's veterinary clinic would be overrun with patients before he ever got there.

With his hands on her shoulders, Mack gently turned his daughter around to face him. "Don't ever think such a thing, Kitty. She loved you and that's why she gave you to me—so I could take good care of you."

Frowning with confusion, Kitty's head tilted to one side. "Why couldn't she take care of me?"

From the moment Kitty had begun to talk and form whole sentences, Mack had learned that one question always led to another. Most of the time his daughter's quest for answers was amusing. But not this morning. Talking about Kitty's mother was like prying the scab off a wound. Not that he regretted having a child with the woman. No. He wouldn't trade Kitty for anything in his life. He only wished, for Kitty's sake, that their relationship had been something more than a meaningless affair.

"Well, because your mommy was different. She was like a bird. To be happy, birds have to fly free—to far-off places."

"But she can't be a bird, Daddy. She can't fly."

Mack bit back a sigh, while at the same time admiring his daughter's ability to see the reality of the situation.

Mack said, "No. She doesn't have wings or anything like that. I only meant that she has to keep traveling. But I promise that she thinks about you."

To his relief a smile spread across her face. "Really?"

"Yes. Really." He patted her cheek. "Now go find your boots and get your red coat. It's going to be colder today."

She jumped off the dressing bench. "Can I wear my red cowboy boots, too? The ones with the stars on the tops?"

"Sure. But don't drag your toes on the concrete."

"Okay." She started toward the closet, then halfway there, turned to look at him. "Daddy?"

"Yes."

"Will I get to see Dr. Grace again?"

The question caught him off guard. Last night after they'd left the clinic, she'd talked briefly about the examination Grace had given her, but after that, she'd not mentioned Grace or anything about the doctor's visit. Mack had assumed his daughter had already dismissed the whole experience.

"I don't think so. Unless you get sick again. And you don't want that to happen, do you?"

"No! I'm going to do like Dr. Grace told me. I'm not gonna think about my tummy!" Momentarily forgetting her father's order to fetch her boots and coat, she took a few steps toward him. "She was really nice and pretty. Did you think so?"

Unfortunately, he'd been thinking those very things and a whole lot more he shouldn't have been thinking. "She's a nice doctor," he said.

Kitty nodded emphatically. "And she smelled extra good, too! I wish I could smell like her."

Oh, yes, Mack had noticed the soft, sultry scent floating around Grace. He'd also noticed how her silky blond hair brushed the tops of her shoulders and the way her black slacks and sweater had clung to her feminine curves. The passing years had been sweet to her, he thought. Even under the harsh fluorescent lighting, her ivory skin had appeared flawless, her blue eyes bright and her pink lips just as full and luscious.

Damn it, he had to be a glutton for punishment, Mack thought. Instead of taking Kitty to one of the other physicians in town, he'd taken her to a doctor he'd been in love with for all of his adult life.

That thought brought him up short. He wasn't still in love with Grace! That part of his life had ended years ago. Now, she was nothing more than a book of bittersweet memories. One that he hadn't cared to open for a long, long while.

He said, "When you get older I'm fairly certain you'll smell as good as Dr. Grace."

Kitty's smile grew wider. "And be smart like her, too."

"Don't worry, Kitty, you're going to be as smart as you need to be. That is, if you get to school on time." He gestured to the closet, where a pile of clothes spilled out of the small enclosure and onto the bedroom floor. "Now, hurry. Get your boots and coat. I'll wait for you in the kitchen."

Thirty minutes later, Mack dropped off his daughter at Canyon Academy, a private elementary school located in the heart of the small town of Beaver. Then he drove to the western edge of the community where for the past six weeks, carpenters, electricians and plumbers had been working nearly nonstop to transform the old feed and grain store into Barlow Animal Hospital.

Before Mack had purchased the vacated property, the large building with lapboard siding had sported peeling, barn-red paint and a rusty tin roof. Now the siding was a soft gray color and the roof was white metal. Corrals and loafing sheds had been erected at the back of the structure to house large animals, while the interior of the building had been partitioned into smaller rooms, consisting of a treatment area with an adjoining recovery room, two kennel rooms and a break room. At the front entrance of the clinic, there was a large waiting area with a tiled floor and plastic chairs, along with a reception counter.

Mack parked his pickup truck at a gravel parking area at the side of the building, then quickly strode toward a private entryway located at the back.

He was stepping beneath the overhang that sheltered the door, when a tall, sandy-haired cowboy with an anxious look on his face hurried to intercept him.

"Man, am I ever glad to see you!" Oren exclaimed.

"There's already a row of vehicles parked out front. Two of them have stock trailers with about eight head of cattle in each one. If we try to do first come, first serve, we'll probably have a riot on our hands."

Three weeks ago, Mack had hired Oren Stratford as his one and only assistant. The young man, who was in his mid-twenties, lived in the nearby town of Miners-ville and had been working for a well-established vet-erinarian in Cedar City. Because he'd been looking for a chance to shorten his commute, he'd answered Mack's ad for an assistant. Knowledgeable and friendly, Mack had already developed a good bond with him. But they needed more help in the worst kind of way.

The number of patients passing through the animal clinic each day was growing at a rapid pace and Mack had yet to hire anyone to fill the job of receptionist. So far Mack and Oren were trying to deal with answer-ing the phone and scheduling appointments, along with treating animals.

"We're going to deal with one thing at a time," Mack told him. "The most critical comes first and then on down the line." He opened the door and headed into a narrow hallway with Oren walking alongside him. "Have any idea who arrived first?"

Oren spoke as he followed Mack into the space he'd designated for his office. "Actually, I can tell you that much. A lady with a cat. He has a cyst on his back and at first glance it looks like it's going to need to be cleaned surgically."

Mack switched on a row of overhead fluorescent lights, then flicked on the computer on his desk. "Okay.

We'll begin with the cat. Sedate and prep him. Have you turned up the thermostat to the rest of the building?"

"Yes. It's already warm. And I've let the customers into the waiting area. I've taken down names, but that's as far as I gotten with the paperwork."

Mack let out a long breath. "Thanks, Oren. I'd be in a heck of a mess without you. Kitty was dawdling this morning or I would've been here sooner. Once you have kids, you're going to understand what that means."

Oren chuckled. "I get it, Mack. Mom said as a kid I was the world's worst at dawdling."

"Thank God you grew out of it," Mack said with an amused grin, then quickly shifted gears. "What about the cattle? What's the reason for their visit to the vet?"

"Two separate owners. Vaccinations for one bunch."

Mack groaned. "Doesn't anyone work their own cattle anymore?"

"It's an old man who walks with a cane. Said he couldn't find anybody to come out to his place and help him do the job."

"That's not surprising," Mack said with a grimace. "And the other trailer load?"

"Cow-calf pairs. Looks to me like they might have shipping fever. The guy hasn't had them long. Said he bought them over in Sevier County. But you're the doctor, Mack—you might have a different diagnosis."

"Lord, help us. If that's the case, we'll have to keep them contained and away from the rest of the animals. I'll look them over while you get the cat ready. Anything else?"

"A dog with a torn ear. Doesn't look like it's worth saving to me."

Mack shot him a stunned glance. "The dog?"

"No. The ear. But I could be wrong."

"I hope you're wrong about the ear and the cattle." The phone began to ring and as Mack reached for the receiver, he jerked a thumb toward the door. "Go on and get the cat ready. I'll deal with this."

More than five hours later, the two men had managed to successfully treat the morning patients and send all of them home except for the cattle with the shipping fever. After they had treated the cow/calf pairs with shots of strong antibiotics and corralled them safely away from the adjoining pens, Mack suggested they take advantage of the time and eat lunch at the Wagon Spoke Café.

Wedged between a saddle shop and an antique shop, the Wagon Spoke had been in business in Beaver for nearly a century. Although, according to the town's history, the eatery moved to its current location after the original building burned down in 1936 from a fire that many old-timers say originated in the kitchen.

Some of Mack's earliest memories were those of his parents bringing him to the café on Saturday nights to eat dinner. Simply furnished, with wooden tables and chairs and one long bar with a green Formica top and matching stools, the place only served ordinary food, but to Mack the outing had always been special for him.

Presently, the front of the old building was sided with a mixture of corrugated iron and asphalt shingles and one large plate glass window overlooking the street. A wide wooden door painted bright green served as the entrance.

As the two men stepped into the busy interior, a cowbell clanged above their heads. To the right, standing behind a long bar, an older waitress with fire-engine-red hair waved to them.

"Seat yourself, boys. Laverne will be with you in a minute."

The two men worked their way through a maze of tables, most of which were occupied with late lunch diners. A couple of men Mack had been acquainted with for years lifted their hands in greeting, while a pair of young women at a nearby table smiled and waved at Oren.

Mack slanted him a sly look. "You obviously have friends here in Beaver."

Oren grinned. "Beaver is only about twenty minutes away from Minersville. And a guy has to do a little socializing. You remember how that is, don't you?"

Mack certainly remembered when he and Grace had been dating. Every minute he'd spent with her had been like a slice of paradise. But after they'd parted, dating or partaking in the social scene had meant little to him.

"I may act old to you, Oren. But I'm not *that* old."

Oren chuckled. "You don't act old, Mack. Just disinterested."

Mack grunted. "Well, Kitty gets what little spare time I have."

The two of them found a vacant table located near the wall at the back of the long room. Once they were seated, Oren looked over at him. "I haven't had a chance to ask you how Kitty is feeling. You were going to take her to the doctor yesterday evening. How did that go?"

If a man liked having scabs ripped off old sores, Mack supposed the appointment had been successful.

But he'd not made the visit to Pine Valley Clinic for himself. It was all for Kitty's health and nothing else.

Mack said, "It went better than I thought. The doctor prescribed a mild medication and suggested the problem was the stress of being away from her friends and having a new teacher. This morning she seemed to feel perfectly fine and since I've not gotten any calls from school yet, I'm keeping my fingers crossed that she's going to remain that way."

Oren said, "Moving can be tough on a kid. When I was about ten Dad moved us up to Spanish Fork. My brother and I hated living in town. We were used to roaming outside and being with our best friends. Thank goodness we weren't there long before we moved back to Minersville."

"Yeah. Moving to a new place is tough on kids. Tough on adults, too." Mack shrugged out of his denim jacket and hung it on the back of his chair.

"You almost sound like you regret moving back here to Beaver. What's wrong? I thought you liked it here," Oren said.

"Getting into the swing of things here hasn't been as easy as I'd hoped." Especially now that he'd come face-to-face with Grace again, he thought ruefully. He'd held the notion that seeing her would be no more than seeing any other old acquaintance. Hell, just how stupid could he get? Just looking at her had been like a hard wham to the side of his head and he still wasn't sure he'd recovered from the blow. "You've heard the old adage you can't go home again? Well, I think that aptly applies to me. I...well, if Dad was still alive it would be different—better."

"If your father was still alive you wouldn't be here, period," Oren reminded him. "You told me you moved back here to take over the Broken B."

"Yeah. That's true. Mom died several years ago, so I'm the only one left now to run the ranch. And for a long time I've been wanting to start my own veterinary business. This move gives me the chance to do both."

Oren opened his mouth to reply when Laverne, a middle-aged waitress with salt-and-pepper hair and a weary smile, walked up to their table and placed plastic-coated menus in front of them.

"You guys look like you could use some coffee," she said.

"Make it hot, Laverne. It's getting colder outside," Oren told her.

"Coming right up."

She left to get the coffee and Mack picked up the menu. A small square of paper with the details of today's special was clipped to the front. As soon as he spotted the words *meat loaf,* he dropped the menu back on the table.

Oren lifted off his cowboy hat, and after placing it in the empty chair next to his, he raked both hands through his hair. "How long has it been since you lived here in Beaver?" he asked.

"About twelve years. Before then, I'd been commuting back and forth from here to college in Cedar City. But after I got my associate degree there, I decided to attend a college in St. George for the rest of my education, so I moved down there. I decided I couldn't do a long commute, attend classes and work a part-time job. I've lived away ever since then. Until Dad died a couple of months ago."

"So you never had the pull to come back here until now?"

Mack supposed most people wouldn't understand his reasoning for staying away. But for a long time he'd associated his hometown with Grace and he'd wanted to forget that idyllic time he'd spent with her. Then later, when his father had told him she'd returned to Beaver from Salt Lake City, he could only think how gut-twisting it would be to see her from afar. At that time he'd never imagined his father would die an early death and send Mack back here to take over his inheritance.

"Kitty and I were just fine down in Nevada," Mack answered. "But we'll be just fine here, too."

Laverne arrived with their coffee and two glasses of ice water. As she placed the beverages on the table, she looked questioningly at Mack.

"Have you hired anyone to be your receptionist?"

No doubt the waitress probably saw an endless number of people pass through the café on a daily basis and heard just as many stories. Mack was surprised the woman remembered he'd mentioned he'd been on the hunt for someone to fill the job of receptionist for his animal hospital.

"A few persons have inquired about the position. But none were suitable," he told her. "You have someone in mind who'd be good at the job?"

"As a matter of fact, I think I do. I don't know why it didn't cross my mind before now. Eleanor Shipman. She retired from her job about three months ago. Worked twenty years as a receptionist for Denver Garwood over at Independent Insurance. I'd say the woman would know how to answer the phone and schedule things. And I know she's as bored as heck sitting home. No husband or kids to keep her busy, you see."

Mack exchanged hopeful looks with Oren.

"Sounds like she might be the answer," Oren said.

"You have her number?" Mack asked. "I'll give her a call."

"I'll get it when I turn in your orders." She pulled out a pad and pencil. "You two decided on what you want?"

"The special for me," Mack told her.

The woman scribbled down the information, then looked pointedly at Oren. "What about you, scrawny? Looks like you could use a double-plate special."

From the very first day Oren had walked into the café with Mack, Laverne had teased him mercilessly and Oren was always trying to get her back. Now he playfully pulled a face at her.

"No meat loaf for me, Laverne. Give me a double-meat, loaded burger, fries and a piece of rhubarb pie."

"We don't have rhubarb today," Laverne said. "We only serve it on Tuesdays and Wednesdays."

"Okay. What do you have on Thursdays?" he asked.

"You want the meringue choices or the fruit?"

"Fruit."

The waitress named off a list of pie flavors until Oren held up a hand to halt her.

"Blueberry, that's it," he told her, then gave her a sassy wink. "And for your information I'm not scrawny. If you saw me without any clothes on, you'd know so."

Mack watched the waitress sweep a skeptical gaze up and down Oren's tall frame.

"Not interested," she said blandly. "But those girls at the table across the room probably would be."

Oren's face turned red and Mack couldn't choke back a laugh.

With her pen still poised above her pad, Laverne asked, "Is that all?"

"That's plenty," Mack told her, then continued to chuckle as the woman turned and headed toward the kitchen.

"Guess I asked for that, didn't I?" Oren muttered.

"Don't try to get ahead of Laverne. It'll never happen. She's been here for years and heard it all. Besides, she picks on you because she likes you."

"I'd hate to hear what she'd have to say if she didn't like me," Oren muttered.

Mack picked up his coffee cup, but only managed to lift it halfway to his mouth when the cell phone inside his shirt pocket began to vibrate.

"An emergency?" Oren asked as Mack pulled out the phone and scanned the screen.

"I don't think so. I wanted to make sure it wasn't the school informing me that Kitty was sick again. Thankfully, it's not the school, so I'll let voice mail deal with the call. Otherwise, I'll not get much of lunch break."

"Yeah. You need to fix the way you operate, Mack. The vet I worked for down in Cedar City let the receptionist deal with all the business calls. Only family or close friends had his personal number."

Mack enjoyed a few sips of coffee before he replied. "You don't need to remind me how we're hurting for help. It would be great if the woman Laverne recommended works out."

Oren didn't reply and Mack glanced over to see he was focused intently on something at the front of the room. In fact, the young man's jaw had dropped to leave his mouth partially gaped.

"Who is *that*?"

The wonderous tone to Oren's question told Mack the object of his attention had to be a woman. "I'm sure I wouldn't know."

"Well, I'd sure like to!"

Curious, Mack gave a cursory glance over his shoulder to see a young, slender woman with short blond hair moving into the maze of dining tables. She looked vaguely familiar and then it dawned on him as to where he'd seen her.

With a wan smile, Mack looked back at Oren. "What a coincidence. We were just talking about receptionists and one walks in."

"You know *her*?"

Mack nodded. "She works the front desk at Pine Valley Clinic. I think her name is Hailey. No, it was Harper...or something like that. I wasn't paying much attention."

He'd been too busy worrying about Kitty and wondering where he was going to find the nerve to face Grace again, Mack thought ruefully.

Oren playfully grabbed one side of his rib cage. "Oh! I just felt an awful pain in my side."

"The blonde doesn't treat patients," Mack pointed out. "She only makes appointments for them."

"Well, in that case I need one." He leaned forward eagerly and snapped his fingers. "Mack, she's the sort of woman you need to hire! Your office would be overrun with male customers."

"Sure! And I'd be spending most of my time chasing my assistant out of the waiting area." Above Oren's shoulder, he spotted Laverne coming their way with a loaded tray of food. "Here comes our lunch. Maybe Laverne can tell you whether Eleanor is a raving beauty."

"Ha! I'm not giving her another chance to make me look like a fool," Oren said.

Years ago, Mack had made a mighty big fool of himself when he'd fallen in love with Grace. But since then he'd learned to never hand over his heart to a woman and, so far, he'd managed to hold fast to the difficult lesson.

Mack grunted. "Women tend to do that to us men, Oren. It's just a fact of life."

Each year on the Monday night before Thanksgiving, the town's business owners provided a free dinner to anyone who wanted to attend. Ever since Grace had returned to Beaver after living a few years in Salt Lake City, she'd always contributed to the charity meal by giving food and helping in the kitchen.

Tonight was no exception. Except that she and Ross were running late as she steered her SUV into the large parking lot located next to the town's civic building. A huge number of vehicles were already taking up the parking slots, forcing Grace to settle for a spot at the far end of the area.

"Gosh, Mom, we're going to have a long walk from here," Ross said as he unsnapped his seat belt. "Couldn't you get any closer?"

"Sorry, lazy bones," Grace told him. "This is the only space left and it won't hurt you to walk."

He groaned. "Yeah, but we have to carry all this food."

Grace climbed out of the vehicle and hurriedly pulled on a gray trench coat to ward off the cold wind sweeping across the parking lot. "That's right. So hurry and jump out and make yourself useful."

Shrugging on a puffy nylon coat, the boy joined his mother at the back of the SUV. "We must be the last ones here. Do you think they've started eating yet?"

"Probably. But don't worry," she told him as she opened the hatch on the SUV. "There will be plenty to go around. Just remember we're here to help others, not ourselves."

She placed a cardboard box holding a ham into Ross's arms, then picked up a two large plastic shopping bags loaded with bakery goods. After closing the hatch and locking the vehicle, mother and son walked toward the redbrick building.

"I imagine you're going to see some of your classmates here tonight," she told him.

"Bobby said he'd be here tonight. And Trevor said he might get to come. I hope he does," Ross said. "It's more fun when you get to eat with friends."

He glanced curiously up at his mother. "Mom, do you have any friends?"

Grace was accustomed to having Ross ask her all kinds of questions, some of which were a bit weird. But this one brought her up short. "Of course, I have friends, Ross. What makes you ask such a thing?"

"'Cause I never see you with any."

She said, "All the women I work with are my friends. And the people we attend church with are all friends."

"Yeah," Ross said. "But you don't have a friend you go places with or do things together."

Her son had noticed that about her? He was definitely growing up, she thought.

"Hmm. Do you mean like a boyfriend?"

"Sorta something like that," he agreed.

And why had Ross been thinking about this sort of thing? Grace wondered. When he'd been smaller, he had often begged her to get him a father. However, now that he'd gotten older and understood a daddy wasn't something his mother could pluck from a tree, he'd quit asking.

"Ross, I don't want a boyfriend. At least, not right now. I'm too busy being a doctor."

He frowned as though her reasoning didn't make sense. "But, Mom, you're always going to be a doctor."

"Yes. I will always be a doctor," she replied, while thinking she'd already tried being a girlfriend and a wife. Neither had worked out the way she'd planned. Yes, she wished more than anything that Ross had a father, but Bradley had been dead five years now and even before his death, she'd obtained a divorce. No. The only father Ross could hope to have now would be a stepfather and so far she'd not met anyone here.

To Grace's relief, they finished the walk to the building without Ross throwing any more dating questions her way, and by the time they stepped into the busy kitchen he'd turned his mind back to eating.

After turning the food over to a pair of kitchen helpers, Ross asked, "Mom, is it okay if I go out to the dining room?"

"Not yet. Just wait over there by that far wall while I speak to Dorothy about helping with the serving. I'll come tell you."

Ross left to do as she instructed and Grace made her way through the bustling workers until she reached a middle-aged woman with a messy bun and harried smile. Grace didn't know how the woman managed to do it, but every year Dorothy successfully orchestrated this whole event for the townspeople.

"Happy Thanksgiving before Thanksgiving!" she said with a little laugh. She gave Grace a brief hug. "I'm glad you could make our dinner tonight."

"I wouldn't have missed it for anything, Dorothy. And I'm ready to help serve," Grace told her. "Just show me what you want me to do."

The woman shook her head. "Honestly, Grace, we already have more help than we need. People are tripping over each other back here. And you've done more than enough by donating food. You and Ross go on and mingle with the townsfolk. We're almost ready to begin serving."

"Are you sure, Dorothy? I'm more than happy to do my part."

With a laugh of dismay, Dorothy patted Grace's arm. "Oh, my, you're one of the hardest-working persons in Beaver, Grace. And believe me, we all appreciate you. So scram. Go enjoy the meal."

Seeing there was no point in arguing with the woman, Grace thanked her and made her way over to where Ross was impatiently shifting his weight from one cowboy boot to the other.

"Dorothy says I'm not needed," Grace told him. "So let's go out to the dining area, where everyone is gathering. Maybe you'll spot Bobby or Trevor."

"Yay! Let's go!"

At the far end of the room, they passed through a pair of open doors and were suddenly faced with a thick crowd blocking the entryway.

"Gosh, Mom, I think everybody in town is here," Ross commented as he tried to peer around a group of men standing in front of them. "Reckon there will be room for us to sit down?"

Going home and cooking a meal for her and Ross might actually be easier than fighting their way through the crowd, Grace thought. But they were already here and she didn't want Ross to view her as a party pooper. Especially since this event was primarily given for the needy townsfolk.

"We'll see how things are after people start going through the serving line," she told him. "Right now let's find a quieter spot to stand."

They were slowly working their way along the wall toward an open space at the back of the room, when Grace felt a hand come down on the back of her shoulder.

Expecting to see a coworker, she was stunned when she turned and found herself staring straight into Mack Barlow's face.

"Hello, Grace."

Nearly two weeks had passed since he and Kitty had come to the clinic. She'd not seen or heard from him since. But that hadn't stopped her from thinking about him. To be honest, she'd thought about little else.

"Good evening, Mack."

As she met his gaze, her heart gave one hard thump, then leaped into such a fast pace that the rush of blood caused her ears to roar.

"Hi, Dr. Grace! My tummy is really good now. Are you gonna eat turkey with us?"

Grace's gaze dropped from Mack to Kitty, who was standing at her father's side, clutching a fold on the leg of his jeans. She was wearing a blue velvet dress with a white Peter Pan collar, and a pair of silver cowboy boots with sparkling rhinestones on the shafts. A wide velvet headband the same color as her dress held her dark hair away from her sweet little face. She looked so adorable that bittersweet tears pricked the back of Grace's eyes.

"Hello, Kitty. I'm very happy to hear your tummy is feeling well. But I—I'm not sure if they'll be enough room for all four of us to sit down together."

"I imagine we can find room enough somewhere," Mack said.

Did he want her and Ross to sit with them? More importantly, did she want to spend this evening in his company?

The questions were running through her mind when she felt Ross tugging on her hand to catch her attention.

Taking him by the shoulders, she said, "Ross, this is Mr. Barlow. He's the new veterinarian in town. And, Mack, this is my son, Ross."

"Nice to meet you, Ross." Mack reached down and shook Ross's hand, then urged Kitty to take a step forward. "This is my daughter, Kitty."

The girl gave Ross a long, critical look then she shot her father an inquiring glance. "Is it okay for me to shake Ross's hand, too?"

Mack nodded. "If it's okay with Ross."

The girl held her hand out to Ross and the hearty shake he gave it put a wide, smile on her face.

"My name is Kitty and I'm five," she told Ross. "How old are you?"

"I'm seven," Ross told her. "Do you go to school?"

Kitty gave him a proud nod. "I'm in kindergarten— at Canyon Academy. Do you go to school?"

Ross shot her mother an amused grin before he answered Kitty's question. "Sure, I do. I go to Canyon Academy, too. I'm in second grade."

Kitty's expression said she was properly impressed. "You must be awful smart."

Ross's face turned a light shade of pink. "I don't know." He cast a doubtful glance at his mother. "Am I, Mom?"

Grace and Mack both laughed.

Clearly amused with his daughter, Mack said, "Kitty admires smartness in a person."

Grace said, "Well, I might have a biased opinion, but I think Ross is smart. He makes good grades."

"I'm gonna make good grades, too," Kitty announced, then directed her next statement to Ross. "I have a horse and a dog. And two cats. Do you have any animals?"

He nodded. "I have a horse. Her name is Penny, 'cause she's red and she's a mare. She stays at my grandpa's ranch. And I have two cats, too. George and Ginger."

Kitty giggled and Grace was a bit surprised that Ross appeared to be totally charmed by the girl's reaction.

"George and Ginger," Kitty repeated. "Those are funny names. I just call my cats *Cat*."

"Why?" Ross asked.

Tilting her head to one side, Kitty contemplated his question. "Because they live in the barn and when I try to play with them they run from me. So I don't think they want names."

Ross stepped closer to Kitty and the children went into a deeper conversation about their cats. While the two of them continued to talk, Grace looked at Mack and smiled.

"Kitty must love animals as much as Ross."

"When we're home on the ranch, I can hardly keep her inside," Mack admitted. "She wants to live at the barn."

"Sounds like she takes after her father. Remember the baby goats you raised on a bottle? You took them on our picnic, just so you wouldn't miss their feeding time. I knew then that you'd be caring for animals the rest of your life."

Mack's gaze met hers and suddenly she was transported back to when the two of them were very young and very much in love. They had spent many days riding and exploring the Broken B and dreaming about making their home on his family ranch. When she thought of those days, she always viewed them through a warm, golden haze of sunshine. Even now, after all these years, it was hard for her to believe he'd wanted their relationship to end. But where Mack was concerned, she'd always been a bit blinded.

A wan smile touched his lips. "Actually, both of those goats are still on the ranch," he told her. "Mildred and Morris are old now, but in good shape for their age."

At least the goats had survived all these years, even if Mack's love for Grace hadn't, she thought.

"Wow. Your father must've taken good care of them."

He shrugged. "Dad made sure they were pampered. Now Kitty loves seeing after them."

As he spoke, his expression shifted subtly and Grace found herself staring at him and wondering. Was that regret she was seeing? Sadness?

No. He'd been talking about goats and nothing else. She needed to quit weighing every expression that crossed his face, each word that rolled out of his mouth.

"I'm sure she does," she said, then, realizing her voice had taken on a husky tone, she cleared her throat and glanced toward the front of the long room. Thankfully, she spotted Dorothy stepping out of the kitchen and ringing the dinner bell.

"Looks like they're going to start serving," Grace announced as the milling crowd began to slowly migrate toward the buffet tables.

Overhearing his mother, Ross exclaimed, "Yay! I'm hungry!"

"Me, too!" Kitty added with eager excitement.

Ross turned to the girl with an all-important question. "Are you going to eat turkey or ham?"

Her little eyebrows pulled together as she contemplated the two choices. "What are you going to eat?" she asked him.

"Ham!"

"Then I'll eat ham, too!" she said happily.

Ross looked hopefully at his mother. "Can we get in line now?"

Grace glanced at Mack. "Are you ready?"

"From the looks of this crowd, better now than later," he agreed.

As the four of them began to head toward the side of the room where a line was already forming, Grace was more than surprised to see Ross reach for Kitty's hand.

"You'd better hang on to me, Kitty," he said to the girl. "Or you might get lost."

Kitty gave him a beaming smile. "I'll hang on real tight," she promised.

While the children moved a few steps in front of their parents, Grace cast a look of amazement at Mack.

"I've never seen him behave this way," she said in a voice too low for Ross to hear. "Does Kitty normally take this quickly to boys?"

He let out a short laugh. "She never takes this quickly to any kid, girl or boy. And that's the biggest smile I've seen on her face since we moved here."

"I'm glad. Hopefully Kitty will get more than a meal out of this evening," Grace said. "She'll get a new friend."

He slanted her a wry smile. "Maybe I'll get more out of this evening, too."

Grace very nearly stumbled. What was he talking about? Spending time with her? No! Her imagination was working far too hard, she thought. She and Mack had been more than friends…once. She'd be silly to think they could ever be more than friends again.

Yet as they maneuvered their way toward the long line of waiting diners, she felt Mack's hand lightly rest against the small of her back. And foolish or not, she realized the contact felt just as good as it had all those years ago.

Don't miss
Rancher to the Rescue *by Stella Bagwell,*
wherever Harlequin® Special Edition
books and ebooks are sold.

www.Harlequin.com

#3001 THE MAVERICK'S SWEETEST CHOICE
Montana Mavericks: Lassoing Love • by Stella Bagwell

Rancher Dale Dalton only planned to buy cupcakes from the local bakery. Yet one look at single mom Kendra Humphrey and it's love at first sight. Or at least lust. Kendra wants more than a footloose playboy for her and her young daughter. But Dale's full-charm offensive may be too tempting and delicious to ignore!

#3002 FAKING A FAIRY TALE
Love, Unveiled • by Teri Wilson

Bridal editor Daphne Ballantyne despises her coworker Jack King. But when a juicy magazine assignment requires going undercover as a blissfully engaged couple, both Daphne and Jack say "I do." If only their intense marriage charade wasn't beginning to feel a lot like love...

#3003 HOME FOR THE CHALLAH DAYS
by Jennifer Wilck

Sarah Abrams is home for Rosh Hashanah...but can't be in the same room as her ex-boyfriend. She broke Aaron Isaacson's heart years ago and he's still deeply hurt. Until targeted acts of vandalism bring the reluctant duo together. And unearth buried—and undeniable—attraction just in time for the holiday.

#3004 A CHARMING DOORSTEP BABY
Charming, Texas • by Heatherly Bell

Dean Hunter's broken childhood still haunts him. So there's no way the retired rodeo star will let his neighbor Maribel Del Toro call social services on a mother who suddenly left her daughter in Maribel's care. They'll *both* care for the baby...and maybe even each other.

#3005 HER OUTBACK RANCHER
The Brands of Montana • by Joanna Sims

Hawk Bowhill's heart is on his family's cattle ranch in Australia. But falling for fiery Montana cowgirl Jessie Brand leads to a bevy of challenges, and geography is the least of them. From two continents to her unexpected pregnancy to her family's vow to keep them apart, will the price of happily-ever-after be too high to pay?

#3006 HIS UNLIKELY HOMECOMING
Small-Town Sweethearts • by Carrie Nichols

Shop owner Libby Taylor isn't fooled by Nick Cabot's tough motorcycle-riding exterior. He helped her daughter find her lost puppy...and melted Libby's guarded emotions in the process. But despite Nick's tender, heroic heart, can she take a chance on love with a man convinced he's unworthy of it?

YOU CAN FIND MORE INFORMATION ON UPCOMING HARLEQUIN TITLES,
FREE EXCERPTS AND MORE AT HARLEQUIN.COM.

Get 3 FREE REWARDS!

We'll send you 2 FREE Books plus a FREE Mystery Gift.

FREE
Value Over
$20

Both the **Harlequin® Special Edition** and **Harlequin® Heartwarming™** series feature compelling novels filled with stories of love and strength where the bonds of friendship, family and community unite.

YES! Please send me 2 FREE novels from the Harlequin Special Edition or Harlequin Heartwarming series and my FREE Gift (gift is worth about $10 retail). After receiving them, if I don't wish to receive any more books, I can return the shipping statement marked "cancel." If I don't cancel, I will receive 6 brand-new Harlequin Special Edition books every month and be billed just $5.49 each in the U.S. or $6.24 each in Canada, a savings of at least 12% off the cover price, or 4 brand-new Harlequin Heartwarming Larger-Print books every month and be billed just $6.24 each in the U.S. or $6.74 each in Canada, a savings of at least 19% off the cover price. It's quite a bargain! Shipping and handling is just 50¢ per book in the U.S. and $1.25 per book in Canada.* I understand that accepting the 2 free books and gift places me under no obligation to buy anything. I can always return a shipment and cancel at any time by calling the number below. The free books and gift are mine to keep no matter what I decide.

Choose one: ☐ **Harlequin Special Edition**
(235/335 BPA GRMK)
☐ **Harlequin Heartwarming Larger-Print**
(161/361 BPA GRMK)
☐ **Or Try Both!**
(235/335 & 161/361 BPA GRPZ)

Name (please print)

Address   Apt. #

City   State/Province   Zip/Postal Code

Email: Please check this box ☐ if you would like to receive newsletters and promotional emails from Harlequin Enterprises ULC and its affiliates. You can unsubscribe anytime.

Mail to the Harlequin Reader Service:
IN U.S.A.: P.O. Box 1341, Buffalo, NY 14240-8531
IN CANADA: P.O. Box 603, Fort Erie, Ontario L2A 5X3

Want to try 2 free books from another series? Call 1-800-873-8635 or visit www.ReaderService.com.

HARLEQUIN
PLUS

Try the best multimedia subscription service for romance readers like you!

Read, Watch and Play.

Experience the easiest way to get the romance content you crave.

Start your **FREE TRIAL** at
<u>www.harlequinplus.com/freetrial</u>.